I0675159

Praise for Jack Cady

"A remarkable talent for translating familiar life rhythms of ordinary people into moving and meaningful writing . . . his style is direct, simple, and natural."
— *Publishers Weekly*

"Jack Cady's knack for golden sentences is an alchemy any other writer has to admire."
—Ivan Doig

"An exceptional writer."
—Joyce Carol Oates

"His structural control and the laconic richness of his style establish Cady in the front ranks of contemporary writers."
—*Library Journal*

"A writer of great, unmistakable integrity and profound feeling."
—Peter Straub

"[Jack Cady is] a lasting voice in modern American literature."
—*Atlanta Constitution*

The Cady Collection

Novels

The Hauntings of Hood Canal
Inagehi
The Jonah Watch
McDowell's Ghost
The Man Who Could Make Things Vanish
The Off Season
Singleton
Street

Dark Dreaming [with Carol Orlock, as Pat Franklin]
Embrace of the Wolf [with Carol Orlock, as Pat Franklin]

Collected Writings

Phantoms
Fathoms
The American Writer

The Man Who Could
Make Things Vanish

The Man Who Could
Make Things Vanish

Jack Cady

FAIRWOOD PRESS
Bonney Lake, WA

THE MAN WHO COULD MAKE THINGS VANISH
A Fairwood Press Book
June 2019
Copyright © 2019 by the Estate of Jack Cady
Introduction © 2016 Dale Bailey
All rights reserved.

No part of this book may be reproduced or transmitted in any form or by any means, electronic or mechanical, including photocopying, recording, or by any information storage and retrieval system, without permission in writing from the publisher.

Fairwood Press
21528 104th Street Court East
Bonney Lake, WA 98391
www.fairwoodpress.com

Series Cover Design by Jennifer Tough
Book Design by Aaron Leis
Collection Editorial Direction by Mark Teppo

ISBN: 978-1-933846-82-8
First Fairwood Press Edition: June 2019
Printed in the United States of America

The first edition of this novel was published by Arbor House in 1983.

To the poet Margaret Shafer.
We're all on that train you wrote of, Peggy.
Chugging and whistling our ways through the universe.

The Muscular Truths of Jack Cady:

An Introduction to

The Man Who Could Make Things Vanish

Dale Bailey

MUSCULAR.

Tasked with writing an introduction to Jack Cady's apocalyptic, quasi-science-fiction novel *The Man Who Could Make Things Vanish*—though it's more pleasure than task—I've been walking around in distraction for the last few days trying to think of a word to characterize the novel, a lesser book in Cady's body of work, but one well worth your time and attention, one that nonetheless exhibits Cady's many virtues. The central attraction, the bait that lures you in, is, as is the case with virtually all of Cady's work, the prose. The man can write. Dear God, how he can write. He is the kind of craftsman that his peers—though he is virtually peerless—often refer to as "a writer's writer," which may be the commercial kiss of death, but is the highest possible praise, because it means that here is a craftsman so skillful that even others who have mastered the trade find much to admire, much that they can learn from. And I think the central and defining characteristic of Cady's prose, that which I most admire, is its muscularity—which, of course, requires definition.

I first encountered Cady when I read "The Sons of Noah" in the pages of *Omni* magazine in 1991, when I was at the Clarion Writers Workshop, making my first real attempt to learn the craft myself. The opening sentence reads, "When darkness edges through this valley, shading the slow figures of cattle moving toward milking barns, last light falls on the weathered steeple of Sons of Noah Church." That sentence nailed me to the page. He next pinned me down two years later in *The Magazine of Fantasy & Science Fiction*, where I read "The Night We Buried Road Dog," which opens this way:

> Brother Jesse buried his '47 Hudson back in '61 and the roads just got that much more lonesome. Highway 2 across north Montana still wailed with engines as reservation cars blew past; and it lay like a tunnel of darkness before headlights of big rigs. Tandems pounded, and the smart crack of downshifts rapped across grassland as trucks swept past the bars at every crossroad. The state put up metal crosses to mark the sites of fatal accidents. Around the bars those crosses sprouted like thickets.

And one more, the opening sentence of his novel *The Jonah Watch*: "On those far northern shores where the wind sets north-northeast, and where the remote lighthouses are haunted by dark tales of men flung upright from the surf—as if the dead rose through spray like pathetic divines—the summer slides in on the memory of ice."

Disparate as these examples are, a careful attention to language unites them—not the kind of language that calls attention to itself, exactly. It's not rococo, or ornate. Their beauty lies not in the exuberant flights of metaphor we associate, say, with a Salman Rushdie, or the fine psychological shadings of a Henry James. It is rather the sure hand of the captain at the tiller, a matter of rhythm and word choice that lets us know we are in the hands of a master, and, most of all, the way the prose echoes and reinforces the cadences of the rural working class that is so often his subject, and displays to high effect their stoic poetry. "Darkness edges" and the "crack of a downshift . . . raps" across the prairie and "summer slides in on the memory of ice." The diction is pared down, everyday, the rhythm memorable, but not ostentatious—read it aloud and you'll see what I mean. This is prose that shoulders up beside you and announces itself a force to be reckoned with.

We see the same kind of prose in the pages of *The Man Who Could Make Things Vanish*. In the opening paragraph—another powerful beginning—we meet a man whose "thoughts were like the thin whistle of wind over the shallow and still ice-enclosed

Montana rivers," and as the novel proceeds, we'll see a breeze moving through "the shadow-knitting leaves"—as accurate a description of that physical phenomenon as I have ever seen, and the most beautiful. A clock is described as "indifferent as history." And we're told that a "chainsaw makes a nice sound if you have your ethics straight," which means, I think, that there is honor in the work if the work is done with integrity. Truth is beauty, beauty truth, Keats tells us. Cady's ethics are straight; the work is honest. When he describes "lonely streets, arc lamps, jukes playing from long ago," the sentiment comes through like the edge of a blade. Another writer might have stopped with the abstraction of "lonely streets." Cady, with his arc lamps and jukeboxes, lends the idea weight and gravity. Showing, not telling, with a single masterful brush stroke.

But prose alone is insufficient to carry any writer through, of course. Fortunately, Cady's work is as muscular, as honest, in other ways, especially in his determination to face the truth of the world. We see this in his depiction of rural working men, as stoic and dedicated in their enterprise as he is in his. Cady brings a lifetime of such experience to the table. His bio for *The Sons of Noah and Other Stories* tells us that he had worked as a "truck driver, a tree high-climber, landscape foreman, auctioneer, and member of the Coast Guard." When he writes of the sea, as in *The Jonah Watch*, he knows the sea. And when he writes of the ragtag crew of loggers in *The Man Who Could Make Things Vanish*, his portrayal rings utterly true. He knows the language of the trade (the most dangerous tree to cut is a "schoolmarm," because it has high branching trunks, called "leaders," which destabilize the tree); he also knows its emotional terrain—the stoic (there's that word again) dignity and courage of men who work constantly in the shadow of danger and death, men who work with their hands, without formal education, but with a deeper, hard-won wisdom. His style does not echo Hemingway's, but Hemingway's doctrine of "grace under pressure" applies.

Further, I can think of few writers who marry the tropes of science fiction and fantasy and the world of rural life with such success—Zenna Henderson and Clifford D. Simak come to mind, though Cady's work is unmarred by their sentimentality. For while *The Man Who Could Make Things Vanish* occasionally veers off into abstraction—especially in its depiction of psychic powers and psychic combat—it is remarkably, frighteningly prescient in the way good science fiction often is. Cady, writing in 1983, foresees everything from drone attacks to the ascension of the one percent and the corporate entities they control and that in turn control us all. Against them neither governments nor individuals can stand. Those who are not bought off are sold like dry goods. "Schools were hired to teach their students to be consumers of corporate goods," he notes in passing, a stunningly accurate indictment of our present day.

Where Cady transcends his deployment of these standard science fiction tropes is in his understanding of the magnitude of the natural forces that envelop us all, their beauty, sure, but also their power and the dangers they pose. He understands the insignificance—but importance—of human enterprise in the face of such power. In this he echoes the naturalists of the 19th Century, among them Stephen Crane and Jack London. His is a world where the ship can sink or the fire go out at any moment by chance or error, leaving you at the mercy of forces that transcend your ability to respond. Some of this comes through in *The Man Who Could Make Things Vanish*. "The sailors were like submariners everywhere," he writes. "They were experts in controlling their imaginations. Most sailors do not allow themselves to think of depth, only of surface"—the implication, of course, being that the truth of the world lies in the crushing depths, not the serene surfaces (though they, too, pose their dangers). We are indeed, as he says in *The Man Who Could Make Things Vanish*, "creatures of smoke"—fleeting and impermanent—but in the work of Jack Cady we are striving, against impossible odds, to endure.

The Man Who Could Make Things Vanish

Author's Note

THREE TOWNS ON THE WASHINGTON PENINSULA MAY, IN ONE OR more ways, resemble the fictional town of Land's End. They are Port Townsend, Port Angeles and Forks. Each town's economy depends largely on fishing and lumber. Two of the towns enjoy at least some elaborate architecture. At least two of the towns have served in the past as centers for smuggling. Thus, the town of Land's End is a fictional construct that is faithful to locale.

No character in this book is based on anyone, living or dead. I have scrupulously avoided portraying any character who might resemble any of my acquaintances on the Washington Peninsula, or elsewhere.

Take a sad song and make it better . . .

—The Beatles

The First Attack

WYOMING AT HIS LEFT HAND, CANADA AT HIS RIGHT, MAX KLEIN SAT IN the 3 a.m. darkness of his small apartment in Billings and waited for the ring of the phone. His thoughts were like the thin whistle of wind over the shallow and still ice-enclosed Montana rivers. Max immersed himself in the thoughts and discarded them one by one, flicking them from his mind as an adroit gambler might flip cards into a hat.

So now it was time to leave. He supposed the direction would be west. During his fifty-two years he had made a slow westward movement from a childhood home in the Southeast. During the three and a half months of this newly started year of 1991 the westward feeling increased, wrapping him easily with its humors and cadences.

Soon the phone would ring. He knew that with the same ease and authority that allowed him to discard useless thoughts, although he had not troubled to uncover the name of the caller. Max felt the familiar apartment about him, the comfort offered by familiar things, and understood that now most of the things were lost. It was time to travel unimpeded. He would miss the books.

The phone rang and he smiled at the smallness of events which change life. He answered.

The direction was west. He had heard Jake Sandiford's voice only once in the last fifteen years, and because it was Jake calling it could only mean that life—his, and probably Jake's—had arrived at some final and important test. There would be great danger. Max considered his age. Fifty-two years were quite a lot.

"Yes," he told Jake. "Yes, friend, I'll prepare to leave quickly." He hung up the phone. It would take a day or two to give away his possessions.

Chapter 1

WE LEFT THE WOODS EARLY, OUR CREW TRUCK JOLTING DOWN THE old logging road that we had regraded. We passed our Kenworth, our yarder and our bulldozer. I was driving. I'm Jake Sandiford. I boss this mess.

I've run this gyppo logging outfit for years. During those years a lot of guys have come and gone, and so has a lot of timber and a few mysteries. Trees fall wrong, sometimes, and sometimes the woods seem haunted. A few years back, one guy even claimed to have seen the ghost of an old Indian. Stuff like that is okay. The woods are just naturally mysterious. No mystery, though, had ever been so frightening that it ran us off the job.

Now we were running scared, and no one was trying to deny it. The cab was stunk up with fear. Behind us, high on that grade, stood a massive and freshly cut stump. Beside that stump should have laid four thousand pounds of fir tree.

The tree was not there. It had vanished before it hit the ground. If it had not vanished, Jim would have been killed.

Jim sat beside me. He was still so weak from shock that his hands did not tremble. Barrows, ancient looking and tranquil, sat beside Mike in the back seat of the crew cab. Barrows was the only one who did not seem afraid. Mike was hunched up, not trusting his nineteen-year-old mouth.

As we left the logging road and got onto the county road I looked at Jim. There was not a scratch on him. The hospital is a long way off, and it charges too much. I decided to drop Jim at his house, in care of his wife. Penny is smart and tough and she loves him.

The truck gathered speed and the lousy road sent vibrations through the cab. We rattled along, and all of us were thinking about mysteries. All day long we had logged on a grade. It was a stinking show.

High elevation. Mostly cleanup. When the big boys, the corporation timber company, came through, they had taken the prime timber. What was left were salvage snags, white fir, some Douglas fir at the lower elevations, and a lot of hemlock. Some of the snags were monsters. We were working two guys on saw, two on wedge, or trading off turns on the saws when there was no need to wedge.

The day had started good and held good until after lunch. Then the stuff began to fall wrong. It happened right away.

Most working men are superstitious. But superstition does not really cover all that you feel in the woods. The snags towered. Those trees had been there before we were born. Our work was going too slow. In a way, I guess we were spooked.

Barrows was on the saw, I was wedging, and the fir began to lean wrong as it fell. The butt of the tree twisted on the stump and the whole tree walked sideways. Barrows and I got free, but the saw's bar was pinched as Barrows tried to jerk it free. The tree hit the saw, and what had been an expensive piece of equipment was now a mess of broken metal that would fit in your shirt pocket. Even as I had collected what was left of the saw, it occurred to me that there had been something wrong with this logging show all along. Barrows and I had no sooner caught our breath than we heard Mike yell. Jim was dancing away from the same kind of mess. The only difference was that he saved his saw.

Those two trees could have been flukes, but none of us were making mistakes. I know this crew. There is not a fool in the bunch. All four of us stopped to figure it out.

We talked, and then I sighted elevations on the grade. Sometimes you think you see a clear lean, or a clear descent, and the grade is fooling you. This time it was not the grade.

"Wasting time," Jim said. He is always quick, but he works accurate. Mike followed him across the grade to the next tree.

"Scrub it," Barrows told me, "or get it figured out."

"We can work the down stuff, bring in the yarder. We can cut again tomorrow."

"I'd be happier if we did." Barrows was looking at the gray sky that misted through the tops. The forest was going dark. Soon there would be wind.

A chain saw makes a nice sound if you have your ethics straight. Use it wrong, like in clear cut on this kind of grade, and it is not much different than a cannon. Jim's saw was going again as Barrows and I talked.

"We'll scrub it after this one," I told Barrows. I was not nearly as worried as he was, but I trust his instincts. Most injury in the woods does not come from falling trees. It comes from carelessness. I never worry about Jim. He was raised with logging.

What happened next sent us home. Sometimes when a tree is young it gets wind damage in the top and throws up two or three or even four main branches, called leaders. Such trees, called schoolmarms, are the most dangerous in the woods. After they have grown for many years, those leaders gain authority. They can make up half the weight of the tree, and they can twist the tree into unpredictable falls. Sometimes I top them before we cut. I always try to top the worst ones.

This tree was no giant, but it was big. It had only two leaders, and one of them was crooked. The leader looked like a shattered and badly twisted arm. Wind damage. Lightning is practically unknown here. The voice of Jim's saw blanketed the woods, running across the tangle of brush and slash that the corporation boy had left. The saw droned low and easy.

We are too money minded. To live on Washington's Olympic Peninsula, you have to accept that there will be times when you are broke. It's been that way for as long as I can remember, even back in the sixties when I was young and the world was interminably old. If Jim had not tried to save that second saw the whole thing would not have happened.

The tree sat back on the saw. The answer is to stand it up with wedges, cut, then wedge it over. Mike laid another wedge.

The tree took a twist. There was a puff of wind, a dirty little laugh of air two hundred feet in the tops. The tree spun. The saw wagged slow like a lazy pup's tail, and Jim went for it. A wedge flipped, dropped under his arm and he missed the saw and stumbled. He was looking at four thousand pounds of death right on top of him. No one screamed. There is never time for that.

Back in the days of movies a big tree always fell slow. In the woods trees rush down like an avalanche. Cedar springs, alder hits with a dead whack, and fir slams like a well-seasoned club. The Pacific Northwest slugger.

This fir slugged the top of a tree down grade, whirled on the stump, and walked off to place the butt squarely in Jim's belly.

That is what I saw.

What I also saw was two tons of tree disappear. It was not there. For an instant it was visually the way a faint echo can exist just on the edge of hearing. It was there and the man was clearly dead. Then it was not there and the man was still alive.

Jim was on his back. His arms flopped. His mouth was open. His chest heaved. There was spastic movement in his hips, and his legs kicked and convulsed. In the ten seconds between the beginning and end of the trouble I was running. I was running toward the tree with no notion of its fall. There was not a thing I could have done.

We got through the wool work shirt and there was no mark on his belly. Whatever his body was doing was caused by his mind, or by the tension that ran through him the instant before the blow that had not arrived.

Mike held Jim's head up, cradling him. Mike acted quite well for a kid who has not had much experience in emergencies. Barrows knelt beside Jim and took one of his hands. Jim's convulsions were slowing. He gasped and sucked at air. He made grabs for words, but the words would not come. In two or three minutes he was sucking air more regular, but letting it go in long and uncontrolled breaths. His face got calm. Then even the calmness disappeared. He was going to live. That meant that Penny was going to live. She is tough and smart, true, but she is dumb about Jim. We were going to catch it from Penny. I watched Jim and thought of the four of us catching hell and almost laughed.

"He'll be all right," Barrows said. "All we can do is wait. "

The pressure was too much. I started giggling, nearly out of control. Mike took one look and began to laugh like he was mindless. The fear smell was on him, but the laughing exploded some of the tension. Barrows smiled.

If a man was going to be hanged, saw the trap thrown, and if the trap stuck and he still stood with the noose around his neck . . . such thoughts brought me from my laughter. Jim had been dead and not dead. He was no Lazarus. There was no resurrection. It was horrible. Mike's laugh choked. The forest was going black, shadowed, the tops dark silhouettes against the sky. Dark towers of solitude.

Trees are more than just lumber. Trees define the sky.

Jim's long, narrowly compacted but tough body finally relaxed. His face was the last part to change. His thin, Scandinavian mouth firmed up. The high forehead showed a wrinkle. His eyes blinked, closed, blinked. He tried to roll over and could not. You expect those eyes to be blue, but they are almost black. In the pale Norwegian face those eyes can be as polished and deep as anthracite.

It took half an hour. In that time all of us looked at the stump. The saw lay with the bar bent like a carcass. The fresh cut was moist and clean. Piles of yellow chips lay at the base of the trunk, and the resiny smell of fir was familiar, almost reassuring.

Down grade and to the left was breakage in the top that had been hit. Limbs dangled. One was knocked from the socket and stuck on other branches. It hung like a disjointed black flag in the gathering mist. Maybe the wind would get it. Otherwise, it would wait to kill some logger.

When Jim rolled over, I expected to see a hole beneath him. Nothing. The forest floor was unmarked. It was that final proof, maybe, that made my fear and Mike's fear return. We did not help Jim walk to the truck, we carried him as fast as we could. Barrows followed along behind us, taking his time, and carrying the broken saw. When Mike and I got Jim settled in the truck, we all headed for home.

Chapter 2

WHEN WE GOT BACK TO TOWN WE DROPPED JIM OFF RIGHT AWAY. Instead of shoving it in gear, I sat watching Jim walk up the path to the log house that he and Penny had just completed. He still wore his corks, but that does not make a man walk in such a dead-footed way. Jim is twenty-seven, Penny is twenty-three, and it came to me as I watched him shuffle that for a while they would both be old. Penny might not understand that she looked at a dead man returned to life. Maybe Jim would not even say anything.

I pulled away when Jim got to his doorway, our truck cruising easily along the nearly deserted streets of this town. There is hardly ever any traffic here in winter anymore.

"Home or drink," I asked Mike.

Mike lit a smoke and watched the tremble in his hand like it was the last interesting thing in the world. The match flame flicked, danced, jumped. Then Mike gave a silly flip with his hand in the direction of home. I drove him to the crossroads store near where he lives. That store is the only place that will sell him beer.

"Drop over to my place later," Barrows said to Mike. "If you want." We all take care of Mike, but Barrows does it best.

"Maybe later." Mike's voice was a whisper.

I know Mike. It was going to be one of those three-liter beer nights. He would not show up at Barrows's. I started to give some good advice, then kept my mouth shut. Daddy Jake. What business did I have telling him not to get sloshed?

"I have to talk to you or I'll bust," I said to Barrows.

Barrows turned to Mike. "I'll either be at my place or with Jake." Mike headed toward the store and Barrows climbed in front with me. I watched Mike. He is a tall guy who moves good. Right now he walked in the same shuffle-footed way as Jim. "You think he'll be all right?"

"Yes," Barrows said. "He was shocked and now he's confused. You'll probably go through the same thing."

"I'm already doing it."

"And don't underestimate Mike," Barrows said. "He is young, but he is not just a kid." Barrows lit a smoke. His hand did not tremble. "Let's go get some coffee. Downtown."

"Sure," I told him, "and let's talk."

There are three restaurants in town. The only good one is by the water on the main drag. It takes five minutes to drive there because it is all the way across town.

"I don't think I'm crazy," I said to Barrows as I parked the truck in front of the restaurant. "There have been some times in the past when I knew I was nuts, but I don't feel that way now."

"A tree vanished. You can't explain it. That doesn't mean that you are crazy." Barrows's voice is usually quiet and firm. This time it was a little loud, like he was trying to sell something.

We climbed from the truck. I walked to the back and covered the broken saws with tarp. No one around here would steal them, even if they were in good shape. I covered the victims because I did not want anyone to see we had that much trouble and ask what had happened. It's an awful small town. When a dog whelps it makes the weekly paper.

The restaurant was steamy from the wet clothing of fishermen who were repairing boats and waiting out the winter. There had been only a little rain, but the weather signs said there would be a lot more. Ann was busy at the grill, but she had time to wave and smile. Ann is slender and girlish, even if her hair is nearly all gray. She moves like a dancer. We poured our own coffee and hunched over the cups at a table near the back of the room.

I slurped coffee. Looked around. It was a real pleasure to be surrounded by familiar faces. The only strangers were a tourist group dressed in flaming polyester. We always get a few of those, even in winter.

"What happened is against all natural laws," I said.

"Do you know all of the natural laws?" Barrows was amused. His deeply lined and bearded face held the slightest touch of laughter.

"Except for a few exotics," I told him. "I know density and gravity and volume and attraction of bodies. I know velocity and boiling points and relativity. I don't know what wins football games."

"All that education, and now you're a gyppo logger."

"You know why," I told him. "You've met dropouts before."

"I know what you've told me. " Barrows was fooling around with a saltshaker. He took the cap off, put it back on, took it off again.

"I've got reasons to be hiding in this town," I said. "Shall I go through them again?"

"Children repeat themselves," he said. "We are not children." He was sure right about that. Barrows is old and I'm forty-eight.

A couple of mill guys came in shaking water from their hats. At my back I could hear waves smacking the bulkheads on the water side of the building.

"I've thought and thought," he said. "There is a dream men have when they are old. Maybe it's a dream men have after they've lived too long." He tipped the saltshaker. The salt poured into a little pile on the table.

It is not like Barrows to mess a place up. "Watch it," he said. "Touch it."

I stirred it with my finger. It was salt. Then it disappeared. The table was clean.

Chapter 3

BARROWS DID NOT KNOW THEN, AND I SURE DIDN'T, BUT WE WERE already up to our eyes in trouble. The attacks on the town were about to begin. One mystery we would have to solve was identifying our attacker.

At the time Barrows made the salt disappear I was optimistic.

I was partly optimistic because I figured things could not get worse. In 1991 most of the population was hungry. The class structure had changed. There was the small corporate upper class, the only slightly larger bureaucratic middle class, and the vast majority of the people were lower class, at least in income. The black market was the only dependable distributor of goods. In urban areas police forces exercised continuing martial law.

So I may have been shocked, but I was optimistic. At the time I just stirred air where the salt had been and looked at Barrows. Then I thought of my reasons for living in this town. Good reasons. I am a dropout ex-theorist who once believed that he could change society and institutions.

I had dreamed the same dream as Barrows. To make things vanish. The dream of men who live too long.

"Give me a minute," I said to Barrows.

"We have more time than we need." He stood and walked to the counter for more coffee. He chatted with Ann. She likes Barrows. You can tell. Both of them are like contradictions to age. Barrows, though gray-haired, moved like a young man.

I watched them and listened to the waves smacking the bulkheads while the wind gusted over dark water and banged against the restaurant. Old feelings returned. They were feelings of the way the world must fit together, how wind and emotion and creatures and rocks and economic systems are all pressed in the same ball of wax.

"I've dreamed your dream," I said to Barrows when he returned. "To make things vanish. I've had fantasies over that dream."

"One big fantasy is our usual way of looking at things." Barrows returned to fooling with the empty saltshaker. "There are other ways."

Behind Barrows the tourists were chirping and clucking about the quaintness of the area. That was bullshit. The Olympic Peninsula was ruined.

"Stop it," Barrows told me. "How can I trust you if you are harsh?"

"Do you also read minds?"

"No," he said, "there's a look you get when you're being stupid."

"Quaint," I said about the tourists. "They're probably from San Francisco."

"I mean it," he told me. "Your constant, deep anger is a real enemy. It has caused you to make some terrible mistakes."

He was right about my temper. It is a bad problem, but I'm tired of phony stuff. And yes, my temper has cost me. More than Barrows knows. A job, a loved woman who is now only a friend, and a couple of close escapes from death. But cheap shit still infuriates me, and cheapness is the stuff of society.

"I planned to work with you for another year or two," Barrows said. "Then I was going to tell you about the power. With Mike and Jim involved the matter becomes complicated."

"They are dependable guys."

"There are a lot of dependable guys." Barrows spun the saltshaker like a man experimenting for the first time with a roulette wheel. "In fact, you are less dependable in some ways than they are." Barrows leaned back, looked toward Ann. His eyes betrayed no emotion, but there was a hint of loneliness in his voice. "Being dependable isn't the point. You can't imagine that I would display this kind of power simply because of friendship." The saltshaker tumbled back and forth in his hands.

"You made the tree vanish. That was a display."

"Yes," he said, "but Mike and Jim don't know who caused that disappearance. But to you, I have consciously shown the power. I have shown you an enormous force."

He was right. The situation was changed. It might be that there was more power sitting across that restaurant table than there was on the rest of the planet.

"How do you know you can trust me?"

"You would have figured it out sooner or later. I know you pretty well." Barrows seemed like he was talking to himself, instead of me. "Beyond your temper you are a decent man." He looked at me with a kind of affection, the way a father might look at a son who had done something smart.

"And," he smiled, "you can accept facts. Even if you do act a little silly at first."

"What do you expect? My whole idea of the world goes flip. Physics blows up in front of my eyes."

"That's right." He was smiling. His face was all creases, the forehead, around the nose. I could imagine that I saw creases beneath the beard. "The first thing you must do is get a handle on that temper."

"I control it."

"Not well." He hitched a thumb over his shoulder toward the water. "Now I'm going to tell you something about the power. There's a submerged sub in the channel. It carries enough firepower to destroy a continent. Six foreign submarines are cruising at points a hundred miles offshore. One concentration of three is below Anchorage. Four from this nation monitor those three, and three others monitor the other six. They chase each other like children playing tag. Their combined arms can destroy the earth."

I sat amazed and wondered if Barrows were insane. "How do you know?"

He did not even bother to give me an answer. He leaned back in his chair. "This is an old building. Trace across the ceiling from the back wall. Come ten feet toward the center of the room. There is a frayed wire against dry tinder and hidden by plaster."

"What will you do? This restaurant is all Ann has to make a living," I told him. "What are you going to do about that wire?"

"Nothing." His voice was friendly. He was trying to teach me something.

"I'II tell her about it."

"Then you'll have to tell her how you knew."

"Quit playing," I said. "This is serious."

"You are the one who has been playing," he told me. "A futile game. I'll take care of Ann's problem and then we'll go to your place."

"Don't bet that my house isn't bugged," I told him. "The feds still check me out every couple of years."

"It isn't bugged." Barrows stood, walked to the door, and as we climbed in the truck the lights in the restaurant went out. I was glad to know that my place was not bugged. Now I would be less self-conscious when Julie and I made love.

Chapter 4

THE FIRST ATTACKS WERE ALREADY BEGINNING TO FORM AS BARROWS and I drove up the hill to my house. We did not know that at the time. We understood it later, when Barrows used his power to investigate. He figured out who was who, and what must have happened.

The attack organization came together slowly. A world that enjoyed instant communication could no longer act instantly. There were endless chains of command out there, endless reasons to pass the buck to someone else.

In Dallas an executive hung up a phone and began to worry. He was afraid to call his superior in Houston, because he knew that it was the dinner hour. At the same time he was afraid not to call. The executive made a decision, picked up the phone. He spoke to his superior in Houston. That man listened, acknowledged, hung up the phone and worried. He made a decision and called his superior, a man named Chester, whose main office was in Louisiana.

In Kansas General of Air/Space Butterfield was not worried. He spoke easily into a phone as he checked the readiness of equipment. He canceled all military leaves.

At the same time, for other reasons, a darkened warehouse in a rundown Philadelphia neighborhood was brilliantly lighted inside. Electronics gear was loaded aboard a truck that was destined for a nearby airfield.

And in our own town, Land's End, our mayor, half-boozed and trembling, arrived home after having spent more than an hour in a phone booth that he knew was not bugged. Our mayor went immediately to his radio and a marine frequency. He spoke a code phrase to the fishing vessel Rose. The mayor did not know about the warehouse, and he had never heard of General Butterfield.

Barrows and I drove the half-mile from the restaurant to the other side of town. The road cuts away from the strait and comes over a hill. There is uptown and downtown. I live uptown, and there are only five thousand people in the entire town. Land's End has not always been small. During the late Victorian period it was a major shipping center. Half of the houses in this town were once mansions, Victorian and gilt.

The wipers of the truck slapped as we arrived at my house. The rain, which had been playing around all day, now misted in the headlights. Wind pushed and snapped at the bare branches of fruit trees surrounding the house.

My house is like a mausoleum for giants. The thing was built in 1888 of western red cedar. It is a three-story firetrap of fifteen rooms with an unfinished attic that looks like a dusty football field. It has fireplaces, four chimneys, and is ornamented with remnants of splendor that were attempted by a rich but unimaginative man in the days when this town was populous and rich.

The house sags in places. Someday it will burn and some other guy will come along and build a log cabin. It is nicer in my mausoleum than it will be in his cabin. There is space here, even space for a wife if that should happen. It won't. Julie is trying too hard to be independent.

My house did not cost much. It is not worth much.

"You can learn from things," Barrows said. When we entered, I had started a fire in the cookstove and in one of the living room fireplaces. We were waiting for water to boil. We live on coffee.

"How do you mean?" I kicked off my boots.

"A place like this tells of the past. A lot of despair and hope have lived here."

"Only for a little over a hundred years," I told him. On one chimney there were three places where brick had been holed, then later plugged and covered with paint. Three different ideas of how to heat when some guy had too much stovepipe or not enough. Voices of the past.

"I'll tell you another dream," Barrows said. "I'm in a boat, drifting slowly down a fogbound river. My feeling is euphoric, what psychologists call the 'oceanic sense.' I feel the mouth of the river ahead. It joins with the ocean at some place in the fog. I will never know the exact moment, and that doesn't matter.

"There are echoes all around. They nudge at the fog. It is like all the people who ever were or ever will be are moving together, either on the water or along the riverbanks. They continue downstream, moving toward the sea."

"It's a nice dream," I said. "Like Zen."

"It isn't Zen," Barrows said, "but it is mystical. Mysticism is the source of my power."

That stopped me. I had not even bothered to ask myself how Barrows had gotten his power.

"My kind of mysticism," I asked, "where groups create a mind that is independent of the group, or Julie's kind that deals with shamans?"

"Neither," he told me. "There are many kinds of mysticism." He stood, walked to a far window and stared into the empty streets. The night was now slick with rain, but the clouds were broken. The moon appeared and disappeared and then returned. I thought about a line from a poem that spoke of uncaring movement "with tremulous cadence slow" and wondered what Barrows was doing here. Not in this room in this house, but in this form on this planet. It is not a new question. I have asked the same about myself.

"To make things vanish," Barrows said, "is not the same as if it didn't happen at all. To make things vanish is to interfere in human affairs."

"You saved Jim's life."

"Yes. And it was an interruption of human affairs. I don't argue against it, but I want you to think about it."

I could see where Barrows's sense of responsibility was taking him, and I was glad it was his problem. Barrows has never shown anything but the deepest respect for other people. Part of that respect allows them to make their own mistakes—to learn. I remembered when Mike first started working with us. He mixed the gas and oil wrong for the chain saw and burnt out the engine. Barrows could have stopped him but he didn't. He knew that once

Mike made that mistake he would never burn up another engine as long as he lived.

I knelt to stir the fire and add wood. The good, pink, salmon color of the fir turned red in the firelight. The heft and feel of the wood, the straight open grain. Fir is beautiful.

"I suspect," I said, "that you have the greatest power in the world. Can you actually sense a ship a thousand miles away?"

"It would be difficult to sense a frayed wire on that ship, but with complete concentration I can even do that."

"Can you make that ship vanish?"

He avoided the question. "There are two separate functions," Barrows said. "The first is the sensing function, and it is fairly harmless. Have you seen Al the fisherman lately?"

"This morning," I said.

"Al is an agent with Interior, which is linked with State, which is linked with Revenue. Al is trying to find out which boat is the big drug smuggler from Canada. That boat is the *Rose*. I know this about Al because I can see identification he carries. He owns test equipment to analyze chemicals."

That got to me. The fire sparked and cooked and sizzled as it hit a gummy place in the fir. The wind rattled a loose window from upstairs and caused a vibration in the house.

"The government doesn't want the drug traffic broken up," I told Barrows. "Al is only a guy being used. Maybe even Al knows that the government is pretending."

"That makes no sense."

"Sure it does," I told him. "Anyone who thinks theoretically can figure that one out. The population of the nation is desperate. When you have a desperate population, then you have to leave escape routes. People escape with drugs, booze and television. There will never be a shortage of those." It seemed to me that Barrows was mighty innocent in a lot of ways.

"Tell me about the tree," I said.

"That's the other function. The tree discorporated on the molecular level. There is a dispersion of molecules and the appearance of space."

It is lonely in this universe. It is lonely in this house. Around here the wind is nearly as constant as clouds, and the dark corners of this house must hold as many whispers, voices, questions, as they hold crumbling plaster and dust.

"Are you talking about parallel universes?"

"I may be," he said.

"You don't know what the hell you're doing?"

"I've thought about it," he said. "Molecular structures may exist in many ways. There might be structures with molecules as big as footballs."

"You really don't know?"

"I really don't care."

"Still, it would be nice to know."

He ignored it. I might as well have made a remark about the weather. Wrinkles in his face seemed deeper. The fire illuminated his face, lit it bronze.

"You could control the world."

He shook his head. "The things I can 't make vanish are fear and hate. If I use my power it will cause fear, and the fear will cause more hate."

I backed my chair away from him, almost unconsciously. "Who are you?" I asked. A feeling of awe came over me. For the first time in a long time I was afraid of someone.

"John Barrows," he said, "and the rest is up for grabs. Don't be afraid. My power comes from a trained human capacity. It is not a common capacity, but it is not unique."

It seemed, looking at him, more wizened in the firelight, that this was the kind of man who sang the first incantation over the hunt, or over the fire, or who first appealed to the spirits of wind and storm.

"Why did you tell me all this," I asked.

He smiled. "After the tree vanished I had little choice, but I was going to tell you at some point. I need you. You are a brilliant theorist, or at least you once were."

"And you figure that even power needs theory?"

He explained, and the explanation told more about Barrows than it did about theory. John Barrows might be the world's most powerful man, but he was also the world's most ethical man. An impossible combination. John Barrows knew that history was about to force his hand. At some near future date he was going to have to take action, and he did not trust his own point of view. He absolutely had to have another trained perspective.

"What is the most effective active group," he asked.

"Small groups of religious conviction. Zealots. Pound for pound there is nothing stronger."

He smiled. "Then we are halfway successful already. We are a small group." He walked back to the window and stared into the wet street. "My dream about the river is true. It's a new beginning. It's got to be that, because the alternative is fire."

"Hellfire?" Surely he was smarter than that.

"Manfire. Technology is not out of hand, but society is. At other times in history when this occurred there has been no totally destructive technology."

He was suddenly morose. His shoulders slumped. "Damn." I have never heard him swear before.

"It's easy to understand your own evil," he said. "But just try wrestling with your own goodness."

=

When Barrows left, dawn was lying red and gray and black across the strait. The mountains and islands bulked blue and gray in the dawn, rapt, beyond change. My mind felt like a force of direct calm that could even soothe the wind. Barrows might be troubled, but I was not. I could see clearly that Barrows's power was a method that could end all wars. Society could have another chance.

If I could make things vanish, there would be high old times. I would vanish every weapon in the world. Then the fat cats could go back to throwing rocks. There is a descending order of life on this planet: Homo Sapiens, lobo sapiens, politicians and businessmen. I would not trust the sincerity of any businessman or politician unless he got on television, took a lie detector test to prove that he was himself, and then slit his own throat.

Chapter 5

As chains of command grow long, and as the buck is passed over greater distances, the chance for error and delay increases. Each time a message is passed there is a chance for distortion. Pass that message often enough and distortion is inevitable. That kind of distortion was going to eventually work against us, but for a few hours it worked for us.

We were in a war, and we did not have the foggiest notion that a war was happening. Barrows didn't know it, or even suspect it. There was no reason why he should have. All he had done was make a tree vanish. None of our crew thought that anyone else knew about it. But, as we would find out later, an enormous political and military machine had swung into action because of that tree. Later on, it would make sense. At the time, had we known of it, it would have made no sense at all.

As we later learned, a plane loaded with electronics gear left Philadelphia on schedule and landed in eastern Washington on schedule. The helicopter which was supposed to connect with the plane and transfer the gear still sat at an airfield fifty miles away. The machine that met the plane was a large attack helicopter that was useless in any covert operation. It took hours before the large and useless helicopter was finally replaced with the one that was small and silent.

I spent those hours in both worry and dream. When Barrows left I was hopeful. At the same time I was scared. My mind was engaged in a curious but not unusual split. This mind split has been happening for years, ever since a couple of cops singled me out as the cause for the world's problems, and tried to cure those problems with nightsticks and boots.

Dawn lay across the strait. In a while it would be time to call Julie, who wakes early. If I was going to help Barrows, then it seemed clear that our lives together, Julie's and mine, would be changed. Maybe better, maybe worse, but changed. It is impossible to deal in power and remain a simpleminded timber jock running a company plagued with bureaucratic rules and lack of money.

I had been working a mind-dulling job. The only good part of the job was the woods. The bad part was the day-to-day solving of problems. Tools that broke, contracts behind, payrolls to figure. The woods sustained me, but not well enough to keep my mind reflective or theoretical. I had to get back in touch with my mind.

In other days, back when it still seemed worthwhile to think, I had developed the custom of walking through my old house. It put me in touch with history, with echoes, and the whisper of old ideas. So, as dawn grew orange over the strait, that is what I did.

The steps from the front hall are showy, like a road to upstairs that divides the house. I climbed them and once more thought of the old merchant who built this house. He was a ship's chandler and a leading criminal. He stepped heavy up these stairs because he was heavy. His picture is in the local museum where ragtags clutter and wait the cataloging that will never come. The museum is in the basement of the courthouse. The courthouse will burn. This town will burn.

I have no obsession with fire. This is an old town that has been burning for a century. Each year we lose a house or two because masonry in chimneys has decayed, the sparks from wood fires freed into the walls, or eddying above roofs in light crosswinds. The roofs are cedar shakes.

That old merchant stepped heavy up this stairway that is like a road, the only road he knew. When our harbor was a jumble of clipper ship masts so thick it looked like a skinned forest, that merchant handled bills of lading from all over the world. Ships bundled in from the sea roads of China, Japan, Hawaii, New York. They offloaded stained glass, silks, rice, copper, lead, staples, bond slaves and the mails. They loaded timber.

Did that old merchant, dealing in Chinese slave contracts, feel any of the urgency and dreams of the men who arrived here—the shanghaied Chinese? Did he ever think of other roads?

There's no way to know, but it was worth thinking about. If I wanted to get my mind working, then a feel for history was a good way to get started. I know so much, or once did, about the way society behaves. Studying society is even a worthwhile thing to do— until you take theory into the streets and end up under the boots of cops.

Men *en masse* are almost always clumsy. The great bulk of history is made up of common man following a plow and breathing platitudes at the ass end of a mule.

I walked through the upstairs rooms, the dusty stained glass, ornate wood work, plaster decoration, peeling paint and sprinkling dust. A society made a decision about the time this house was built. These crazy-quilt facades and bulky ornamentation in dull gold leaf are like symbols of a dedication to rape. In the 1880s land, resources and the human mind were despoiled. The Victorians followed trite and destructive styles. These ornate houses are symbols of the avoidance of facts. Pissed off and bitter I might be. Yet I found, walking these old rooms, that I was still ridden by the worst thing a man can have clawing at his back. I still had hope.

It occurred to me that may be society still had hope. Maybe that was the reason it had not taken up arms against the police.

What kind of hope? Forget those white plastic magic consoles where men pushed buttons to feed, clothe and educate the population. Forget the dreams of efficient modular transportation systems. Forget the idea of turning the world into a garden that meant paradise on earth. Those hopes were gone, but it seemed that society must still have hope. I know that I did.

Because, no matter how bad the world was, there was still some courtesy left out there. There was still the palette of human dreams. Maybe, in helping Barrows, there was still something I could say or do that would help somebody else, sometime.

It would soon be time to call Julie. I turned back toward the steps that would take me into that troubled and tumultuous world where there are still dreams. I had some hope this time, but damn, damn, there had been hope on all of those other times as well.

Chapter 6

I LIKE THE WAY HER HAIR FALLS OVER NARROW SHOULDERS, HOW HER breasts move beneath her shirt as she walks, and the way she smiles. She smiles a lot, and the rest of the time she worries. Life is no sleigh ride for Julie.

Her hair is brown, her hands move as if they weave charms. When she is in my house it fills with echoes. The shades of Victorian ladies in long dresses seem to float through the upper halls.

I called her early.

"Something to tell you," I said. "How is Jim?"

Our secret had not lasted the night. None of our crew, not even Mike if he was drunk, would have said anything about that tree vanishing.

"What have you heard?"

"Mystery stuff," she said. "Spooks and goblins and things that go bump." She actually giggled. "Where did you hide that tree?"

"I'll call and ask about Jim," I told her. "Meanwhile, can you take some time off?"

"If it is really important, and if it doesn't get important too often. I talked to Penny last night. Jim was okay then."

Julie is an anthropologist surviving on occasional small grants and part-time office work. Shamans and medicine men and sacred formulas are subjects she considers all the time. Barrows's power would be no surprise to Julie. Julie's life is a forceful following after mystery, contradicted by a Midwest go-to-church upbringing. Even if she is young, she is awfully knowledgeable. She has worked in the Southwest for a year, and did a one-year independent study among some maverick Klingits in Alaska.

When our conversation was finished I hung up, made coffee, and called Jim. Penny answered, and she answered brisk.

"Is Jim okay?" I asked.

"Is this Jake?"

"Sure. How is Jim?"

"In much better shape than you're going to be when I catch you." She hung up.

I poured coffee into a thermos and actually felt pleased. Penny was just doing her front number. When Jim was ready he would get in touch.

High clouds, mixed sunlight and sometimes a spatter of rain; a day for the windy, cold beaches along the strait. Julie, Julie, how did you get so smart when so many are so dumb. I think of you. Sometimes too often and too much. I think Julie cares for me because of my ideals. There's nothing else I can figure. She is thirty-three and beautiful, while I'm going bald. I move okay. Anyone moves good if he works out of doors. There was Barrows . . . I did not even want to know how old he was.

Barrows. I had time to walk around before meeting Julie. Winter was nearly over. When the rain popped in splatters it was different from winter rain. It rarely freezes here. It rarely snows.

My mind was still engaged in that split which has been happening ever since those cops beat the shit out of me in a street demonstration. My mind walked my body through the sunlight, and I appreciated the new green poking through the soil; crocuses never learn. They always come up too early. At the same time the dark side of my mind was working. It was like lying on a sunny beach while listening to recorded testimony from the Nuremberg trials.

=

"The race is doomed."

Barrows had said that last night.

"I think you 're right," I had told him. It had been late. "If they throw the big stuff then I know you're right. Maybe in a few back areas, where there are caverns or mines, a few people may survive."

"Those weapons will be used," he said. "Other weapons that are even worse will be used."

"Slow down," I told him. It had been about twelve hours since the tree vanished, about three hours before he would shrug into his jacket and leave in the dawn. I had leaned back in my chair and looked through the stained-glass windows at the moon. The moon was weird, changeable, remote. It was austere or funny depending on the color of stained glass I chose. The moon changed from green to orange to nearly black.

"All positions have the same conclusions," Barrows said. "Fundamentalists believe in the end of the world. Evolutionists say that through genetic manipulation the race will change. Visionaries say that man will enter and settle out in space."

"In which case," I told him, "there is no chance for human psychology to remain as it is. If the psychological rut changes, there will be evolutionary change. I know that sounds crazy."

"Not nearly as crazy as UFOs belonging to corporations, which they do; or that the first successful experiment in anti-gravity has been suppressed since the 1950s."

Anti-gravity. And the moon was weird. I jockeyed around to look through a blue pane of glass. The moon was green. Wind started to pop again from the strait. Wind comes from a single direction here, sometimes. It blows like a pack of hunting wolves. I watched the moon. There was a question I had to ask.

"Can you stop a bunch of infantile politicians from throwing bombs?"

"I could stop most of their bombs," Barrows said. "Two or three people with my ability could stop all of the bombs."

My fatigue had begun to move away. Barrows had watched my reaction.

"That is only one alternative," he said.

"I'd admire to hear the others."

He told me. He had a vague idea about gradually restructuring society. He actually believed that government and business might cooperate if he used his powers to get rid of pollution and end the arms race. Hopelessly idealistic, I thought, or hopelessly innocent.

Still, he was on the right track. I listened to all he said, and thought about it after he left; and I thought about it now, on my way to talk to Julie, walking in sunlight. I had been up for twenty-seven hours and my legs were good, my mind clear even if it was split. It is amazing how strong we can be when we are pressed by great ideas and hopes.

Winter, summer, sun or storm, Julie and I like the beach because there are no cosmetics. It is elemental. The tide pools churn with life and death. The wind tears at rocks. The surf crashes and sprays. Nature is indifferent.

On the beach there are no critics. The Ladies' Aid, the VFW and the Chamber of Commerce are lapping tea or booze and licking at each other in parlors and churches and bars of this town. When people meet on the beach there is a chance for civilization. If one of those people is Julie the chances increase. In forty-eight years I've met a few people who will not lie about anything to anyone. One is Julie, another is a friend of mine named Max, another is a friend named Dolores, and I don't think Barrows lies either.

Julie came toward me with her hair blowing in tangles and with more authority in her manner than an ambassador at a dinner party. Julie is almost always confident and in control. Sometimes, not often, but sometimes, she can become confused and helpless. That usually happens when she gets in a situation she does not like. I wondered quickly how she was going to handle the news of Barrows and his power.

The sun highlighted blue eyes and the oval contour of her face so often obscured by her long hair. The snowcapped mountain range was at her back.

"You've made this week for a lot of people." She hugged me and we headed for the lee of a big rock. "How is Jim?"

"Married."

"At least it's to Penny." She reached for the thermos. "Yum. Are you going to tell me what happened?"

"Didn't Penny?"

"You know her better."

"Then you know it was a secret. How in the hell it ever got out . . ."

"This is a small town," she said. "What do you expect? I heard," she said, and she counted each rumor off on her fingers, "that Jim got trapped by a tree and the tree disappeared . Then I heard that

Jim was crazy. Then I heard that you tried to kill him. Then I heard that Barrows was a Communist. Then I heard that the manx at the boatshop had seven kittens . . . three gray-stripey ones, three yellow ones, and one that's fluffy black. Four have tails and three haven't, but I don't know who has what."

"I love living in this hick town . . ."

"And then," she said, "I heard that the state agencies are going to enjoin your job."

"What?"

"You didn't file some report or other."

"I did."

"Very probably you didn't. Then I heard that Ann has to rewire her building because the wiring burned up."

"I filed every one of their crap reports."

"You probably didn't." She giggled. "Then I heard that Dolores finally got an almost new truck for her lab, and the only way a single girl can get a truck like that in this town is to sin a lot in some other town . . . which in Dolores's case might be true but in her case is not sin . . . and then I heard that Sandy's bar is putting in linoleum tile so they can give dances." She began laughing outright. "You didn't file the report," she said. "You bitched so hard and long about it that you thought you'd filed it."

"The old gossips have really been bending your ear."

"It's getting serious," she said, "because it wastes so much time."

"Mrs. McKenzie?"

"Yep. And Mrs. Porter and old Sam Johnson, the whole tongue-wagging crew. There isn't a phone in town that isn't overheated. This is very good coffee."

"Barrows caused that tree to vanish," I said. "The important thing is that the town thinks we were either drunk or lying."

"If it helps," Julie said, "the consensus is that you were drunk *and* lying."

"Good," I said. "The old sonsabitches."

I could see her pain. Julie is not a counterpuncher. She is the eternal peace seeker.

"Let's walk," she said. "The world makes me sad and you mad."

When we walk it is always serious. Two or three miles up the beach and return, or cut off through a pasture and return along country roads. That is for a cold and windy day. On warm days a walk can find us unrolling sleeping bags in the dark. Sometimes we talk. Sometimes we are silent together for hours. This was a day for talk.

Barrows was psychic. We discussed that.

"It's more common than you might think," Julie said. "Most people have some psychic ability. I've seen it time and time again in tribes."

"Do tribal peoples train their psychic ability?"

"Not often," she said. "Mostly they just use it without thinking about it. It's almost uncanny. I've seen a man leave home in the morning, drift around half the day, and get talked in to going fishing. If you ask his wife where he is, she will know, although no messages have been passed."

"That's telepathy. Powerful stuff."

"It's old news to a lot of native people," she said. "I figure that Barrows must have worked for years to perfect his ability."

"He does not want to play at being God," I told Julie. "It's a good thing. He could nearly control the world."

"A god has to make things appear, not make them vanish."

"That's one point he made," I said, "but some kind of creative factor is working. What he makes appear is space."

"Where do the things go?"

"He doesn't know. I figure they are either displaced in time, or that he pulls space out of inner space."

"To which . . . I say good. And you can just slow down. C'mere." She pulled close. The wind did nice things with her hair, laying it across her face and across mine. We stood in the wind and simply held each other. It was not sex or love but the warm affirmation that comes from long experience with both. Sometimes we stand together content with our experience.

"I am a kind of mystic," she said finally, "and I am first of all an anthropologist. God knows what Barrows is. Explain slowly."

"I am old and wise . . ."

"And copping a feel."

"Uh huh."

"Sleeping bag weather, though." She snuggled closer. "Now put your hand . . . yes, well trained." She was smiling and there was that easy, and easy-to-make-grown hunger in her eyes.

The hell with Barrows, with society, with things that vanish. Sooner or later it all vanishes.

"I always love this next line," she said. "My place or yours?"

"Yours is closer. "

"Keen intellect. Keen." The wind kept doing all of those nice things with her hair. "Tell me about inner space."

"Walk or carry."

We headed up the beach toward her house. The hopefulness of a new chance for society was all mixed in with loving her. I thought at the time that Barrows had been right when he said that we had more time than we needed.

Chapter 7

MILITARY DOCTRINES COME AND GO, BUT THROUGH THE CENTURIES some things have remained constant. Even in these days of electronic gear that can see and hear through brick walls, the military still likes to mount a major attack in daylight. It likes to run its covert operations at night. The military is still as superstitious as those old barbarians who attacked in daylight so that their souls could find heaven if they were killed.

Since covert operations were called against the town of Land's End, the attack was delayed until dark. There were other reasons as well. Our mayor had to wait for the banks to open. He had to draw out money, make a little trip, and get that money out front before any of his part of the business could get moving. A couple of hit men in Boston missed one regularly scheduled flight and had to wait in a coffee shop for another.

We in Land's End believed that we had as much time as we needed. We expected no attack.

In this year of 1991 the U.S. had learned nothing from recent experience. I was born forty-eight years ago, during World War II. I was a kid during Korea, prime cannon age during Vietnam. During those years I watched a fat-minded civilization compete against itself to grab the last cookie in the jar.

George Orwell's predictions for 1984 did not miss by much, and they did not come fully true for one reason. Industrial nations depleted resources at a rate that allowed for elaborate social control in places, but no control in others. Figuratively speaking, the fat cats ran out of gas. There were only so many resources, and as they declined, government and business had to use them to help maintain an otherwise dying economy. There were not enough spare resources to spend on elaborate police structures. In some places in the nation people lived in a police state. In other places they had no police or government at all. American greed did not save America from becoming a police state, but the cookie jar mentality did. Still, in 1991, the police state was becoming well formed.

Julie and I made love, slow, confident. Then we lay together and talked.

"Barrows has inconceivable power," she said.

"Not if you think of parallel universes."

"Don't give me that, baby. The Navajos already told me all about that."

"That's the anthropologist talking."

"That's the scared lady talking." She lay naked beside me, and already her body seemed under some tension. She was afraid, and I could not understand why.

"Science won't help you with this one," Julie told me. "The sooner you forget science, the better off you'll be."

In a way she was right. Unless science could set up controls, and duplicate phenomena, most scientists would insist that phenomena do not exist. The social sciences, if they are sciences, which they are not, are among the worst offenders. Science would not believe in Barrows's power in the first place.

"I depend on no science but my own," I told her. "Every time I depend on another's science, I either lose a friend or a job."

"I hope you won't lose me." She did not say it like a threat, but her sadness and fear were apparent.

"I'll tell you a story," I said.

"For many years I've had a friend who reminds me of Barrows, except that Max is only three years older than I am. He seems somehow happier than Barrows. Max and I were fired from the same university for different reasons.

"My own reason was because I took political action to the streets when I was already on the shit list. I asked strenuous questions of the wrong people, people in power. Max made the list by remaining silent in the face of technicians who believed that the end of inquiry had been achieved by computers.

"If Barrows made things vanish, it was no more than other people have done at other times. There is documented proof that people can walk on fire. Those people know that ash buildup is an insulation against heat. They have thick calluses. Sometimes they get burned. Still, some walk on impossible fires. There are reliable reports of vanishment. Telepathy can sometimes be demonstrated. The old Rhine Institute used to demonstrate telepathy, but it was abandoned in the eighties for lack of funds.

"Max and I were interested in this unexplained phenomena, because we thought it related to another idea that we were trying to understand. We were interested in the creative power of groups. Somewhere between August Compte's idea of the group mind, and Ralph Emerson's idea of the Oversoul, there was a valid force that operated in history. Whether it was closer to Compte's 'mind of a people' or Emerson's 'creative energy,' we did not know, but it was not just mob psychology. When it created, it mostly created hell— like the Nazis. Max and I thought that groups could also create positive things."

"I've not talked about it." I watched Julie. She seemed not quite as tense. She was interested.

"There is such a mind in tribes," she said. "I'm not talking about consensus. "

"Me either. You want lunch?"

"I wanta stay here and be naked with you."

She pretended a pout. Grinned. Stopped. "Where is Max now?"

"Works at a department store in Billings."

"I'm pretty scared," she said. "I am really no kidding pretty scared."

I understood her. "You're scared because you think I might do something, take some action?"

"Baby, I know you. Of course you'll do something, whether you know it yet or not. I'm going to have to try to stop you." She shook her head back and forth, back and forth. Determination. "Good intentions and ends and means . . . they end up causing trouble."

"But, with Barrows . . ."

She interrupted me. "He should find a woman."

That was the go-to-church Julie talking. Maybe Barrows should find a woman.

"He was married once," I said. "Maybe he got cured." It went right past her. She was thinking of something else.

"You're really going to do it, even with that bad temper. You're going to do something." She sat up and her narrow shoulders and full breasts and wonderful, lovely hands were enough to make me want to say the hell with the whole thing. Take care of Julie first. Who was more important than Julie?

"I love you," I told her. A truly inept thing to say.

"Me too. I love you. If I don't love you later, I really and truly love you now."

We got it smooth before I left, her fear calmed, my anger close-hauled. When we were feeling together again, it was time for her to go back to work and for me to leave.

I did not go directly home, which is probably a good thing. A nasty little electronic device had been planted near my house. If I had gone directly home, the thing would have had an additional hour with which to work me over. I walked a little way up the beach. There is a trail that leads over to a country road. The long way home. But scenic.

Chapter 8

THE TRAIL TO THE COUNTY ROAD IS NARROW AND TANGLED WITH salal and Oregon grape. I pushed through the brush and began to understand Julie's fear. I had some fear of my own.

Barrows was too great to handle. He might say that he needed my advice, and he might believe it, but he held ultimate control.

Julie feared that I would take action. The only action I could take was as an advisor. Being an advisor is taking one whale of a lot of action. History is just stinking with advisors who gave the wrong advice. We would never have had World War II with the Japanese if Roosevelt's advisors had told him to assure Japan that it would always have an oil supply. Japan was afraid of China, the U.S. cut back oil, and Japan had to strike in an attempt to control oil fields to the south.

Barrows could choose to use his power. He could choose not to use it. Maybe he would end up using me as nothing but a tool. Julie might turn from me. If I was not careful I would end up a lonely old man.

On the other hand, if I was careful, then it probably meant that I already was a lonely old man. There are no guarantees.

Three or four times a week the rain flows in from the Pacific to lay a gray shroud over the Washington Peninsula. The forests take the gray sky and reflect green darkness. The Strait of Juan de Fuca goes from silver to gray to gray-black, returning then to silver. The darkness comes and goes, and it does it winter, summer and all the time. The rain flows and undulates. It damps fires and throws up smoke and mystery. Magic seems never very far away. Barrows would not be the first to show me that the mysterious does not always speak an unknown language.

I kicked through the salal and was glad for life and afraid of love. Julie can do that to me.

I understood her fear. Barrows's power was so great that anything he did would bring big consequences. As an anthropologist, Julie had seen enough cultures ruined because someone from another culture had tried to do good. Anthropologists and missionaries have probably done more to destroy other cultures and peoples than did the conquistadores in South America.

The old gossips in town who bothered Julie were tough, not timid. They were survivors. Some were born just after World War I and Roza McKenzie before then. If they had lived that long, there was not much that even a degraded and dying government could show them. There is not much practical illusion here. The wind surrounds, the rain meshes, and life can be hard.

The weather, the elements, are part of the reason most people cannot stand it here. The timid people need comfortable illusions: neon memories, twenty-four-hour pharmacies and instant fried chicken. They need police sirens calling in the night to tell them their protectors are awake.

=

It's a long hike to town because the road loops. It follows the beach but breaks away toward what used to be a series of homesteads. In the old days the road was built to and for the people. Now the people from those homesteads are gone, but the road is unchanged. I came to this place because I like echoes and I dislike crap. The crap level in this place is pretty low.

I came to get away from Out There. Out There is just about every other place in the country.

Out There is why a man gets bitter, and the question is how anyone raised to American tradition would not be bitter. The stink is too high. Free enterprise died with World War II and the rise of the corporate state. Even the myth of individualism died in the choking coils of bureaucratic red tape. The government became warlord, vengeful master after Nuremberg and the political excesses of the sixties and seventies.

Barrows said I had to get a handle on my temper. Mike is nineteen. Every time anyone I care about gets to be nineteen, some political or corporate jackass brays about national pride and historic necessity and sends them off to war.

=

A beat-up old panel truck pulled alongside. Gimp Sam offered me a ride. Sam has one short leg, a thin beard, and he makes a living by fishing or picking up work here and there. Sometimes he works with us when we're on a tight schedule. He's a nice guy when he's sober. When he's drunk he throws things. Down from Alaska. God knows where before that.

"Thanks Sam," I said as I climbed out in front of my house.

"You guys working or drinking?"

"So-so."

"If you need any help."

"I'll get in touch." I turned toward the house. If I needed help I could hire fifty men in five minutes. This town is like a ghetto when it comes to people needing work.

In the house a stack of money lay on the kitchen table. I sat down and looked at it. A note from Barrows said replace the saws. I flipped through the bucks. Eight thousand. We only needed one saw and one bar. If he wanted, Barrows could conceptualize a laser-sized space through the base of a tree and the sonovabitch would fall down by itself.

I didn't want to think about money and economics, but I did. Out There it was certain that at least four million people would starve in the next year. Another half million would die in assorted wars. Hundreds of thousands would die through industrial accidents or industrial wars. The clash of high-priced corporate machines against other corporate machines.

Damn. Damn. The economist Malthus showed that when population grows beyond the available food supply the positive checks of war, famine and disease come into play. What he didn't know, back in those days, is that lack of transportation and distribution can also bring that about.

I called Mike and told him to come over. His voice was steady. It didn't sound as if he were drinking.

I called Jim. Penny answered. "Don't hang up."

"Of course not, Jake." Something had happened. Penny was talking sweet.

"Is Jim okay?"

"Sleeping again. He's slept one whole hell of a lot." Penny can out cuss a fisherman. "Barrows is here."

"Put him on." As I talked to Barrows the rumble of Mike's ice-cold hot rod came from the drive. The door slammed, and I heard Mike climb through the back entrance. I wanted to call a meeting. Barrows was reserved. "Not a meeting. I'll drop by your place tonight."

"About this money?"

"Don't worry." His voice was gentle, like he explained something to a child that had been explained a dozen times. "You've been up thirty-six hours. Get some sleep."

How did he know? Of course he knew. With his ability he could see anyone at any time. That meant the end of privacy.

"You keeping track of me?" I was pissed.

"No," he said, "I just know you pretty well."

"Eight o'clock?"

"Get some sleep."

I turned to find Mike staring reverently at the stack of bills. Mike is tall and muscular, big features, heavy brows, big nose. He wears his hair to the shoulders and ties it back in the woods. Sometimes he grows a beard and sometimes he gets disgusted and shaves. For the last couple of weeks he had shaved.

"You rob the bank," he asked.

"Barrows came up with the bucks."

He believed me. When you are young you have to believe plenty. Later it changes.

"Is that junk running?"

He was hurt. I should not talk bad about his car, even if it is a ragged-out heap. He nodded.

"Get gas from the company tank and go to Seattle. Buy two saws and a bar like we've been using. We'll have a spare." Lumber is an essential industry. We usually get as much fuel as we need."

"Why not here?"

"Even on the black market it would take three weeks, and people would talk. Where would we get this kind of money? People would want to know." I counted out four thousand. "Two saws, trip expense, chow and music."

He did not even say wow.

"Take a girl."

"She's already there."

"I didn't know that."

"I ain't met her yet."

"You get mashed last night?"

"Got up this morning feeling fine."

"Seen Barrows?"

"No."

"Got yesterday figured out?"

"Kinda."

"You're holding out." When he goes monosyllabic it means that he is not saying anything about his feelings.

"Two saws."

"And work tomorrow. Have fun."

"I'll keep it to myself." He eased backward out the doorway and I wanted to go after him and tell him it was just life. It would be over pretty soon. It was just youth, and that also passes. The starter turned and turned, his shit box came alive and rumbled off. The fatigue was working me over. I headed for the sack. While I slept the first attack began.

Chapter 9

When I woke I urgently needed to get laid. Boobs and legs and hot mouths knotted in my imagination. I wanted Julie, but if not Julie then Dolores. Dolores and I lived together once . . . push that one away, that hurts . . . I have experienced these feelings before and know why they come. They come from frustration and a feeling of helplessness.

It was not quite dark. The days were getting longer. In deep winter here we go to work in the dark, return in the dark, and are lucky to see seven hours of light. In much of this Northwest you cannot work in winter. We are in the rain shadow of the Olympic Mountains, but when it rains it rains hard.

The last light gave the stained glass windows a dull glow. The room was cold. There was no fire in the heating stove. There was none in the kitchen. Daylight would last long enough for me to bring in wood and get coffee started.

My mind jumped back and forth like toads in a garden. The sex urge pulsed. I forced myself to think of making things vanish. I thought of the consternation that would be rampant if all weapons disappeared. How I needed to get laid. I picked up an armload of kindling and returned to the house. The kitchen range is old. It may have been the original stove in this house. I laid a fire, flipped a match, and in a minute the stove began to pop as the cedar took hold. How many days of fire has that stove seen?

Fire, fire, fire. It throbbed in my testicles and knotted the back of my neck. When I feel good about life I think of loving, not screwing. Fury starts deep and builds until it finally breaks. A man lives with hope and gets old. He dreams and acts and believes he can make the world a better place. Instead, the world gets worse. My fury lay just beneath the surface. A memory of good sense told me to say this to Barrows.

There were light footsteps in the hall. A normal, fairly rapid pace. A woman. I waited for a knock on the door and none came. Things like that happen in this house, and they happen in human minds that are under stress.

The stove popped, spit, was settling into the hum of a working fire. Four, maybe five generations of women have stood before this stove. Women in love, women in hate. Mothers, wives, spinsters standing in front of a stove where now stood an aging guy hearing things that were invisible.

Generations of women. Daughters and lesbians and mistresses, grandmothers and sisters and old maids. Role and definition.

A good thought occurred. Barrows was going to arrive at eight, and he would stay late. When Barrows left I would call Max. That would give me two perspectives. It would do Max good to be dragged from the sack at two or three in the morning to hear a voice from his past. I could see his bleary eyes and unshaven mug, his Yid face and the black hair streaked with gray. It made me laugh and the laugh was hysterical.

Clearly I was nuts. After a man lives long enough he can read the signs. The fire hummed. The room seemed to shrink. My mind felt compressed, in pain; the fine reasoning power of the mind fading. A scatter of problems hit. Bills to pay. The state might enjoin the job. Julie might not love me. I was old, old. Barrows was going to use me.

The phone rang. I staggered across the kitchen, across the bigger of the living rooms that seemed as long as a barn, fumbled for the phone.

A voice as gentle as Julie's hands said, "Dear friend, dear Jake, be careful."

"Max?" It couldn't be Max.

It was Max.

"He is a troubled man, this Barrows."

"Max, dammit."

There was a buzz of dial tone. No click. No hum.

Footsteps in the hall. I lurched to the door to capture my ghost, to wring sense from the invisible. From the deserted second floor came the sound of a child running, romping, and now from the hall the low voice of a woman. "Jake, are you there? Are you there?" I opened the door. No one.

A man's voice from upstairs, distant, harassing the child. It did not sound like Max.

"Come out of it." Barrows was there, like a man who had stepped through an invisible doorway. He led me to a chair. I felt different pressures in my mind, felt the madness dissolve like the scatter of water drops dancing on a hot stove. The room held an indefinite and changing variety of shapes. I did not recognize the room.

I closed my eyes, opened them. It was the same old room and Barrows was there. The firm hand that guided me to the chair was on my shoulder. He gave me a small shake, then turned to drag up a chair.

"Tell me." His voice was gentle, but it was not easy. Trouble in his voice said that this was more than simple concern for a friend. The room was cold. There were no sounds from the kitchen. The fire was out.

"What time is it?"

"Eight."

"The time is off. I had a fire started. I've lost at least an hour."

"What happened?"

I told him all of it—the invisible voices and echoes. I told him of Max. An impossible phone call. Hallucination.

"It was like being walked over by a wave. It was like being engulfed."

"Can you account for it?"

"I haven't taken any drugs, if that's what you mean."

"I'm trying to rule out possibilities," he said. "I'm afraid we have attracted trouble."

It bothered me that the room was still cold. I wanted to be moving, doing.

"We can talk when it's warm." I stood to point myself at the kitchen.

"This is urgent. You seem to have been attacked."

"Who from?"

"I'm trying to figure that out." He looked kind of ashamed. I could not understand why he should look that way.

"Empty your mind," he said.

I stood before the stove, closed my eyes, tried not to think. The image of a naked woman danced, faded, flicked back and departed. There was a whisper, unintelligible, fading.

"Residuals." I told him what had happened.

"Let's get out of here. I want you on neutral ground."

Downtown the low cloud cover still hung in back of the mountains, and the strait lay calm. Lights from the finger piers, from the moored Coast Guard cutter, from buoys and fishing boats, lay like narrow paths in the water. I pulled the truck into a parking spot on the main drag. The street was nearly empty.

There are four bars in town. I was parked so I could see three of them. There is a bar for freaks. Another is for business types and the local power elite. A third is for youth, Indians, and small-town hoods. The other is a redneck bar for loggers.

I am a logger but not a redneck, which makes me one of the working freaks. I was entitled to spend bar evenings with a good poet, some painters, a few musicians, and one hell of a lot of burned out hulks. Mike would be welcome at the hood bar if he wasn't carded. Jim would go to the redneck bar. Barrows doesn't drink.

"I ate nothing," I told Barrows. "No one could have slipped me any drugs. May be the psychological pressure and the fatigue were more than I imagined."

"I hope so, but I doubt it." Barrows seemed less urgent. Barrows has no sense of formality or informality. Right now he leaned half against the seat and half against the door of the truck. One knee was propped against the dash. The ember of his cigarette occasionally illuminated his face. The face was crinkled, shadowed, a broken crisscross in the light of the cigarette and the half-light shining through the windshield from the bar sign.

"Try again."

I closed my eyes, emptied my mind, but it would not stay empty. Thoughts of Julie, thoughts of the next day's work, little worry thoughts about whether Mike would get back safe from Seattle.

"Normal."

"At your house I had a strong sense of something mechanical present."

"You didn't examine it?"

"I only located it and got rid of it. I rarely examine anything."

"Why?"

"Most of it is none of my business." He dragged on the smoke, rolled the window, flipped the butt into the gutter. "In this case I didn't want to waste time. I just wanted rid of the thing."

"Thing?"

"Some kind of sound transmitter," he said. He paused. "The other reason I rarely examine things is because I don't want to get overloaded."

"You can take care of yourself."

"One way I do that is not to get overloaded. Do you know any big city police?"

"A couple of them beat the shit out of me once. I know something about criminology."

He sat up straight, then half tucked his beard into his chest and watched the street. We were parked close to the freak bar. Two dogs were tied by the doorway. They sniffed each other in the same way they had probably sniffed on a hundred nights while waiting for their human connections to stop drinking.

"I try not to get overloaded, the way a big city policeman gets overloaded," said Barrows. "The worst part of their job is the day to day dealing with seamy matters. The mind can only take so much."

"So you can read minds."

"I've never tried. Partly self-protection. Partly morals."

What he said was easy to understand. Barrows is an ethical man who did not want to pry. I do not value society, but do value human dignity. Privacy is required, especially privacy of thought.

"A long time ago," Barrows said, "I took on a responsibility. From the first I was opposed." He lit another smoke. I restarted the engine to run the heater. Mist was forming on the windshield.

"I thought the opposition was dead," Barrows told me. "Now I think the opposition has quietly kept track of me all along."

"Why?"

"No one in our crew said a word about that tree, yet the story is all over town."

"There was no one on that grade but us."

"We were surely observed."

"You want a beer while you explain that one?"

"I'll watch you drink one, and I'll tell you the story."

I cut the engine and we climbed from the truck. The mist was beginning to roll in. On the strait the lighted pathways were dim. The water lapped, ran, popped against bulkheads. When we got to the bar it was nearly deserted. Two hulks felt each other up in a booth. They were both male. Residue. Minds burned out from acid, speed, smack. A woman sat at the bar, bored, an untouched glass of wine before her. She had a wide bottom that spread beyond the barstool, but her hair was long and smooth and Indian black and that was nice. The guy tending bar startled. He hid the joint.

"Hey, Jake." He drew a beer. Barrows and I took a booth away from the lovers.

"Sometimes I interfere," Barrows said. "Last night Mike was dangerously drunk. I entered his system and gradually removed the alcohol as he slept. It isn't unusual."

"I hope Mike can handle this."

"I hope we all can." The urgency was gone from his voice, but not entirely from his manner.

"This started after Reconstruction," he said. "There were other times when things like this started, but it was not until after the Civil War that technology could handle the situation. A group of men decided to control the world."

"That's not new." I looked around the dump. The bar is on the ground floor of a Victorian building. It used to be a combination hotel, shipping agency and warehouse. That accounts for the twenty-foot high ceilings, for the heavy rafters to hold rigging that could move tons of freight from lighters moored at the rear of the building. Beneath the building is a now un-secret passage where shanghaied Chinese, drifters, loggers and whores were channeled to various destinations and fates.

"It was only technology," Barrows said. "The feelings of superiority were no different."

"Rich men."

"The rich do not believe they are superior. They know it."

"And they write amused essays to each other about the masses . . ."

I was so filled with concealed fury that I could not continue. I looked at the woman who still sat unmoving before her glass. The reason this town supports a freak bar is because street people from the sixties and seventies drifted here from Seattle and San Francisco.

That girl was maybe superior in the days before acid and speed. Now she was only rich with hair. I was willing to bet that she brushed it twice a day, smiling at a mirror that did not show her wide butt and thick legs, a mirror that showed a wino face encompassed with a wealth of hair, a mind as dreamless as a desert.

"All kinds of contempt," Barrows said. "There is also the contempt of the military."

"That one I know about."

Barrows looked at the oak bar, the high ceilings, seemed listening to the mutter from the high-backed booth where the hulks might still be feeling each other. "A lot of things happened after Reconstruction," he said.

"The big rip off."

"Railways. Shipping. Experiments in light and sound. As late as the 1880s and 90s there was a craze called mental science or mental dynamics."

"Mary Baker Eddy," I said. "I despise religion, but at least she was not afraid of the mystical."

"You are going too fast." Barrows seemed nearly impatient. "Both you and Julie use that term 'mystical' pretty loosely . . ."

He was suddenly alert. He did not seem nervous, but the sense of urgency was back.

"What's the matter?"

"Visitors. Stop talking." He leaned back and closed his eyes. "Mike is all right."

"Julie?"

"Is safe. Jim . . . something is wrong up there. Sit tight."

From the street came the sound of motorcycle engines. The engines shut off. Silence. Then a thump. A dog screamed, yelped, cried. More thumps. Heavy.

The fury lying in my mind became a singing and celebrating thing. It poised, about to come loose now.

More thumps. A second dog screamed and the door banged open, swung hard, kicked to help it along. Two bikers followed the door like an explosion. They had no business here. They belonged in the joint down the street.

They were the usual variety of pet goons. Two-bit pirates. Their filthy jackets were marked with lube and faded club emblems. They had heavy shoulders, slim hips, busted-up hands and hair greasy enough to match their jackets. These were from a Seattle club. Sometimes the mills hire them to trash the union. Sometimes the union hires them to trash its own members.

"Man," said one of the hulks, "man, that was muh dog." He stood, a blond guy with weak eyes who was afraid. The girl turned around on the barstool, looked at the bikers, sat silent. The bartender was moving slow like he was going for something, an illegal gun. The bikers stood in the middle of the room and watched him. The bartender stopped moving, fiddled around like he was checking the cash register, gave up and turned back with empty hands.

"My dog, man." The hulk would not let it be. One biker turned, bored, walked to him with the quick spring and hit, and indifference in the hit that made it efficient. The hulk went against a booth, bounced, was hit again, fell and was kicked.

The fury hummed in my mind. I watched the biker. I almost loved the son of a bitch. He was a dead man and I was going to help him be that way.

The hulk lay silent. Outside a dog moaned. The girl started to scream, choked it, held her hands over her mouth.

I got set.

"Ease off," Barrows told me. He still had his eyes closed.

"You," the biker said to Barrows.

I came from the booth yelling. As I came, time suspended the way it does in a fight. I threw my empty beer glass into his face, the glass arcing slow, timeless, collapsing in a shatter against his forehead. The leather cap flying away, the dark dago face erupting blood that was black in the badly lighted bar. Behind the face, high on the wall and indifferent as history, an antique, neon-circled clock stood over his head like a halo. I was going to kill this man. The beer glass did a good job. It missed the eye, though. You can get one free shot with a biker if you move quick. I could have wished for a better shot.

A table was in the way. The slow shatter of glass spread across it, bounced and the biker followed, moving forward and shoving the table into me so I was off balance and pushed backward.

He was across the table and on me. There was no halo now, the clock turned sideways or I was. I caught his shoulder to make him brace and spread his legs, got a knee in his crotch, threw him sideways and watched him catch his balance and return. The guy must have an iron jock. My fury still sang, and I deliberately took a hard one under the heart to get at his throat, chopping against the first pain and quick exhaustion. He backed away, started to get set and I moved to grab his slick head and get a thumb in his eye. It worked, and then he was away. He was slick with blood. I followed, caught three hard, fast shots. He was good. I had not expected him to be that good. I pushed away.

The guy backed, bent, and then the dumb shit went for his boot. His hand rose arcing and my foot caught him in the throat right where it is supposed to go. His knife sailed from his hand, passed my hip and bounced from a table behind us. The guy fell, twisting, rolling away, and I caught my balance and leaned against a table. He choked and I checked the other dude.

The hit guy rolled, gasped, started to come back . . . and my gut and heart were sick from the way he rolled away like that . . . The neon was a thin glow on the wall or in space. My eyes were not working good. The neon was out there somewhere.

It had been a good shot. The biker got to his knees, hacked like a death rattle. He fell forward, gasped, flopped.

Now I was afraid that I really had killed him. The fury was drained. The girl was screaming, and now the bartender was moving.

"Don't do it." Barrows was talking to the second biker. His voice was easy, like he was asking the guy if he wanted doughnuts and coffee.

I did not want to have to take another one, but I was set. I was too old for this kind of foolishness. The second biker started for his boot, saw the bartender coming with an ax handle and thought better of it. The guy was sure no Hell's Angel. He was confused. He could not understand how they could have lost.

"Out," the bartender said. The second biker walked to the one who was still choking, pulled him to his feet and started to walk. He said nothing. He had said nothing. Usually they tell you they'll be back. He just looked around, looked at faces, and then shoved the first guy across the room and through the doorway.

"Take care of him." Barrows pointed to the blond guy who was still down. The bartender went to him. So did the girl. His buddy hid in the booth, whimpering. Outside the bikes kicked on. The engines cracked like sharp words. They pulled away, but they pulled away real slow.

"Let's go." Barrows was already moving. I pushed away from the table, nearly fell on my ass, got steady and walked.

"Thanks, Jake." The bartender had the blond guy on his feet.

"Next time get a bigger ax handle."

I was moving okay. Nothing broke. What a stupid way to live. Stupid. Stupid.

The mist was thicker. It seemed trying to bury the street. Lights from the other bars, from the bank, from a restaurant were dim in the mist. I fumbled for the keys and passed them to Barrows. "You drive."

"Yes," he said. "You did not have to do that, and we're headed for Jim's house. If it helps any, we've won the first round ."

"I did it for me."

"We've got a mystery," Barrows said, and his voice was grim. "It's one I don't like."

"What?"

"We seem to be dealing with real power. Some power out there has the most sophisticated equipment in the world. Why would any organization that powerful bother to hire a couple of hoodlums?"

"Is Jim all right?"

"One more piece of electronics gear has vanished from the world," said Barrows. He climbed in the truck. We traveled a lot faster than the mist would allow. It came to me that the dogs must have been pretty badly broken up. Neither had been outside. That was the sort of kindness you could expect from Barrows. The blond guy would think his dog had broken loose and run away.

Chapter 10

WE MADE A MISTAKE, BARROWS AND I, AS WE DROVE TOWARD JIM'S house. We assumed that the attacks were either under control, or over. We assumed that we knew the nature of the attacks. Sound waves and thugs. I can forgive Barrows for making those assumptions because he is dumb about attack situations. I cannot forgive myself.

We pulled up to Jim's house, bailed out of the truck, and walked quickly to the door. Knocked. If I had been on the ball, we would have run to that door and begun searching for the real enemy.

When she opened the door, Penny was steaming mad. At some other time it might have been almost funny. Penny cannot weigh more than eighty-five pounds, but a bobcat is not very big, either. When she isn't a bobcat, she is more like an inflamed skunk .

She comes from eastern Oregon, where kids are raised knowing about horses. Penny's family is made up of cowboys and cowgirls who live by the rule that says if you have to punch a cop, then punch him good.

She looked at the blood on my face and gave a little sniff that was close to contempt. "What happened to you."

"What happened to Jim?"

"How did you know?"

"At least let us inside. "

She stepped back and Barrows and I followed. The new house smelled of caulk, fresh cedar, wax and paint. Jim and Penny put it up without much help from the rest of us. The girl is like steel cable. She's also pretty. Wears her hair long. Narrow face, narrow nose, narrow all over, and the long hair does not make her look taller.

They built a conventional log house. It is modern with an odd accumulation of furniture. They managed to get hold of some new stuff that was actually usable from the black market. The place looked nothing at all like the ranch where Penny was raised, or the logging camps where Jim came up.

"He'll live," Penny said. "Do something."

Jim sat in the most comfortable chair and seemed to be staring at space. Barrows walked to him.

"Wash your face." Penny was actually behind me and pushing me. It felt okay. Sometimes you like for someone to be practical.

It was mostly the biker's blood on my face and shirt. He had opened me up on one cheekbone. Going for my nose. You can really slow a man if you can break his nose.

I looked at the bathroom mirror. Stupid. My stupid face looked back. The thin jaw, the balding dome. It was a long, Englishy-looking snoot that should have been easy to break.

"Toss me a shirt." I began to strip. There was blood on the under-shirt beneath the armpit. When the beer glass shattered against that biker, a piece of it had somehow come my way.

I started to wash the cut. Penny came in to the bathroom with one of Jim's work shirts. She looked at my naked front. Whistled. An act. If anyone but Jim touched her, she would go off like a dynamite cap. Penny is as conventional as Julie is not. Julie does what she wants. Penny does what she is supposed to want. Dolores takes it as it comes. For a moment I was lonely for Dolores. Not Julie. Dolores might understand how a fight is sometimes inevitable.

"What happened?" I pulled on the shirt and began to snap it up.

She unsnapped it. "Bandage first." She got tape and gauze.

"The dumb shit tried to kill himself." Her face is always set. She drives life ahead of her like she was driving cattle. There was fear in her eyes. Penny has her whole life tied up in that guy. It isn't bright.

That makes two of us. Me with Julie. Penny with Jim. She is my short partner in idiocy.

Barrows had Jim talking by the time I was dressed and back in the living room.

"Like I was being swallowed up," Jim said. "All I could think was I was supposed to be dead."

"We spoke of that this afternoon," Barrows told him. "I showed you that these things are not predestined."

"I've been around timber all my life." Jim leaned back, stared at the ceiling, then looked at the dead eye of the television. He looked at the log walls of his new house, at the carpets, at a couple of prints and paintings given them by friends. A lot of artists and crafts people have moved here to get away from Out There.

"What difference does that make?" Now Penny was verbally punching him.

"Honey, it does. I don't know how to say it."

"I can say it," I told him. "I haven't been around timber all my life. For me, what happened was at least a possible miracle."

He looked weak and sick.

"What happened?"

"I was feeling bad. Nervous like," Penny said. "Then he got the rifle and started talking like he was in church. I conked him with a bottle." Penny looked at Barrows. "Make it right."

Jim is lucky. Lucky.

Barrows looked at me. "Are you steady enough to drive?"

"Sure."

"Mike was turned back at the ferry. He didn't get to Seattle. Go to the main road and stop him. He's about twenty miles out of town."

"Sober?"

"He won't need coffee." Barrows turned to Penny. "Walk to Julie's house and bring her back. I'll take care of Jim."

"Nope," I said. "Julie isn't in this."

"I'm sorry, Jake. She's in it. We all are. I know now what we are dealing with."

We all trusted him. I nodded to Penny. "I'll give you a ride partway."

"I'll have you covered," Barrows said.

"You know what it is?"

"I'm afraid I know what it has to be." Barrows never had seemed so sad.

"This isn't your fault."

"Get going."

Penny came along but she was reluctant. She was silent as I drove. The mist was rising. It was well over a hundred feet above the channel. It rolled over the bluff and surrounded houses that sat bulky behind dark hedges. I looked at my watch. A little past ten. Not surprising that Mike was turned back. The ferries have lots of breakdowns.

When we arrived at the top of the road to Julie's house, I pulled over. Penny did not move.

"You better hold me for a minute."

I hugged her.

"No. Hold me, kid. I'm scared." It was one of the best things any person has ever done for me. Jim knew this feeling of being with a lady who could trust that much. She stayed close for probably two minutes.

"Thanks, kid."

"Thank you."

"Will it be okay?"

It has not been okay for a long time, whatever it is . . . not just society, but spirit. For thirty years, no, more like forty, the nation has gotten more ugly and stupid.

"It will be okay between you and your guy."

"Yeh, if we've just got that."

"No trouble, is there?"

"Barrows," she said. "Barrows is trouble, sure as a cat craps in alleys."

"I don't know," I told her. "We're different. To me Barrows is the best hope for all of the things we want."

"You know why I haven't had a kid?"

"No."

"I'm afraid. Not about having it, not afraid for me."

She was only twenty-three. She had such a long time to live. "Got to get moving," I said. "Get Mike. I love you too."

"It works that way." She opened the door and stepped into the mist. A tiny figure disappearing into mist as I pulled away and across the top of the hill.

The night was silent except for foghorns. Lights shone dim from a few houses. At times like this I love the town, have the feeling and sense that it is not difficult for humans to live peaceably together.

The mist was so thick I kept the wipers going. We are lucky to have good equipment, for God knows when we will get more. I had money saved when I came here. If it wasn't for Jim's knowledge and Barrows's steadiness, we would have been broke in six months.

We are all partners. That keeps the union away. If the union does not break the gyppo, then it comes from government, or when one of the big timber companies lies. They call it corporate reevaluation. That means that they put you into a shit show at high elevation, then jockey the rates or pull the show. Because we have a bulldozer we can build our own roads. It's the ability to make your own roads without paying union time that keeps us alive.

I eased along the top of the hill and passed a parked police car. The cop waved. It was old Pete, who doesn't sleep much and takes most of the night shifts. There are only four cops. Each does six hours on the street and two hours with paper work. Their wives help with dispatch and paper work.

Past the fire station, the red night light wispy in the mist. Past the movie. Past one of our eleven churches. Maybe God was hiding someplace in the mist. Maybe God was lost in the mist, trying to home in on the foghorns.

I rolled the truck down the hill easy and pushed through the town. The restaurants were closed. The freak bar was closed. The stores had darkened windows. The lumberyard, the docks, the boatyard. A boat crane stood in the mist and did not look like a crane at all. It looked like a stork. Hulls, masts, and then the road turns and heads back up another hill and out of town. I would meet Mike at the comer store where you turn off to the mill.

His crate has headlights that slant weak beams into the trees. He should adjust them, he never does. When I saw him coming off the far curve, like he was coming from a tunnel of trees, I pulled to the shoulder and waited, the truck pointing back to town.

When he was a hundred yards away I started popping the brake lights. He cruised up, recognized the truck, pulled ahead of me and stopped. Got out. Walked back. Mike. Mike. I can't even take care of myself.

He came like he was afraid. I don't blame him. He might figure I had been sitting there for hours, and was prepared to sit for hours. That would have to mean something bad. I rolled the window.

"How's it going?" We have this way of talking. I tell him everything is under control by being innocuous. This time it did not
work.

"You ain't sitting here to ask me that."

"We got a couple of problems. Get up to Jim's place."

"He okay?"

"Sure."

"I didn't get across."

"I know. We'll try again next week. Hang on to the bucks."

He looked at me like he loved me. He was proud. To be trusted
like that, with that money. And it was nothing but goddamn lousy
fucking stupid shitass money. I wanted to bawl.

"I'll follow you," I told him. My banged-up face must have shown
in the lights from the dash. He looked me over, turned, went back
to the car that was still churning exhaust into the mist, a red swirl
in the taillights. Black shadows of mist encroaching on the red.

Chapter 11

THE TOWN OF LAND'S END WAS HIT BY THREE SEPARATE OPENING attacks. Barrows should have anticipated trouble and did not. He had information at the time that he did not tell me until later. If he had, those attacks could have been neutralized.

The first attack was the two-bit attempt at hitting Barrows with the bikers. The second was an electronic attack calculated to wipe out one or more of the people nearest to Barrows. The third was standard, covert infiltration that had terrorism as its object.

So far as I could make out, as Mike and I drove up the hill to Jim's house, two ordinary looking workboats were feeling their way through the fog that covered the strait. The boats showed no running lights.

At the same time, at the county airport a small van was pulling onto the empty runway, which was illuminated by a minimum number of lights. As some men climbed from the van and approached the small, unlighted tower, other men began to unload explosives. In less than five minutes the runway lights winked out.

In the town of Land's End the explosives were carried beneath the jackets of men who were dressed like fishermen. The men embarked from another van at the edge of town. They moved quietly, unseen, as they headed for various destinations, while from two darkened automobiles a half-dozen men emerged. They were lightly but effectively armed. They did not whisper to each other. They spread out across the abandoned golf course and moved toward the streets of Land's End. Beneath one streetlight, as one of the men approached, a small dog sat on his haunches and barked. Distant barks of dogs from across town were muffled in the mist. The small dog barked, perhaps for the sheer enjoyment of joining the muffled chorus. A sharp sound, like a light slap, came from the night. The dog was thrown sideways by the high-velocity bullet, its head a puddle of splintered bone and brain as the body rolled.

Barrows, with all of his chicks gathered beneath his wing, was not watching out for the town.

Mike and I entered Jim's house, looked around, and advanced into the room. I thought that we looked like a bunch of refugees, but refugees who had been granted a little breathing time between salvos. Julie has this crazy nightdress ornamented like an Apache shirt. It was given to her by an Apache, but I doubt if any Apache ever made the thing. It probably came from Hong Kong. She was wearing that, her outdoors jacket, and her hiking boots. Penny had done a first-rate job on moving Julie. Julie's hair needed brushing. It tangled around a sleepy face that turned into a frightened face when Mike and I entered the living room. She walked to me quick.

"I'm all right," I told her.

Barrows looked older than prophecy, but he looked strong. He looked like a claw-footed Victorian antique in the chintzy living room. The rug was blue, the armchairs were off-red, gold, brown. There were knickknacks and colored burlap curtains. The log walls were still shiny with preservative and clear lacquer. The wrinkles in Barrows's face looked carved.

Jim looked better but still spaced. Mike stood confused. Only Penny continued to kick right along. Penny arranged us like she was a seven-year-old playing with dolls. She pushed Mike at a chair, shoved me at another . . . grabbed me before I could sit. She felt the shirt over the bandaged cut.

"Don't bleed." It was one of the new chairs. I decided it would be nice to let someone else run the show. I sat down, leaned back, waited.

"I don't want to complain . . ." Julie can complain bitterly. That really happens big when she feels dowdy as a rag shop.

"Then don't," Penny told her. "Until you got something to bitch about." Penny was shoving Jim across the room. "Don't just stand there."

Barrows looked at Mike. "Have any trouble?"

"Not until I got here." Mike pointed at Jim. "What's with him?" He looked around. "Matter of fact, what is biting all you people?"

"Nothing," Penny told him. "They are drinkin' and dancin' and fuckin' and fightin' like usual. Pretty, ain't they?"

Julie giggled. Even Barrows smiled. Mike was puzzled. He sat and probably wished he had made it to Seattle.

Penny walked to Barrows, who looked like he had emotions that were about to get out of control. They were not good emotions. You could tell. Penny sat on the arm of the chair, put her arm around his neck and hugged him.

"You look like cow plop," she said. "Nobody got a right to look that way in my house."

Barrows began to look better. I could never remember anyone hugging Barrows. It would be like trying to hug a monument.

"Get this straight so we can get some sleep," Penny told him. "You started it. Straight it up or make it go away."

"Not fair," I said.

"Shut up," she told me. "It's fair enough for now." She hugged Barrows again. "I'll start it for you. Just look around at these good folk and say something idiotic like, 'I expect you all wonder why . . . ' Go to it, champ."

I watched Penny. She was working on Barrows and keeping an eye on Jim. Those eyes. They are darker than brown, more painful than black. Long lashes that combine and work with the narrow shoulders, the narrow hands, the almost miniature figures. Those eyes seem to have a thousand invisible wrinkles, and Penny has earned every one of them.

"I don't understand all of it yet," Barrows said, "but I can now guess who has attacked us." He turned to Mike. "You weren't here. I'll fill you in. First Jake, then Jim, were attacked by sound equipment."

Mike looked puzzled. So, for that matter, did I.

Barrows almost seemed to be musing. "I knew," he said to the room in general, "that some really vicious weapons were being developed. In a way, sound equipment is even worse than chemical warfare." He seemed lost in some kind of dream, a dream of horror. "The sounds were not audible," he said. "They were infrasonic and more or less directional. Had they been nondirectional it would have taken me more time to discover the source of the transmitter."

"If you can't hear it. . ." Mike changed his mind and shut up.

"The idea of using sound as a weapon is not new," Barrows said. "The transmitter that was used was Japanese, and similar equipment has been around for twenty-five years. The main research on sound waves as weapons has been done in France." He still seemed to be musing, to be on the threshold of some enormous grief simply because such weapons existed. "There are two kinds. Ultrasonics and infrasonics. What these infrasonic waves did was intensify the preoccupations that were already in Jim's and Jake's minds."

"I can do that drinking," Mike told him, "and I don't know anything about what you're talking about."

"Ultrasonics are a range of short sound waves so high that you can't hear them. Infrasonics are a range of long sound waves so low that you can't hear them. The right combination of ultrasonics can destroy human tissue. They can kill. The right combination of infrasonics can actually disrupt the geology of the earth."

"The town's still standing." Mike was not going to be put off with theory. Mike is not a theoretical guy.

"This was a narrow range of infrasonics," Barrows said. "Our attackers wanted to keep this quiet. They tried to get Jake and Jim to kill themselves."

"If you say so."

"You weren't here," Barrows told Mike. "Jake was nearly catatonic. Jim was suicidal."

I had not realized that it was that bad. Mike was looking at me like I was something in a zoo.

"Anybody can gawk," I told him. "Even jerks."

It stopped him. I never talk to him that way. His eyes showed hurt. "I'm sorry, man," I said. "It must have been worse than I thought."

"Experiments in sound have been going on since 1893," Barrows said. He looked at Mike. "Everyone here already knows that it was me who made that tree disappear. Can you handle that?"

Mike nodded. He did not exactly believe it, but he looked relieved. He had probably figured he was going nuts. At least this made everyone equally nuts.

"Now you all have some more to handle," Barrows said. "I'm sorry. No one deserves this." He looked at Julie and Penny.

"I'll judge it myself." There was no confusion in Julie's manner. Her mouth was no longer lax.

"Then these are the reasons why we are here." Barrows began to talk, and we all sat on the new chairs in the new house and each of us knew that we were becoming younger and dumber by the minute. John Barrows was born during a time of chaos. He did not know that. When you are little the world moves low and long, days of heat and sunshine, summers of storm. In Barrows's case the storms yearly swept the Ohio River Valley. The storms were greater than human wrath above a river that moved like a measuring tape of time. The summer storms rolled and thundered like the Old Testament God. John Barrows was not allowed to go close to the river when he was little, but he learned that he lived on the Kentucky side. He learned that Kentucky was the greatest state in the greatest union of states that the world had ever seen. Later, there would be more talk about that union. He learned of universal judgment, the second coming, the place in society of men who were white, men who were black, the place of women. He would learn of rifles and axes, plows and flatboats. Days of hot and humid sun. Days of chaos. Days of storm.

He grew and learned other things that were secret, like the feel of the land. And he learned of the depth of the great river and how sometimes it was bottomless as a dark heart or an engulfing belly. Somewhere and somehow he had learned to protest that which is insane.

On January 19, 1862, when he was older than Mike and younger than Penny, he saw his first battlefield. Razorback hogs were in the brush, and razorbacks are the greyhounds of brush. They are fast, lean, tough, and they will eat that which is dead and kill that which is wounded.

The union forces of Thomas met the confederate forces of Zollicoffer in slick, deep mud to the sounds of curses and the screaming and grunt of hogs. John Barrows walked onto the battlefield at Mill Spring. The rifle he carried weighed exactly nine pounds. It was loaded from the muzzle and fired by a cap. It was four feet eight inches long and it delivered a .58 caliber minié ball that could kill at half a mile. John Barrows took one look at war, quietly laid down the rifle and quietly walked away. He expected at any moment to be shot for desertion. He walked.

Zollicoffer was soon dead. The mud was slick and deep, the fine-grained and water-saturated clay like a mouth to suck away souls. The hogs screamed in the brush.

The union would be at low tide by the time Barrows arrived in Oregon. He had walked east and north, caught a ship, and arrived in Oregon from seaward on December 15. Behind him 17,962 human beings lay dead on the plains before Fredricksburg. The victor of the Battle of Fredricksburg, Robert E. Lee, mourned and said: "It is well that war is so terrible, or we should grow too fond of it."

As Barrows talked my disbelief turned not to belief, but to the knowledge that I listened to the absolute courage and truth of a man's life. Barrows was a hundred and fifty years old. He was more than that, though. He was an idealist, and his ideals were easily explained. Barrows was a pacifist, maybe one of the world's great pacifists.

That made me shudder. Barrows was a peace seeker. No peace seeker can ever be a good peacekeeper . . . I interrupted my thought, told myself to shut up.

Barrows spoke easily. The simplicity of his speech made the facts he told us as stark as that battle scene must have been when he walked away and went west. His words displayed something that Barrows did not mean to tell. They displayed courage.

It was not only the great courage that it takes to walk away from a battle. Barrows's courage was even greater. He had exercised the kind of courage that it takes to stay alive in body and mind while engulfed in loneliness. This man before us had already lived the length of two lives. He had arrived here still an idealist. He carried the heat of his belief in his heart, yet his words spoke of the frigidity of his loneliness. Barrows was alone. He was as alone as a rock at the bottom of the sea, but he was not a rock.

I mentally flipped through my knowledge of the Civil War. Mill Spring had been one of the first of the western engagements. I could not remember if Zollicoffer had been unlucky or a fool. Thomas outlasted the war. I did not know what had happened to Thomas, but here before us was John Barrows.

It is all one war when you are that kind of idealist. During the late sixties I was a member of that war. They, Out There, called me a peacenik, a longhair, a traitor.

In that war, when Barrows laid down his rifle to go west, he was called an emigrant. Had he gone to Canada, as many did during the Civil War, he would have been called a skeedadler, a traitor—and I am going bald and cut trees for a living. Today we measure our cut with the word stumpage. During the Civil War the cut was called wood-clip. Conscientious objectors were called defeatists then— and I am going bald. I do stupid and dirty battle with a biker in a cruddy joint that caters to burned-out acidheads.

I looked at Penny and Mike. They wanted to understand but they did not understand. There was no way in the world that they could understand a pacifist. Mike is young and male and full of the responsibility for being that way. Penny was brought up to be able to punch cops.

"You're singin' a hard song," I told Barrows. "Are you bitter and hiding it, or are we in the presence of a saint."

"I am not bitter and I am hardly a saint."

He was looking better. I do not know if he trusted us, but his situation made him have a try. Having told us about himself, he seemed a little less lonely. He had lived so long in silence.

"How do you do it," I asked. "There was a time when I understood why you do it, and maybe that time is coming again. But for now, how do you preserve your life?"

"The aging process is mostly chemical," Barrows said. "It is also conditioned. People get old because they expect to get old."

"Or they get tired and say to hell with it."

"True," he said. "People get tired." His face was creased and gaunt, like crumpled paper.

"Is this a private conversation?" Julie's voice sounded like she was trying to control tears. She wanted to weep because of Barrows's loneliness. "How do you keep from getting old?"

"Don't be fooled," Barrows said. "I am old. I interrupt the chemical process. I reach into my own body with the power. It is possible to remove disease."

"Is that all?"

"Heredity and nutrition and mental attitude play a big part."

"I know of ages over 120." Julie seemed trying to do a fast recall, lost the information, remembered part. "The record in this area is 126."

"And that person did not have the ability to make things vanish." Barrows seemed to take consolation from the fact, like it made him not such a rare beast. His face still looked crumpled. His eyes showed his fatigue. I hoped that after so many years of endurance he was not going to allow himself to come apart.

"How long can you continue to live," Julie asked. Her voice was kind, but her question was objective, the way an anthropologist should question.

"As long as I have to."

"How long is that?" There was awe in Mike's voice. Mike did not understand that Barrows had kept himself alive because of an idealism that Mike could not understand, either. Mike did not know how much courage it takes to walk away from a battle. He did not know anything about the fatigue of years, or how time weighs a man down.

"That's another of the reasons why we are here." Barrows's voice was nearly timid.

Everyone was quiet. At first, no one understood what he meant. Then it seemed that all of us understood it at the same time. I do not want to die, but goddamn, I do not want to live forever, either. Jim finally got it moving.

"You want to check out," he said to Barrows. "You want to pass the buck to one of us. You want somebody else to take your clout and live forever. Well, pass the buck to Jake." Jim looked around his living room, looked at Penny, and then began to look spaced again. I could understand his resentment. They built this small house, he and Penny. It was chintzy, maybe, but it was Jim's chintz and Penny's. Jim did not want something timeless in his place. It would make his place seem not as important. And Barrows was timeless. Jim smoothed his hair with his hands, looked at Barrows like he wanted to apologize.

"I ain't gonna do it," Penny said. "All I want is to have a kid and be a regular people." She looked at Barrows like she might smack him. "You piss me off, and I don't even know why."

"I can guess why," Barrows said, "but I won't inflict you with it."

"What is going on? What is?" Mike was getting confused.

"Forgive me," Barrows said. "I should not ask anyone to take on such a thing. It's just that my situation is harder than you think." The pain in his eyes was unmasked. It spoke an old anguish that for Barrows was never to be old. Later I would understand, for later he would tell me of his wife, would speak in a way that I could not exactly understand about the mystery of *being* that had once risen between two nineteenth-century people who had other ideas of love and sex and romance. His anguish had begun before any of us were born, back when his wife died.

Still, at the time he said nothing about it. His eyes only reflected pain. We all saw the pain, but doubtless Julie saw it best. I know that because I know Julie.

"We can only deal with this when we know everything," she said. "We still don't know what we are up against."

"So much to tell . . ." Barrows paused. "I am not just talking about this afternoon or yesterday or last year."

"We understand. Take your time. I think we are not in danger with you here."

"That's true," he said, "but it's also true that there would be no danger if I had not mixed in with your lives."

"But Jim would have been killed if you didn't." Penny stood to go to the kitchen. "I'm gonna make coffee and tea and some sandwiches." She looked at Mike. "C'mon, lunkhead, you can at least spread peanut butter." It may be that Penny is a great woman.

Chapter 12

WE ALL SAT AT JIM'S HOUSE WHILE THE DEADLY MOVEMENT OF professional killers spread through our streets. We just sat, talking.

At the time I thought that the whole business was goofy. I thought about what Barrows was telling us and never dreamed that anything was happening in our streets.

Yet, not four blocks away a tough but decent cop named Pridham answered a knock on his door. He died with a bullet in his face before the door was fully open. The sound of the shot was little more than a hum from the silenced pistol. The door was shoved fully open. A woman, together with her son and daughter, sat before a fireplace, startled, not even realizing what was happening. They died quickly, as the pistol hummed. The exploding splat of bullets in flesh made large and indecent sounds compared to the low hum of the pistol. The bodies were flung. They writhed, choked, and were almost instantly dead. By the time they were dead the door was already closed and the killer moved elsewhere.

The skull of a baby girl exploded, passing from sleep to death on the voice of a hum. The child's mother lay faceless across her kitchen table. As the pistols continued to hum, legs of victims kicked sporadically, like beheaded chickens flopping and pumping blood. The killers were quiet and efficient. There were no screams, and there were no wounded. The bullets hit faces or hearts, and the bullets were dispassionate.

While we sat talking.

Mobilier was the outfit that was trying to destroy us, and one tentacle of Mobilier was in our streets.

Mobilier. It sounded like some kind of crazy oil company, and to an extent it was. Which is to say that it had commandeered energy complexes on its rise to power.

Mobilier. Barrows explained. What was horrible was that Mobilier was nearly as old as Barrows.

During the second presidential term of Grant, Mobilier was associated with railroads. The Credit Mobilier, as it was known in those days, was originally organized to build the Union Pacific. The first organizers, including a guy named Oakes Ames who was in Congress, could not have cared less about the railroad. What they cared about was the high profit that could be made from building the railroad.

Mobilier bought Congress. It was not as expensive in those days as it would be in our time, although Congress had always been surprisingly easy and cheap. The Credit Mobilier bought congressional votes by using a stock deal with the proposed railroad's stock. In December of 1872 the scandal hit. Mobilier did not disband in the face of the scandal. It went underground. The presidential election of 1876 was the dirtiest in American history. It was bought in favor of Rutherford Hayes. A lot of the men who did the buying of votes were the men of Mobilier.

Hell was popping and had been. The list of criminals from those days carries names that read like a list of what are now called America's "first families." Those bastards were first, all right. They were ruthless, violent, and on any human scale they were depraved.

They fought among themselves like cats. When opposed by government they bought the courts. When opposed by the courts they bought government. The cream of a nation's resources was wet on their whiskers. No one, not even Barrows, knew at exactly what time or which men organized to own the world.

Mobilier. A hundred and eighteen years later the founders were long dead but the organization was strong.

"How big are they?" I asked Barrows. I looked around the room, looking at all of the people I cared for. These were normal people. They had no business being mixed up in this kind of mess.

"I don't know how big they are," Barrows said. "I thought in the growth of other groups that this group had died out. "

"You're sure you have the right outfit?"

"It is the only organization it can be," Barrows said. "I've kept the secret of my power well in this century. I made some mistakes in 1898. My mistakes frightened me into silence."

"Mistakes?"

"I displayed the power in a small way. Only two members of Mobilier knew about that display. In all the world, only two men."

"What happened?"

The fatigue that had been on Barrows's face deepened. Mixed with the fatigue was sorrow, and with sorrow, guilt.

"Two things happened," Barrows said. "First, I was approached by the military. My power is an ultimate weapon. No other weapon can stand against it."

"So the military jocks wanted to use you for a weapon." I almost felt sorry for Barrows, but not quite. He seemed nearly too innocent to be real. "Of course," I said, "Mobilier owned the military jocks."

"Yes."

"What else happened?"

"I ran away and hid where they could not find me."

"Here?"

"I've been here ever since." He rubbed the side of his face, like he was trying to iron his wrinkles flat. He attempted to look strong and managed to look only slightly pathetic. "I'm afraid it has happened again. This afternoon I was approached by a man who wanted to make a deal. "

I was shocked. Stopped. He should have told me sooner. He should have told me that right away.

"Aw, naw, Barrows. Naw."

"There can be no harm," he said. "I told him no."

"You told him no ..." I choked, was nearly speechless. "Didn't you buy time, tell him you would give him an answer in a couple of days?"

"No."

"Do you know what this means?" I looked around, looking at all of them: Penny, Jim, Julie, Mike. None of them were catching on.

Barrows did not answer. "It means," I said, "that their next move will be force. They are going to try to intimidate you."

"They would not dare."

Barrows sure as stink was not just innocent, he was stupid. Of course, maybe Barrows did not know the military mind.

"I can check them out," he said timidly. "I last knew of the organization in Chicago and Albany."

"Check them fast. It's urgent. Disappear the bastards." I walked to the door, anxious, unable to sit and talk. I had to be moving, in action. My heart was cold, nearly sick with what I knew must surely be about to happen. I turned back from the door, paused. "I forgot to get smokes. Anyone else?" What I really wanted to do was get outside, move, think and plan.

"Me," Jim said. "I'll come along."

"Is it safe?" Julie was watching me like I was a three-year-old kid threatening to jump off a roof.

"It's safe." Barrows leaned back and closed his eyes. "I'll start checking Albany, but I'll keep you in view."

We went to the truck. The mist was so thick I felt it settling in my face. There are times around here when you can take a walk and return looking like you've been under water, with never a drop of rain. I started the engine and then sat looking at the house.

Barrows was old, okay. I was only middle age. But middle age is a time when you find yourself beginning to be alone. Maybe all people are always alone, but in middle age you know it. The young dreams and young friends are gone. The parents die. If you have brothers and sisters, they have moved someplace else. When this country was mostly agricultural that did not happen. Now, in the cities, even families are fragmented. The police surveillance is more intensive in this country as you move toward the eastern seaboard.

Inside that house was a woman I loved. She was young. She did not know that in fifteen or twenty years she too would have to remanufacture a world. In fifteen or twenty years I would be dead. She would have to find a man, discover how to live with him.

Inside that house was a kid whom I can't really talk to. I can't help Mike be less a kid or more of an adult. Everything I know is of no use to Mike. He's nineteen.

Jim is my friend. Penny is my friend. Barrows is my friend.

And that is it. Except for Max and Dolores, that is my whole world. Take a cannon and blow that house to pieces and I have no world. My world is a small, important place that gets smaller and more important every year. I am like a hobo bumming his way through life, a few useful things tied in a bag slung on a stick.

Jim was also looking at the house. Maybe he was feeling bad. "You going to sit here all night?"

"Going for smokes." I dropped it in gear.

"Hold on a minute." He rolled the window. His face looked pale in the dashlights and against the gray mist. "Something's wrong."

"What?"

He sat concentrating. Then he almost jumped. "The foghorns have stopped."

I listened. Not a sound.

"Maybe the channel has cleared. We still have the fog up here. That happens sometimes."

"There are four horns. I never heard of it all going clear at once."

"Must have."

"Makes me feel right funny." He opened the door, hesitated, decided not to get out and slammed the door shut. "Go to one of the joints downtown. I'll feel better when I see it."

I pulled along the back of the hill, circling across the top of the town and eased toward downtown. We said nothing. It seemed like we should be talking.

I am too serious. That is also a part of middle age. Light friendships mean nothing, only real friendships. Except for those I love, life seems like a little play. People trot back and forth across the stage of this town. They read bright lines to each other. I no longer understand.

"Too soon old . . ."

"Huh?" Jim was leaning back against the door the way Barrows had leaned.

"Nothing. Thinking to myself," I told him.

"Then think something interesting." Jim sat up straight and peered through the windshield. We both saw the flashing blue light of Pete's squad car at the same time. It was pulled to the curb. I coasted toward the center of the street. If someone was walking around in front of the car, I wanted to be clear. The lights laid flat panels of blue through the mist. When we passed the squad car we saw it was sitting alone. That was not surprising. Most police work in this town has little to do with traffic. Unless they have a job connected with some essential industry, people do not buy cars. Too much money. Black market financing is scary.

"Did you see Pete?" I asked Jim.

"No."

"He's old."

"He sure as hell is. Maybe he's in trouble."

I stopped the truck, then began to back up. I figured Pete was probably just making sure that a drunk got home.

"He's laying across the wheel." Jim already had the door open and was moving.

I started to scream. Choked. Managed a harsh imitation of a command voice. "Stay low," I told him. "Goddammit, stay low."

It was happening. I knew it. Before I even got around the rear of the truck to old Pete, I knew it was happening . Jim stood looking down at old Pete, and Jim was helpless. He could not believe what he saw. Pretty soon, when he caught on, Jim might do something dumb. He might rush into the mist looking for someone to kill.

I did not know then how many people Mobilier had killed. All I knew is that Mobilier had killed old Pete.

The sons of bitches had no right to do that. He was a good man. He'd been a cop in this town all his life, taking care of drunks, of kids restless in the big car days when they took their heat to the road. Pete had put up with fussy city councils, with tourists, with out-of-towners who move here to get away from Out There and then immediately call for more police protection. Pete had stood up to the drunken loggers, drunken bikers, to the wharf scum that drifts into town every summer following the yacht money. He had taken care of women who were having kids while their old men were offshore fishing. He had done it all, and now he was hunched over the wheel with a hole in his back and his lap full of blood. The transmitter of the radio dangled where it had dropped from his hand.

Jim stepped back slow. He was still trying to figure it out. I looked at old Pete, reached for his wrist, and it was no longer an emergency. I walked around the car, keeping low, climbed in and picked up the mike. Then I laid the mike back down. I did not know who would be standing guard on the police radio. Maybe Pete's wife.

That rifle might still be out there in the mist. That killer was surely out there somewhere.

"Get the hell out of here," I told Jim. He knows about logging emergencies. Nothing about murder.

"You reckon this is part of what's happening to us?" He stood, still confused.

"Get out of here. Get back to Barrows. Call help."

"What about you?" He was reluctant to move.

"Get out of here." My command voice was working just fine. "I'm okay, but you get the hell out. Stay low. Crouch." I reached across Pete's lap full of blood to get the headlights. They put sharp beams into the mist, the beams swallowed completely at a hundred feet.

"Goddammit," I told him, "you've got a wife. Don't walk in front of the lights."

Jim turned and walked around the back of the truck with as much attempt to stay low as a giraffe. He turned back.

"Come with me."

"Get out of here." At any moment I expected to see him fold beneath a bullet. He climbed in the truck and pulled away slow, like he was thinking about all this. The shot came. There was a crack, light and sharp, so sharp that even the distortion of the mist could not conceal it. It came from down the street and to the right. I had my man, but I guessed that he had Jim.

The truck hung a left and continued under control and at the same speed. The killer had missed. Impossible.

I sat beside Pete for exactly two seconds to grieve. This had been a good man. Now he was punctured back and front. That was a small caliber, high-powered beast of a rifle out there. Accurate. At five hundred yards you could about light matches with the thing. A perfect assassin's rifle, but the mist had the guy screwed. I looked at Pete slumped over the wheel. He was a grotesque silhouette before the background of the blue flashing mist. He had been hit and had enough life to make it back to the car. It had not happened long ago. The blood was still not fully drained from the top of the body.

Pete's gun was still holstered. I unsnapped it. It was like a million other pistols. A .38 police special. I tested the action. It was smooth.

I was willing to bet it had never been fired except in practice. The last time Pete took a gun from anyone was five years ago. Some jerk had been waving one in a bar. Pete took his own gun off before going in. It was a town legend.

I looked at the gun. When I was younger I knew insecure guys who could not live without one of these. I am willing to bet that there are still a lot of these buggered hunks of steel wrapped in soft cloth high in people's closets. Of course the poor bastards dream of using them.

I shoved the pistol back in Pete's holster. A lousy .38 was going to make no difference. All it could do would be get me killed.

Pete's car was not custody rigged. There was no steel mesh between front and back. I came from my crouch in front of the dash, jumped and rolled into the back seat. I eased the back door open, rolled out and closed it quiet. Then I rolled under the car. I had the advantage. I know this town, all of its places for hiding, its slopes and its places of concealment. That guy out there had to be an import.

If he had fired, then he had to move, even with that quiet rifle. I knew he was a pro. He would at least know the main features of the terrain. He would move deliberately and not far, if his job was still unfinished. Apparently he was still working. He had hung around using old Pete for bait.

The facts started their own talk, confirming what my heart and belly already knew. This was terrorist stuff. That killer was after anybody. The mist cover saved us, even if that killer had a sniper scope. The flashing blue lights and the headlights had caused some distortion.

Terrorism. Wounds count in terrorism, but what really counts is death. And the thing that counts most is the fear instilled by blind ferocity and indifference and meaninglessness.

The killer would have to move to another field of fire. That simplified things. He could nest between houses, which is chancy unless you know who keeps dogs and who can't sleep nights. The best cover is shrubbery, and the next best is beside a public building. There is a recreation center in this block that must have been his original cover. There is a playground, a little park and some commercial buildings across the street in the next block. I would find him half a block away, three points off the rear of the car, at the corner of the park. He might already be in position.

That boy had his problems. I did the usual stuff. Unload the pockets, turn the belt buckle to the back of the pants, daub the face with grease from beneath Pete's car, ease out of the boots and stand to move in to the mist. Another lousy spy movie.

I estimated the distance a moving figure could be seen, then added twenty percent. It took three minutes to circle behind where he had to be.

You could just bet he was not prone. Two inches from the ground the mist was solid. I expected to find him crouched and found him that way. It was not even especially good stalking.

There is shrubbery at one corner of the park. If he were a pro, he would pick that over a building or other planed surface. The formlessness of shrubbery lets you fade right in.

The night was so quiet you could almost hear the mist. At any minute I expected Jim to make contact with the cops or the fire station. A siren would go off. My boy would fade. He would be tough to handle if that happened.

There was no movement in the shrubbery. It bulked dark and concentrated in the mist. I eased close, maybe forty feet out, and waited. If a siren did go off, there was at least a fifty percent chance that the guy would come my way.

He had a clear field of fire from any position in the shrubbery. I closed my eyes. I pass this corner every day. The mind remembers configurations. You just have to take time to listen to what you know. I did not think of the shapes of the shrubbery, just let it come to me. I opened my eyes. He was close. Forty or fifty feet to my left and forward. I watched, eased toward him, watched.

A straight line appeared where no straight line should be. The line ran slantwise to the ground. He was kneeling on one knee. If you catch one line, or one feature, the rest fills in. I eased forward, rushed the last three steps and kicked hard where the neck joins the spine. It was so fast he didn't know I was there. The rifle tipped away, the guy went on his face, and I landed hard in the middle of his back. Something gave, rib most likely, and he was out. The body flopped a little. He was not dead. I did not want him dead. I picked up the rifle and shucked the bolt.

The rifle was empty.

The guy lay there and I stood above him, two killers gathered in silent communion in the mist. I had to give Barrows credit. Barrows was just knocking the shit out of both of us when it came to a sense of accomplishment.

This guy had not missed Jim. The bullet had not arrived. Barrows had made it vanish, and then he had vanished the bullets in the guy's rifle. The guy had taken position assuming that he still had a loaded rifle.

The guy was not big. I dragged him around the kids' swing that stood like a toothpick house in the mist, around the sliding board, the wheel, the jungle bars, past a concrete toadstool. I took him to the police car, found old Pete's handcuffs and cuffed the guy to Pete. I leaned his lousy rifle across his lap, unloaded Pete's pistol and pulled on my boots. The mist was thick enough to confuse a cat.

There was going to be some real crap come down over this.

I just stood there to gather myself, the breathing in heavy gulps, the fatigue crawling over me like an infestation. I felt such sorrow. Sorrow for Pete, sorrow for the guy lying handcuffed to his last job—because no one was going to buy this punk off—and sorrow, but not pity, for myself. Pity is a crummy thing, but sorrow is real.

Then the feelings changed. The old hurt came back, and the fury. I stood looking at the punk and the *up* feeling I needed a few minutes ago started in the wake of the revulsion. This was me, here, and it was him, there. All it took was one quick move with the hand and he was a dead man. It is so personal, that *up* feeling. The key to violence is ego. If there is such a thing as dispassionate violence, then I don't know about it. The violence came twisting at me like it had in the past, and then it went away because I remembered something bad. I remembered the first time I ever killed a man.

Pete was as dead as he would ever be. There was nothing I could do. That was the logic of the thing. Stick to the logic. I wanted to get back to Jim's house, but I did not want to draw any more trouble down on those people. I did not know the situation, and besides, my house is closer.

On top of that I did not want to talk to them. Because it would have been easy to kill that man. It was a masterpiece job that he was still alive, a masterpiece of self-control. I wanted all of them at Jim's house to keep their illusions, to believe in their sloppy and comfortable way that stuff like this was not as common as those millions of acres of scrub trees out there on the mountainsides.

It would not be the first time I felt this dirty. Maybe if I called first, and Barrows said it was okay, then I could go to Jim's house after a while.

Still, there were going to be some bad cops coming around on this one. We were going to get federal cops on this one. This one already had one dead cop in it.

It was just too much. A feeling of horror and loss hit me hard. It was not so much a feeling of premonition. It was more the feeling that something already had happened, something irrevocable, and in its center was total destruction.

Time to get moving. Go home, wash off the outside dirt, call Barrows to see which way the game was running. I leaned over to recover my keys and small change, then walked away. Somebody else could sweep up my litter. It has pretty much always been that way.

Chapter 13

"A list of the dead includes Peter Braca (67) patrolman, John Alley (27) patrolman, John Tupper (36) patrolman, George Pridham (47) chief of police, Grace Pridham (43), Nancy Pridham (18), George Pridham, Jr. (20), Sarge Luczkowski (29) deputy, Samuel Banks (51) sheriff, Joan Godwin (23), Patty Godwin (14), Stan Larsen (38), Don Morris (33), Eugenia Swope Lane (81), Mike Swenson (21), Solomon Katz (55), Jan Thompson (13), Candace Hough (14), Anita Smith (14),—Smith and Hough were visiting at the Thompson residence—Paul Thompson (37), Mary Thompson (36), Richard Downs (24) U.S. Coast Guard, Paul Paley (28), Lena Paley (29), Jon Hamilton (47), Tammy Hamilton (47), Alma Smith (about 25), James Carpenter (25), Joe Gomez (17), George Pouget (63), Marie Pouget (48), their adopted daughter Kim (16), unidentified male (about 30). Unidentified male (about 50). Unidentified male (about 50), who was handcuffed to the body of patrolman Alley. Unidentified female (about 20).

"Extent of damage is not fully known. Destruction was complete against aids to navigation, and the lighthouse sustained heavy blast damage. There were, however, no injuries to personnel. Bombs were placed at the Catholic, Presbyterian and Baptist churches, which sustained moderate to heavy damage. While the downtown commercial district was spared, bombs exploded at the boatyard and the airport. One boat crane was destroyed, and four aircraft. The airport tower burned. Speed Miller, who runs the airport, was *visiting friends, and so the facility was deserted.*

"The town will continue under martial law until federal agents determine that all explosive devices have been located."

—From the *Land's End News Clarion,*
April 4th, 1991

WE WERE PUNISHED. IT WAS CHILD SIMPLE, AND I HAD KNOWN IT was happening even before I called Barrows after leaving old Pete. I knew it because of the sharp, cracking bomb blast that came from the direction of the Presbyterian church. The newspaper report was old news before it even got printed.

"Sit tight," Barrows told me when I called. His voice was full of sorrow and desperation. "Don't go on the streets," he told me.

"What's happening, dammit."

"The town is being raided. A lot of people have been killed. The raiders are leaving now."

There was no reason to be shocked, and I was not. I had already figured out that we had suffered a terrorist attack. Even as Barrows spoke, my mind was matching up facts, balancing information and making tactical decisions. My mind was cold, the way it ought to be in battle. I listened to Barrows, to his blubbering, while I evaluated the situation.

"Barrows," I said, "you aren't going to like this, but you have to do exactly what I say."

"Yes."

"Kill them. Do it now."

"No." His voice was shocked, like he had been hit hard with a fist. Then he whispered. "You know me better than that, surely you do."

"This is the situation," I said, and I didn't give a damn for his scruples. "If you let them get by with it, then there will be another raid. If you don't kill a few now, you'll end up killing a lot more later." It was true. Mobilier had to learn and learn fast. Any weakness on Barrows's part was an invitation to catastrophe for all of us. If he did not wipe out those attackers, more would be on the way.

I know these power-hungry bastards, these businessmen and politicians who run outfits like Mobilier. If they can't make a deal, they will force a deal. They would keep hitting us until Barrows gave up and agreed to use his power to help them.

"I can't talk anymore," Barrows said. His voice was nearly choked with grief, and maybe with indignation over what I had asked him to do. "I'll call you later." He hung up.

I had to take it for that. Barrows either would or would not act. I had no power, unless, of course, I sneaked away and caught one or two of the bastards. I could scrag them quick, and I needed no weapons except my hands. I sat and considered the possibility. It was a bad idea. Either we had to kill all of them or none of them. If I just took a couple of them out it would only be a provocative act.

Then, for the first time, I felt real fear. I sat and evaluated the situation some more. What I came up with stank with horror.

The opposition had moved too quickly. The punishing forces must have started coming together within an hour after the disappearance of that tree. That meant that we had at least one informer in this town. It also meant that a man, not a committee, was in control. Some single individual had punched the button that released the attacks against us. There was still one mystery that I could not figure out, although I would figure it out later. Why, after all these years, had Mobilier overreacted? Barrows had made the tree vanish, thus showing that he could and would use the power. Mobilier had reacted as if Barrows had made a major attack. All the dumb bastard had done was vanish a tree.

What was frightening was that Mobilier was totally without fear. That was terrifying. Sure, there had been rumors of corporate vengeance for years, but they had only been rumors. You never read about stuff like this in the newspapers. Of course, the press was controlled. The corporations owned the press.

Whoever punched the button on us did not care about military intelligence, the FBIA or anything else. Whoever punched the button was in charge of the greatest force in the world. Either that, or they were insane. Either that, or the button puncher owned majority stock in the very agencies that would be doing the investigating. The agents who would investigate would not know who owned them, but surely they were owned.

This looked like more of the corporate wars that had plagued the world during the late eighties. This was not crude motorcycle stuff. No corporation, to my knowledge, had yet actually fielded an army which flew the corporation flag. Of course, how could I know? The corporations owned the press.

If I thought I was afraid, at least I had company. The fear was on the faces of the federal cops when they came without knocking at four AM. They rousted me out of bed, and the talk started. I was back on the streets by eleven the next morning, and most of that time had been spent around the green table. Four tough cops walking all over me with questions, trying to trip me up; and all four of them had fear in their eyes.

I give them credit. The hit had started at eleven-thirty and lasted fifteen or twenty minutes. The feds arrived at one. It would have taken them an hour to get here even in floatplanes. They had my file by the time they picked me up.

They tried to pin the whole shitting mess on me, but it was a futile hope. They tried because they knew that they were not going to solve this one, so they were looking for someone to hang. It was a good thing that I had left so many fingerprints on Pete's car and on the assassin's rifle. Of the bunch they salvaged two. That's pretty good salvaging. Usually you do not get that many identifiable examples. When the feds bumped my story against my file, they figured I was telling the truth. They did not even charge me with the murder of the guy I had cold cocked and handcuffed to Pete. They knew, the same as I knew, that somebody on the guy's own team had shot him on their way out of town.

So, I was back on the streets by eleven the next morning. I could not leave town, but no one else could, either. The only road out was blocked unless you could prove legitimate business. Even delivery trucks from Seattle were being unloaded and searched before entering the city limits.

And by eleven, when I was back on the streets, a small contingent of Army jocks had arrived to enforce martial law. There were a couple of squad-sized groups of M.P.s, and an infantry made up mostly of a bunch of kids. They walked around trying to look tough; but they were actually scared shitless. I figured it was the first time they had ever actually had live ammunition in their rifles.

The federal cops may have been scared, but at least they got to ask the questions. They, like myself, had never run into an outfit so ruthless that it would actually single out a one-and-a-half-year-old child for shooting. Sure, terrorist groups will kill anybody with their bombs, but to actually blow away Patty Godwin with a pistol was more than any of us had seen. It had been a heavy caliber pistol, too. Patty was dead, her mother Joan was dead. I wished that the killers had killed Les Godwin, too. Les had been at sea on the *Rose*, busy smuggling drugs. Les is a real emotional guy. He would have to be watched if he made it back to town.

A terrorist group without motive is almost unknown. Even the sporadic rapist clubs in the big cities are politically motivated. I knew the motives, of course, but the feds did not. The feds did not know anything about Barrows or his power. Those feds were working in a vacuum.

They were efficient. Unless you knew what to look for, it was not easy to see that the feds were uncertain. They commandeered some local automobiles and trucks, including ours, but they were not driving them much. There was little movement in our streets.

Those few people who came from their houses walked around in a state of disbelief and shock. The mental paralysis of shock covered the town. Except for the unknowns who had been crashed in rooms above the freak bar, and the guy I had hit, the dead were all friends. Everyone in town knew them.

I have seen the same kind of mental paralysis before. Back in the sixties the people who walked around in a state of paralysis were Viets. No American town has been quite this way since the Civil War. It is painful to see that aimless, zombielike walk. In the face of unexplainable violence, all life seems stripped of meaning.

In a way, even the feds were more defenseless on that first day than any pros ever should be. The blind, motiveless, insane ferocity threw everything off. If there was going to be a second hit, I expected it to happen during this time, the time that lies between the violence and the time when life starts moving again. It is the right psychological moment. All defenses are no more than tokens or shams. Any Army officer who knows two cents about his business will tell you that this is the time to strike. From a strictly psychological, demoralizing point of view, another good time to strike is three days later. By then, everyone is beginning to feel relief, like they have awakened from a bad nightmare. The problem with hitting three days later is that the enemy's defenses are back up. You risk losing more of your own people.

Populations are so easy to manipulate. Anybody with a brain in his head can twist a population around his little finger at any time he wants.

The time in between is surrealistic. You make the usual actions. You build a fire in the stove, slurp coffee, mutter old plans, while underneath you feel everything is absolutely meaningless.

When one of the feds dropped me home, I asked him in for coffee. I was sure not going to contact Barrows or Julie.

The fed came along. Those cops had been decent about their interrogation. There had been some rough shit, but nothing too physical. The fed came mostly because he wanted coffee and had nothing better to do. There was no need for him to look around. The place had already been combed.

He was a heavy, black-haired, Mafia-looking guy, but the looks were where the resemblance ended. We sat at the kitchen table. The bucks Barrows had come up with were gone. Seized as evidence of something. I had a receipt in my pocket, but it would be a year or maybe twenty before the bureaucracy got around to returning them.

And then I swear this happened next. A wimpy little guy with a sharp nose pounded on the door. He was employed by the lately great state of Washington. He had a cease and desist order on our timber job.

I took the papers and gave the wimp coffee. I asked him if he wanted a good deal on a used bulldozer. He didn't get it. The fed didn't understand it, either, but at least he laughed.

The wimp was one of those suited little bureaucrats who do not wear glasses. They wear specs. I put the papers where the cash had been. It was unreal. Time meant nothing. The punk meant nothing. I felt almost companionable with the fed. At least we could talk to each other. There was nothing to hide. I had already been grilled like a Fourth of July hot dog.

The wimp would not leave it be. He wanted to know when I was going to make report corrections.

I told him I would correct matters by kicking his ass. The fed laughed.

The wimp advised me of my rights. It is illegal to threaten a deputy, and all wimps are state deputies.

The fed asked the wimp how he was going to prove that there had been a threat. Then the fed asked the wimp how he would like it if he just went off somewhere and fucked himself.

The wimp got stuffy. The fed laughed. My heart wasn't in it, and I was glad when they both left.

I sat staring at the cease and desist and thought that I was still out of cigarettes.

That was something to do. Walk downtown, buy smokes. The bars would be closed, but you could bet that the grocery would be open even if the feds had to run it with impressed labor.

It takes seven minutes to walk downtown, and twelve to walk back. You have to climb the hill. This time it took an hour. I was watching everyone and how they were acting. Barrows no doubt had them covered. In fact, I was willing to bet that he was covering the town like a momma hen on a nest. Having totally screwed up once, his guilt would be making him overprotective. For myself, I was still enough of a pro to be getting up for the next hit. None of that aimless wandering.

I wondered how Barrows was actually handling his guilt. For that matter, I wondered how good he was at the vanishing business.

How to understand John Barrows? The pacifist is different from people who call themselves nonviolent. Barrows and Julie are pacifists. That means that they actually have a fully decked out philosophy that goes with their actions, or failures to act. Me, I'm a theoretician and that's different. I tell myself that I am nonviolent. And there's the world's biggest goddamn laugh.

The pacifist philosophy is complicated. Among pacifists can be found true philosophers and idealists. Some of them are even saints. You will mostly find religious nuts, insecure egos, death wishes, and masked killers who, given the power, would destroy that part of the world they don't like in order to force their notion of heaven on the rest. That type of killer nut is no different from the Communist party in 1917, or maybe poor old Rubashov in the book *Darkness at Noon*. Or those masturbating little drugstore cowboys like Reagan in the early eighties.

I am not fooled by pacifists or messiahs. A sincere and thoughtful and sometimes religious few really are superior beings. Most of them are nothing but sadistic bandits.

For my own part, I'm a trained killer. It happened during that cruddy little war to keep the world safe for corporate enterprise. Kennedy and Johnson and Nixon were the presidents during Vietnam, and I still cannot figure out how they managed to get sucked into that one.

What I did in that war taught me to try to be a nonviolent. I did not have the sense of John Barrows. I did not lay down my rifle the first time I saw war.

The grocery store was the center of the action when I got downtown. In ominous times women always buy bread. They also buy eggs, whether they need them or not. There is a Freudian explanation for that, but I don't want to think about it.

The people walked like zombies. Even the old gossips were moving slow and not talking much. True, old Roza McKenzie was eating more produce than she was buying, which is usual—put two grapes in a sack, eat three. Old Sam Johnson is not allowed to drink, but he had a lousy bottle of wine tucked beneath his coat, masked by a cabbage. The cabbage rode right on top of his potbelly as he held it close to the wine bottle. There were no sales of liquor, but the terrorist attack gave Sam an excuse to drink and he was not going to lose it. Marcy was on the checkout counter. The automatics were broken again, so the check stands were on manual. Either Marcy did not care about Sam's bottle or she was being compassionate. Old Sam was as bad at being devious as he was good at talking.

Dolores drifted toward me like flotsam. She is a beautiful woman and knows it. Dark brown hair, dark brown eyes, lots of mouth and breast and legs that can open in the most confident and eager way. I get all mixed up thinking about Dolores. She was so nice to live with, but somehow we didn't take. Marine biologist, she is brilliant. I can't help thinking of her sexually. As long as she's happy—but right now she was not happy. She was not sexual. She was not even beautiful. Her full mouth was slack.

"Are you okay?"

"Sure. Are you okay?"

"Sure."

It was a great conversation. A beaut. I bought cigarettes and got out. Fat old Mrs. Chambers bumped me with her grocery cart. At least someone was acting normal.

The average guy, if he saw the results of a battle, would get sick to his stomach. He would smell tangled, torn and decaying corpses and would feel horror and revulsion. I would feel insane anger. Barrows would feel sorrow. That is the difference between inexperience, experience, and philosophy.

Barrows had managed to tell us a few things before the attacks began. I had a handle on part of what he said.

Simple-minded Barrows still believed that he lived in a world where the individual person was important. Simple-minded Barrows believed that you could not even interfere with the rights of people to make fools of themselves. He believed people had to achieve their own dignity.

Dumb-ass Barrows did not separate the idea of an individual person from the idea of a group. He thought government and corporations were nothing but expressions of united individual expression. That's a traditional point of view, all right. Dumb-ass Barrows grew up in a time when you were supposed to be grateful to your employer, and proud to be working for him.

I walked down the street and told myself that I was awful, awful tired. It seemed like there was a world conspiracy to keep me from getting some sleep. A federal cop cruised by. He drove one of our two police cars. Somebody would be mopping the remains of old Pete from the other police car. Mopping up old Pete would be a crappy job, but I figured that the fed had a job that was even more crappy. Imagine having to drive up and down the main drag in a cop car so that all of the citizens would feel secure. The fat serenity of authority: these cops actually believed that if people saw a cop car they would feel safe.

Old-fashioned Barrows was missing just about everything when it came to how society works.

Still, a society can be made to work. You don't have to have a society where the citizen is only a worker for the state, like in Russia. Or a worker for the corporation, like in America. You don't have to have a society which says that people are just like bees in a hive.

But, who cares? Most people want to be bees in a hive. Look at that wimp who delivered the cease and desist. That putrid little prick could not even exist unless he was a bee in a hive. Oh, yes, oh, yes.

My mind was flipping back and forth. It was going from one thing to another, searching, trying to find answers to questions when I was not even sure of the question. I don't like having been a specialist in killing. What I did with the army had to do with war, but it was around the edges where things were tense. I got concussed with a premature explosion, got discharged and then went back to school and into the streets. The feds had my file, all of it. Maybe they did not like me much, but nobody was talking down to anybody. They treated me like a pro.

I was born during World War II. I was a teenager when McCarthy screamed Commie and we tore up Korea. I was a veteran of the cold war before I ever saw a hot one. I was raised on war, on the yeah, rah, rah American bullshit of gold star mothers, the killing and cheap patriotism of the American Legion and the D.A.R.

What the Viet war taught me was to get back into school and try to figure out why people behave as they do.

How the mind jumps. Here I was, walking the main drag of my adopted town while a fed in a cop car drove back and forth, back and forth, like a catfish snagged on a trotline. People slumped as they walked beside me, their eyes dull, their minds dull from shock. I looked back on a life that had intended so much and done so little.

I was almost fifty. Life would not last much longer. Five years, maybe. Maybe twenty. Then it would be over, and so would all the dreams and good intentions. Death did not seem bad, and dying did not seem too bad, but having life end with no meaning was terrible.

It came to me, as I walked the main street, that Barrows had probably once felt the same way. He also wanted to do good. When he was young, back in 1875, he had been smart enough to get behind the facades of popular psychology. He discovered how to discorporate matter, how to make things vanish. He had dreamed of building a utopian world. He had even joined a group of pacifists, and had met about every kind of cluck that can be found in such groups.

He withdrew. The one person he had going for him was his wife. She must have been a great woman. The raw and naked pain on Barrows's face was because of her. I was willing to bet that he had lived so long with the memory of her that it was impossible for him to seriously think of any other woman. They had lived quietly in the east while Barrows studied. Then they came west. On the frontier he hoped that he might be able to use his power to help construct a perfect world.

An idea hit me hard. That's why Barrows needed me; he needed another perspective. The damned fool had lived a hundred and fifty years and did not realize something that was obvious. My thought stunned me so much that it almost knocked me from the sidewalk. If everybody else was not whipped around in their heads, people would have thought I was drunk. As it was I almost bumped into Grace McCloud. That would have been bad. Grace is the town bulldog. She has the looks of a bulldog. She sinks her teeth like a bulldog. She runs an antique shop and a political hate group. She hangs a wreath on soldiers' monuments on Veteran's Day. I'll bet she even starches her lousy flag.

The fed cruised by in the cop car. Old Jamison and Clete Simpson stood outside the respectable bar, and they looked seedy and sad. Generally they just look seedy. The Coast Guard cutter was moored with its flag at half-mast because one of its crew was murdered. Dick had been a good seaman. The officer in charge of the cutter was probably breaking regulations by lowering that flag and did not give a damn.

Now one of the fire trucks cruised by. It was not going to a fire. It was just for show, like the cop car. I guessed that the town must be in worse shape than I thought. The depressed feelings must be really deep, the fears as sharp as lasers. None of our preachers were on the street. Probably they were uptown with the dead.

Our mayor leaned against a stack of fertilizer bags outside the hardware store. Our mayor resembles a tourist's car. He is shiny and fat and well lubricated at all times. Except today.

"Jake," he said.

"Hi, mayor."

"I had nothing to do with this, Jake." He picked at his tie like there was a bug on it. His forehead was scrunched up and tight.

"Of course not, mayor." I walked on, not even thinking much about the guy . The poor pudding. It seemed to me that not even a government could take him seriously.

I realized Barrows had to act, for a lot of reasons. First of all, it still seemed possible to him that a perfect society could be put together. Second, he had to act before we were all killed by Mobilier. He had to do unto Mobilier before we got done unto.

I headed up the hill. The minute I could be sure the phone was not tapped, or could get to one that was clean, I was going to call Max. This situation needed all the originality and brains that I could gather together. It needed guys helping each other.

Barrows was okay. Just kind of innocent. He was a decent man, the kind I still hoped to become. And I had to admit that Barrows sure did honor people. He had not even saved his wife in 1917, when she contracted influenza. She had asked him to let her go.

The Second Attack

Chapter 14

Federal cops are so dumb at abstracting that they will tie you up for days over the most insignificant point. Federal cops are so dumb they would enjoy eating dog shit if you told them it was a chocolate banana. And they have no sense of humor.

For that reason I stayed away from Julie and Barrows. If the cops caught on to the fact that we were friends, then they would snoop around and snoop around. They would make a big deal out of nothing.

Besides, Julie was afraid. She did not send word for me to stay away from her, but she sure did not send word for me to come see her, either.

I went through a week of hard times. The weather was raw. My emotions were just as raw. My past rose up to slug me. All around me the house creaked and seemed to talk to itself. The wind kicked through the trees and sucked at chimney tops like it was a mouth slurping smoke. The fires had fantastic draft. My stoves have never kept the house so warm, and the house has never seemed more filled with ghosts.

The dreams were the worst. They kept coming back, and maybe it was the heat, and maybe the kettle on the stove put enough extra moisture into the air; but as hard as I tried to think of other things, the dreams would catch me. Dreams of summer always seem most real. In spite of the rain and cold and slop of that year in 'Nam, it was the summer I remembered.

The worst time I ever killed a man was the first time. It was not bad just because it was first. It was bad because I saw the guy's eyes.

I was twenty-two, well trained but expendable, and knew it. What you are told and how you are taught to think count for a lot. My training was good, but not good enough. I was not able to get *up* for that job. When you are really *up*, you have the same kind of mindless concentration that it takes to be good at sports. The difference is that you do not check your ferocity. You do not let the guy get back up for the next play.

The job itself was nothing. All I had to do was walk down a busy street of markets, like another army jock, touristing because he was tired of drinking and fucking.

My man came toward me. We knew he would be there, and somebody who gave orders even knew why. I had my own orders. As the guy passed me from the opposite direction, I blew him away with a pistol. He saw it coming a second before it happened. His eyes got wide but not scared. He did not even have time to get scared. There is a little comfort in that.

The job was nothing, and the guy was nothing. He did not even dress Western, and he was not Cong. Later I found out that he was a black market punk on the wrong side of somebody's dealing. I killed a man over some smuggling issue that had nothing to do with offense or defense in war. It had to do with placating some part of the economic power twist that a jock general was running in Vietnam.

The pistol sounded flat in the busy street. The guy just fell away on an oblique angle and started to flop. I just continued touristing along, and though lots of people saw it happen, nobody stopped me. The market was heavy smelling with sweat and dirt, with wilted vegetables, and there was no fresh smell anywhere in the afternoon.

The second time was technically worse, but I did not dream about it much. The second time I did not see the man's eyes. It was a dark night, and when I cut the guy he started squeaking funny. I had been nervous and done it wrong. So I started hitting with my fists until he was quiet. Like you would club a wounded rabbit or a hooked fish.

These dreams kept coming. The third/fourth/fifth/sixth times were explosive, and I really was up, but the charge went off a little early. I killed my men, but the explosion rolled me out as well. Then there was hospital and home and discharge and school—and let me tell you something, patriots, you Legionnaires and vets of foreign whores and assorted flag snappers.

This is the payoff for your tinfoil patriotism and your stinking flag, which is only an emblem of your dead crotches and disappointed minds.

I *do* believe in you. The way I believe in cockroaches.

After two nights I could not stand it. I walked out of town the back way, hiked across country to the main road and walked the road until I found a store. I called Max collect. He promised to come right away. There's friends for you. Max and I have not seen each other in fifteen years, although we have been writing back and forth. His letters have been nice, but sometimes abstract. Mine have been mostly news. It made my hike home a lot easier to have thoughts of such a friend. Cross-country travel at night is tough, even if you have a compass.

I got home at daylight and none of the feds looked me up. That told me that the feds figured me for a has-been. The human ego being what it is, that hurt my feelings. At the same time, from a tactical standpoint, it made me glad. The winds dropped off but the rains returned.

I did everything I could to look normal and unthreatening to the feds. One especially good way to look normal was to attend the mass funeral.

About five hundred people showed up to skid around in the slick, clumpy grass of the graveyard. Dick Peterson owns a backhoe and shovel loader. Instead of graves he cut a long trench. A lot of the bodies, husbands and wives and children, were jammed together in single coffins. All of the bodies, even the freaks and the gunman, at least had boxes.

The services were held right there. I watched the crowd press together in the cold rain like it was trying to get warm; like the water splashing on the boxes and filling the trench was an extra force of cold to reach out to the living. Julie's face hovered like a small moon of pallor and fear between the drawn faces of Barrows and Jim. Penny was there. Small and tough. Mike was not, and that made me glad. The crowd pressed back and forth, and the three preachers divided the service. One wept, one sounded like Jesus's little lamb, and one got mad and scorned the army M.P.s who were standing around showing the flag. It did no good and he should have held it in, but it looked to me like he was just one more guy who was too smart to be a preacher. None of the dead arose. I hadn't counted on it.

Anger spread after the funeral. That is a normal crowd response. Emotions get so heavy that a crowd will feel what it is told to feel, and the angry preacher was the only one who made any sense. The crowd anger would last two days if the bars stayed closed. It would last one day if the bars opened; but if the bars were open there was danger of the crowd blowing up. Anybody who studies group responses could predict that. Even the stupid feds could predict that. I figured the booze joints would be open again in seventy-two hours, and the feds would be gone in ninety-six. That is exactly what happened.

Later, when the feds left, they left a couple of their guys in town. I figured we could expect to see a few new faces for a long while, and those new faces would not belong to tourists. By the end of the week, though, the whole event of raid and murders was history.

At the time of the funeral, though, I just watched Barrows and Julie. There was such deep sadness on Barrows's face. From time to time there were strong expressions of guilt. He still did not have the situation figured out.

I had it figured out. It wasn't even very tough figuring. Anyone who knows anything about bureaucracy and business could have figured it out.

At some time, maybe a long, long time ago, Barrows attracted the interest of the army. He had even told us that the army had approached him, wanting to use his power. He had run away and hid, but the information did not run away.

Files do not disappear. Once it is written down on paper, it is there forever. Anyone who believes that the military or the feds destroy records—just because they say they do—does not understand bureaucracy. Records never disappear, they just get buried from public view. Sometimes the paper disappears, but the record is still somewhere, on some computer. I'll bet if you went into the records of the FBIA right now, sooner or later you could find the file of everyone who was considered subversive during World War I.

Records do not disappear, because in a bureaucracy no individual wants to take responsibility. Bureaucracies do not like to go on record, not public record. They do not like to countermand decisions. Once a decision is made, and is written down, no one will take the responsibility to change the decision. That is true of every bureaucracy all the way back to ancient China.

So, in an abstract way of speaking, we had been attacked and our neighbors had been killed by a piece of paper.

Of course, it was more than that. We had an informer in town. He was probably not a very smart informer; just some jerk who was supposed to report anything unusual. He would be the kind of jerk who would be keeping an eye on me because I had a file with the feds.

The informer had sent word to Mobilier, and Mobilier's computers had coughed up Barrows—some strange old goat suddenly appearing from history. That Mobilier had tried to make a deal with Barrows before the attack showed just how little information on Barrows Mobilier really had. Because Mobilier was in the dark, it had overreacted. That is the way the bureaucracy of business, of government, and of the military operates.

I wanted to tell all of this to Barrows, and I wanted to talk to Julie because her fear was so great. It was like Julie sensed that something terrible was going to happen, and that it pointed right at her. She takes things so personally. The problem is that she was right—at least about terrible things happening—and we were going to have to move fast to avoid them.

Maybe I made a mistake in staying away from Barrows and Julie. Maybe I was being too careful. At the same time, I know governments. They will murder on the basis of nothing more than suspicion. This business had already proven itself to be a kill matter. Because of my record I was moderately hot. Probably no one cared, but I still did not want to take chances or increase Julie's fear.

Dolores did not care. She has as much imagination as Julie, but she is more objective. When I left the funeral, Dolores and I fell in side by side without even thinking about it. The walk from the cemetery is long. The feds had commandeered her truck as well as

JACK CADY

ours. The rain was in front of a stiff wind. That was okay. I work
with timber and she works with marine biology. We know about
weather.

Somewhere between the graveyard and my house I knew that
Dolores and I were going home to spend the day and night. It was a
human enough response. People do that sort of thing after funerals.

We walked, and by the time we got to my place we were pretty
wet. I went to the bedroom for a couple of robes, and we shucked
out in front of the cookstove.

"Did Julie ask you to come?" It was an inelegant question, but I
did not want to feel like a charity case. Julie might have.

Dolores began poking at the fire. She is not as tall as Julie, but
proportionately they are much alike. Both are quiet and attractive.
Both are smarter than I am, but Dolores is smarter than just about
anybody. The big difference is that Dolores has strong emotions
and laughs at them. Julie doesn't laugh.

"Are you deliberately trying to be a jerk?"

"I'm sorry," I told her, "the last few days have been screwy."

"You did not kill that man, that assassin?"

"I just knocked him out and handcuffed him."

"This whole situation will end badly."

"It sure as hell has started badly."

When she smiles, which is pretty often, her full mouth has a kind
of softness that denies the sometimes harsh way she has of looking
at life. Sometimes, and this was one of those times, there is also
tenderness in the smile. It is not sexual and it is not motherly. Just
full and human. I love her, and we lived together for a long time. I
did not stop loving her just because I began living with Julie.

"Do you know why we are no longer together?" Her quiet voice
was filled with the reasonableness and severity that had been hard
for me to deal with at other times. But she was still smiling.

"I thought about it a lot. Then I had to stop, because thinking
about it hurt."

"Because with the best theoretical ability you still take things
personally." She was still smiling. "At your worst you are an angry,
tinhorn messiah." Behind the smile her voice was even a little sad.

"And," she said, "at your best you are the finest and most gentle
man I know."

104

I do not handle nice things said about me very well. It was kind of breathtaking to realize that she had not stopped loving me, either. We have been around each other so little in the last couple of years.

"What exactly is happening?" Her smile was gone now. She was looking for facts, ready to analyze what she heard.

I told her what was happening and could see her balance the information. She was making tentative conclusions and then revising her conclusions as she heard more facts. Her sadness increased. She seemed to know that we were in a fatal situation.

"You have a nondirectional and immense force, which is Mobilier. It is in conflict with a judgmental, all-powerful force, which is Barrows."

"Looks like it," I said. She surprised me. She was boiling the situation down a lot finer than I could have done at the time.

"And the last time that happened," she said.

"It has never happened before in history."

"Noah and the Flood," she said. "It's happened at least once."

I could see her point. If Barrows ever lost control, and really cut loose, then his power would be a flood every bit as great as the flood of the Old Testament story.

"Whether we get out of this or not depends on Barrows," Dolores said. "Or rather, it all depends on you in your relation to Barrows."

I didn't get it.

"You must convince Barrows to use his power, but you must not allow him to use or misuse the power."

"I can't even get the dumb son of a bitch to listen," I told her.

"You'd better get him to listen." She was wearing her analytic look, a look that I trust. "If Barrows acts, really acts, then Mobilier is a paper tiger, a straw man. It cannot stand against that kind of power. If Barrows does not act, then everyone in this town is doomed." She said it quiet, and she did not seem particularly angry or emotional. Only analytic. "Get Barrows to negotiate," she told me . "As long as there is communication, there's a chance that there will be no more murders."

She's brilliant, but she's a marine biologist. She knows very little about power structures.

"A huge organization has been set in motion," I told her. "If the head of that organization calls this whole thing off, the tail will whip around for a few weeks. Another attack is coming. Count on it."

"Then it is stupid to stay here." There was still no fear about her. She was still analytic.

"Makes no difference," I said. "With the kind of surveillance they own, it is futile to leave."

"Are you prepared to take some losses? Are you prepared to lose some more of our people?"

"No," I told her. "There was a time when I understood that militarily, but I don't understand it anymore."

"Then, baby, you had better take action quick."

And there it was. She knew. I knew. Barrows sat with his thumb up his ass thinking great, humane and mystical thoughts. Max was going to be a help. Max could tell me a lot more about these specimens who call themselves mystics.

Another attack came all right, and it was a surprise attack because it did not come directly at us.

While Dolores and I spent the afternoon and night together, while Max was getting ready to leave Billings and while Julie crouched at Penny and Jim's house, Mobilier made what looked like a random hit.

Like hell it was random. The town of Nighthawk, Montana, had exactly the same population as the town of Land's End. Mobilier destroyed Nighthawk. Mobilier did it to show Barrows that he had better come over to their side, or Land's End was really and truly doomed. It was straight-out blackmail.

The people of Nighthawk never knew what hit them, but they sure knew that it was hitting them, because of the pain.

Through the darkness silently running hovercraft whirred and whipped like a blanket over the town, which was illumi-nated by the moon in a cloudless sky. No doubt one cop was awake. Maybe some old people who could not sleep heard the muted sounds of the engines. A few dogs barked. Then the dogs screamed, twisted and died; while in their beds the population of Nighthawk did the same. It was silent murder, or nearly. No one heard the saturating range of ultrasonic sounds, although maybe the dogs heard them. The sounds were no different from knives disrupting cellular tissues. The only thing that could have been heard was the purr of the hovercraft. The purr must have gone on for hours, because Mobilier wanted to be sure that there was total destruction. Death came painfully to Nighthawk, and in too many cases it also came slow.

=

Ageless and indifferent, the rains rise from the western ocean above the turbulence of the Japanese current which drives warm water northward into the encroaching arctic seas. Clouds form and roll away from the vacuum between the current and the Russian, American and Canadian coasts. Above trawlers and trollers and purse seiners flying a variety of flags, carrying fisher folk of a dozen nations following a trade that was ancient in the days of Babylon. The sea lifts and tosses the boats, makes the flags worn and faded and paltry, and touches singly the heart of each man and woman of the sea. And those hearts, fearful as only the sea can cause, courageous in a way that the sea requires, in their genius of wants and necessity, name their boats Archangel *or* Rose *or* Jeanne d' Arc—*to uncover with the bobbing name on the gray sea a spot of consciousness like a spark glowing through the vast and indifferent rains.*

Through the Alaskan southeast, across Vancouver Island and into Puget Sound, the clouds flow roiling and wind driven to carry the indifferent rain. Against the mountains, the Canadian Rockies, the Olympics and the Cascades, the clouds sweep like a green hand to give heat and life to the fecund Pacific Northwest.

Then they rise. Beyond the summits of the ranges, the clouds boil and seem to refuse passage. They lift, high sailing and cold as they cross the short grass prairies of Washington, Idaho and Montana, where wintering beasts huddle. The short grass prairies are harsh and stark and beautiful beneath the high sailing clouds. The land seems as clean as a purified intellect, a mind of grace.

Max Klein carried a suitcase filled with work clothes, a briefcase of books and a small cardboard box of food. He rode a bus that moved antlike across the winter plains that were covered with snow that was icy and even thinner than his possessions.

Chapter 15

THERE WAS A NOTE ON THE KITCHEN TABLE WHEN I GOT UP THE NEXT morning.

"You don't know what love means, because you still believe there is such a thing. If we are happy together, you and I, that is fine. It does not make history, though, and it does not make the future. Maybe someday I will meet someone who can laugh at his own self, and who will be able to laugh at my own self. If I do, then maybe I'll learn more.

"Jake, there is no salvation for you. You theorize, but you are at the bottom—and I don't mean in the crotch-experiential. You have to get cold and logical, Jake, or you will not be able to handle this."

=

Dolores left that, a fresh pot of coffee, a good fire in the stove. When I next saw her we would be old friends again. The warmth and glow and passion of the night would be as if they never existed. Maybe she's right. Maybe nothing is real except what is happening right now, but God, I hate to believe that.

She sure was right about one thing. If I was going to do anything useful, I had to get cold. I had to be objective and not take everything personal. It would be a mistake to get flaming mad. The problem is that I'm a sucker for government and business. The lying cruds.

It was a good thing we did not know what happened in Nighthawk for a couple of days. That gave me time to try to be objective. Max was going to be a big help, but he could not help if my own knowledge was slight. For those two days I reviewed the changes I had seen, contemplated how the country was structured, and projected what might be done to change things for the better.

As the 1990s opened, the best way to describe America was to say that it was gray, with occasional bright streaks of arterial blood.

A new class structure had emerged. Politics and politicians no longer amounted to anything, although politicians still thought they did. When push came to shove, though, government no longer held power. There was only one justification for government. It served as the chief market for goods. It was only useful for business.

I could explain how all this happened. Lord, Lord, I could go back in history and show how the American mind began to form in Europe a hundred years before the Pilgrims ever came to Plymouth plantation.

I could, but who gives a damn? As the years pass, fewer and fewer people care.

And my knowledge gets all mixed up with this man who is me. I get so sad. Stupid Jake tried to care, but stupid Jake never could get it through his thick skull that no one else cared. I watched my beloved nation die, and the more I explained, the more everyone yawned.

When I was a killer everybody thought I was a great guy. When I tried to explain the good reasons for not killing people, my nation decided that I was a perverted intellectual freak. Fuck it. Flush it.

The new class in America looked like the commissars of Russia during the 1950s. The new class was a party elite.

What had once been the middle class was now the government bureaucracy. It made up about twenty-five percent of the working population.

The lower class, the rest of us, made up about seventy percent of the population.

That top five percent, that new class, was made up of high government and corporate officials.

The new class was insanely rich. It was more vulgar than old-time Texas oilmen. The new class had every mechanical toy that a dying civilization could provide. It owned automobiles that were longer than a nun's nightshirt, yachts that looked like converted destroyers and sometimes were; and that class ate steak for breakfast while the cities starved. It was a status-conscious class, subject to fads. For the last few years one of those fads had been tourism. The new class globe trotted in an ostentatious display of waste. It was considered status to blow off two thousand gallons of aircraft fuel to have dinner in Mexico, or a day's shopping in Spain. This, despite the fact that in moderate weather areas such as ours, heat was a luxury unless you burned wood. The new class was aristocratic, in that churlish, irresponsible sense that always attends the dying days of nations. The fall of America looked no different from the fall of Rome.

The bureaucracy, which had once been the middle class, was pretty much nothing. It lived in reduced circumstances. Some smart jock economist had figured the level of income required to keep the bureaucracy at a point where it could hope to better itself. That was politically smart. As long as a segment of a population feels hope for betterment under the going system, then revolution is unlikely.

The bureaucrats made just enough money that they could partly compete on the black market for consumer goods. The rest of us, the poor people, were on a subsistence level. Some places were better than others. Our town of Land's End was remote. It was directly related to production of fish, wood and tourist facilities. More money came through our town than happened in most places. Some of the money rubbed off on local trade. Our town is so small that it is not really worth policing.

In the cities, though, life was awful. Police were everywhere. People starved. Although soybeans and fishmeal were main ingredients of most available food, there was a growing protein deficiency among people in the cities. That was especially true for small children. Their systems do not handle vegetable protein very well.

What had happened? I think of what used to be, and how it has changed. I look at this old house, haunted, like it held the collective voices of a century that are strutting and pontificating about progress and wealth. Those voices are sad and unhappy, now. What went wrong? I'll even bet that one of those voices belongs to the old merchant who built this house. I suppose the sorry son of a bitch actually thought he was doing right in the eyes of society and God. Almost everyone in the nineteenth century would have told him he was.

To understand the 1990s you really have to look at the 1890s.

Mike dropped by while I was working. I had been reading, and when the sound of his shit box rumbled in the drive, it was easy to lay the book aside and put on water for coffee.

He came in looking different. Usually Mike sort of slides through a doorway so that he won't bump into anything. As he grows bigger and gets more filled out, he has to constantly relearn how to handle that frame. This time he just walked right in. I could feel him getting pushy before he said a word. When he did say something, it was only hello.

He had a lot to say. I could tell that. His problem was that he was wordless. Words never seem like very powerful medicine until they are the only medicine that works. Mike was a product of the educational needs of his time. The schools were allowed to teach him to read, but only barely. That low-grade ability to read means that a person has a low-grade ability to think. In other words, the schools were hired to teach their students to be consumers of corporate goods. If one cannot read well, then his wordlessness gets changed into a vague wish to buy things. The most subversive thing I've ever done is to try to teach Mike how to think.

"Seen Julie?"

"She's okay." He looked directly at me, like a challenge. Then he looked away.

"How about yourself?"

"Yeah." He said it, and we both knew it was bullshit.

Something was not bullshit, though. Mike was moving differently. He took possession of a chair, rather than just easing down to sit on it. He actually looked like a punk executive preening his aggressions for a tough business meeting.

"I'm not okay," I told him. "I've been everywhere in my head since the killings."

That eased him a little. If I was not pretending, then he would not have to pretend. I guessed that he wanted to talk about the killings. Mike had known all of those kids who were murdered.

"Been drinking?"

"Some." He could admit to that. It is socially okay. The alcoholism rate among we poor people is not known, but if it is under twenty percent, I'm surprised.

So he had been drinking. Mike was the corporation's New Citizen.

The pliable, anesthetized creature with vague desires and low, generalized ability. The problem for those corporations was that Mike was something more. He was decent, gentle, and he had a good mind that had never been trained.

"They were all friends," I said.

"I'm going to kill the bastards." He was quiet with it, not making a big deal. There was no sense in asking which bastards he meant. He could start just about anywhere with someone who wore a business suit.

"Not the way to do it," I told him. "It looks like it ought to be a good way, but it doesn't work."

He is slow to temper, but he was hot now. Any moment I expected him to get self-righteous and start yelling.

Something else was different about Mike, and it was scary. He was dressed in clean clothes and he looked almost prim. His hair was washed and tied back. He looked like a man who had prepared himself for some goddamned holy cause. Oh, Mike. Mike.

"Nancy?" Nancy Pridham had been about his age.

If he had been weeping, there were no tears now. There was only quiet resolution. He had decided to kill some people, and he had already decided that no one was going to talk him out of it. He sat quietly, and the coffee started to perk. I knew what he was feeling, and I knew how stupid the feelings were. He was so godawful ignorant, and yet in a way he was correct. Sometimes in history the only answer is to start a revolution. Did I have any answers for him that were better? Wind kicked the windows. The house rattled like it would fall down, and, of course, someday it would.

For a shocking moment the kid looked like a priest. There was a tranquil purpose on his face. Mike seemed like he had just been born. The killings had thrown him into an emotional crisis, and the crisis had put him through some cruddy rite of passage. Mike felt himself fully a man.

It made me happy for him, but it also made me tired and sick. It was brand new stuff to him, but it was older than the Rock of Ages to me.

"It doesn't work that way. It won't."

He still said nothing. I thought that he wanted to talk, but he could not get far enough away from his feelings. His thoughts would not take shape.

"How much do you know about me?"

He still said nothing. Eyes sincere and new, visions of truth, maybe; the rise of a new day, the toast to the fall of tyrants—drink to it, boys—oh, Mike.

So I told him all about myself. The army and the killings, then the street leadership and the demonstrations. I was not proud of it, even the last, because the last had been done badly. I started out to tell him one thing, and damn if I didn't end up telling him not to do it if he did it badly.

"That's why it won't work." I finished up, and my argument sounded lame and weak even as I said it.

He was going to protect his newfound authority. He was not going to allow the bright, shining sense of himself to be blown away by my bum experience. At the same time, he was interested. Mike can't read very well, but he's smart. He figured he would learn from my mistakes.

And the crazy thing was that the wind was still blowing. On the strait the water tumbled as it had tumbled since the last ice age. Beyond the windows the fruit trees had swelling buds. Nature was going on the way it always had, regulated and sensible.

I looked at Mike and thought about revolution. I could see how those old eighteenth-century revolutionaries in France and America figured that they could make a society that was as perfect as nature.

They failed, of course, the way Mike was going to fail. They did not take into account the ancient human problems of ego and insecurity and roles and institutions.

So I told him more. If Mike had been born into a violent and vicious world, that still did not mean that there weren't kindness and hope and valor all around him. He had to focus on that, the way I had to focus on that. We had to remember the good parts. If we could not see that the hard stuff was impersonal, then he would become a killer—and maybe me too. I just know that when you kill, the person you kill most is yourself.

Mike was a citizen of a dying nation. That has never been easy. I tried to explain to him what was happening.

In 1991 most of us lived badly because over the years the economic structures had changed. They changed because corporations had finally figured out a different way of viewing the marketplace. It was the third new view in American history.

The first view climaxed in the 1890s. Back in those days, business saw its workers as people who should be exploited. The worker was underpaid and overworked. Business sold its goods on the international market, and to that part of the American class structure which had money.

Then, in the early twentieth century, the labor unions came along and the second view of markets entered American history. Business discovered that well-paid workers were the best kind of customers. Business geared up to sell goods to the American working class. This idea, combined with union demands, eventually gave rise to the large American middle class.

I had to keep it simple, so that Mike would not get confused. I kept politics out of it. I did not say a word about old melodrama John Dulles, or old fart-sniffer Joe McCarthy.

The third new way of looking at the marketplace spelled the end for the middle class. Business finally realized that its best customers were governments. Then the honeymoon was over for most Americans.

It is a gray world, but it is a hot one.

Things really started to go to hell in the mid-eighties. The resources started to dry up. It was not a question of fuel as much as it was a question of copper, lead, uranium, and especially water.

The West had been on a declining water scale for a century. As energy corporations commandeered water to process coal, Montana, Wyoming, Colorado, New Mexico and Texas were turned into dust bowls. The food production capacity of the U.S. dropped about twenty percent.

As resources dried up, corporations made war on each other. The wars were first fought behind the facade of the legal system;

and those kinds of wars had been going on through the whole twentieth century, anyway.

Finally, the courts redefined the concept of "eminent domain." Corporations were named the true protectors of America, and the function of government was declared to be administrative. True, governments still owned armies, but the corporations owned the governments.

Then the corporations turned their attention to manipulation. They attacked the public mind. The public had been used to receiving its opinions from news analysts on television for thirty years. Now the corporations owned the televisions and the press.

Where there were remaining resources, television and the press were used to incite the workers to demonstrate and riot. The news people persuaded the workers that the only way to retain jobs was to rebel against government control of resources.

As scarcities grew, the conflict became more blatant. Battle lines formed. The unions, themselves a major industry, announced their support of corporations. Government was forced to send its armies where the corporations wanted.

Of course, that was nothing new.

Some things, though, *were* new, and they were horrible. One was that the corporations were no longer American. They were international, with no loyalty to any nation. The corporations carved the world and the nations into spheres of influence. In cities they fought with hired gangs. They trained and fielded their own armies in the guise of private police forces.

On the face of it, it appeared as if one corporation and its subsidiaries owned a city like Detroit. Another conglomerate owned Chicago. That was just on the face of it, because at the time I was explaining all of this to Mike, we still did not know the power of Mobilier.

How you lived in America depended on where you lived. Some corporations were more interested in social control than others. In Chicago, which was ostensibly owned by a combination of energy, insurance and publication industries, social control was nearly absolute. Many of George Orwell's predictions for 1984 did not miss by much.

In Chicago workers were constantly under surveillance on the job, if not always in the home. Mandatory attendance at corporation functions was standard. The Chicago police force constituted the most effective small army that the world had ever seen. It was equipped with sophisticated technology, and it practiced social control in most of the ways that had been discovered by earlier totalitarian states. Like the Nazis, the Chicago police practiced something called "social atomization." That meant that the police tried to make each citizen afraid of his neighbor. Suspicion and fear were taught to children in the schools. Political worship was also taught, but the American mind did not produce someone called Big Brother. It just produced one more goddamned Daddy Warbucks.

. . . I just broke it off for a minute. It seemed like Mike was going to overload. He was mad and getting madder. What I was telling him was making him feel kind of hopeless. His newfound authority was sliding away.

His brown eyes grew darker. They were alive in a different way, now. They were filled with pain. He was beginning to realize that there was no answer to our problems. He was feeling helpless, and before I started talking he had felt powerful.

I just let him sit there and feel all the crap he was feeling. Meanwhile, I picked up a broom and kind of swept around a little. When you burn wood you are constantly sweeping. The red, scented splinters of cedar kindling, the chips of alder and fir bark combine with wood dust and stove smoke. Burning wood is an okay thing. It gives good sights, and good smells, but you have to clean up about twice a day.

Cedar ran out on the Olympic Peninsula in the late seventies. In a couple of years there will be none left in the national forest. There is a lot of young growth, of course, but I do not think Mike's kids—if he lives to have any—will ever see a two-hundred-foot cedar.

In Montana there was not a stick of wood left. The people over there had a terrible time trying to burn coal for heat. That Montana coal is lignite with a high flash bead. It is not much better than trying to burn dirt .

In the useless West, corporate control was lax. The population was free to try to subsist without interruption. Utah and Idaho and Eastern Washington were owned by the Mormon corporation. Parts of the South, especially Texas and Louisiana, were organized by fuel companies that ruled as strictly as the Fascists had once ruled in Italy. Hawaii was owned by the black market, Alaska by extracting industries, and the East Coast was the damndest mess in all of history. From Philadelphia northward the East Coast was collectivized under the most intricate system of corporate spit swapping that could be contrived. It was an economic and political showcase. Washington, D.C., was second rate, and only the president and other cheap shit politicians were ever seen there.

The corporations divided up the East Coast. The corporate wars blazed across the nation, but the head warriors played it chummy in New York.

"I don't know how to tell you," I said to Mike. "In the nineteen years since you were born, everything changed so fast."

Then I had what I thought was a good idea. "We are going to be attacked again," I told him. "Right now, somewhere, some son of a bitch is working up the next attack plan. If you want to do something useful, then get ready to defend this town, or at least learn some first aid."

Maybe it was a good idea, but it was not the idea he had in mind. He still wanted to go out and blow away some poor jerk in a business suit. He wanted to attack, not defend.

"Man," I told him, "why the hell didn't you get this mad before." He said nothing.

"Because you didn't know any better. You didn't know how bad things were, because for as long as you've lived they've always been bad. You had nothing to compare with."

He didn't get it.

"You don't have to compare nothing to get mad."

On his way to learning how to be gentle, on his way to learning how to be kind, this nice kid was also on his way to becoming a killer.

He makes me want to cry. He wanted to be effective, to do well. People can make me want to cry sometimes. Because, when you stop to think about it, it doesn't make much difference what people do. It's the meaning that they hope for, strive for.

I had a couple more things that I had to tell Mike, but it was necessary to tell them fast.

A horrible development had come about since the day he was born. The corporate shareholder had disappeared. Even the corporate rich were mostly employees. The corporation had become the final monster that corporations could become. When there were still shareholders, there was still the possibility of some ethics. Now the corporations owned each other, and so they were totally amoral.

There was one final but interesting twist. That was the black market.

The black market originally had its roots in the Mafia, but for years it had been legitimate. It was a separately functioning economic system within the larger system. The black market originally came into being because government and business had worked out no effective way to distribute drugs. In America there was a kind of "doublethink" about drugs. They were as necessary as alcohol. At the same time enough American prudery was left to make them questionable. The black market rose on the back of the need for drugs.

As it rose, it expanded. Finally the black market was encouraged because it could supply goods and services that other corporations could not. The best customers of the black market were the corporate rich. The mediocrity of corporate production was so all-pervading that you could depend on most things to break. When Mike went to Seattle to buy the saws, he would not have bought them from a chain saw dealer. It would have taken weeks to get them, and once we got them we would have spent a lot of time rebuilding them. On the black market, though, you could still buy tools that worked.

"All you do when you kill people is nothing," I told Mike. "If you kill a killer, then society produces three more killers—it produces you, and two guys to replace the one you hit. It's like picking noses. The stuff just keeps building."

"I'm not just going to sit on my ass." He meant it. He was still mad, but at least he was friendlier now. He had gotten it through his head that I was not trying to con him.

What could I tell him? The kid had himself at stake. If action, even futile action, made him alive instead of being only a pablum citizen of the corporate nineties, then we were on the right track. I told him to wait for two weeks. If at the end of that time he was still hot to go out and cause a few eruptions, then I would show him various ways to construct bombs, teach him a few other skills.

I knew that a skilled anarchist does not get caught, or rarely. Especially if he operates alone. Police and government will tell you otherwise, but to believe it you would have to have your thumb in your butt and your head in a crapper—and there is no sense joining government in its usual position.

It's all wrong. It's all wrong. I should be able to protect Mike, help him, show him that you do not need violence to keep your ego alive. The split in my mind seemed like it was working overtime. My other thought was that it was too bad Mike couldn't blow up every bank in the world. Then all the chintzy power mongers could go back to swapping radishes.

After all, Mike was their creature. If there was a flaw in their corporate plans, then surely the fat bellies would want to know about it. There was no damage Mike could do that would one percent touch what those dudes had done in the name of God and country.

=

The myriad dreams and theologies of the human creature pulse through the sliding frames of time like pictures on a strip of movie film that change as more film rolls.

One single frame is a tale of the Hassidic Jews which goes:

Before there was a world, God filled the universe like a fat man filling every niche and corner of a room. Poor God. Especially so fat. This God did not know who he was.

So he sucked in his gut—whoosh—and there was extra space in the universe and He built things: mountains and trees and animals and people and beer kegs, it shouldn't matter. Into each of the things He placed a little piece of Himself, and then He sat back to watch what all of the things did. That was so God could know who He was.

Chapter 16

TWO DAYS PASSED WHILE BARROWS ISOLATED HIMSELF. HE CLAIMED to be tracing the power structure of Mobilier. Knowing Barrows, though, it was likely that he was spending a lot of that time just sitting around and feeling guilty or mystical.

During those two days, apparently, General of Air/Space George Butterfield reviewed a set of orders that made little sense to him. Butterfield was about to prove that he was a genius as a general officer, and he would do it in spite of the orders.

The orders told him to reduce the town of Land's End if those orders had not been countermanded by a given date. Butterfield did not know it, and Barrows didn't, but Mobilier had made a cut-off decision. The guy who was pushing the button on us, an oilman named Chester, had decided that if negotiations with Barrows did not get any results by that date, then the only safe move was to wipe Barrows's slate. In order to do that, he was going to have to kill Land's End. Chester did not know how much of Barrows's ability might have been taught to other people in Land's End. All he knew was that any individual in the town might present a threat.

Butterfield was puzzled because the orders advised him to be aware that he might face "extraordinary weapons." That made no sense, not to a general. That was bureaucratic crap, and he must have known it.

There are a couple of other things that he must have either known or guessed.

First, he had to have guessed that his orders came from some civilian. Military headquarters had been told what to say.

Second, he must have guessed that he was not trusted. If a military man had originated the orders, then the entire tactical situation would have been given. Instead, there was only that vague reference to "extraordinary weapons." He was not being given information that he needed. That meant that he was not even trusted to keep a secret.

It also meant, and Butterfield was too sharp to have missed it, that he and his forces were already written off. They were not expendable, they were already expended. I reckon he figured that that was one hell of a way to treat a general.

Meanwhile, Max was due in town. I swung by Jim's house, picked up Julie, and she hugged me a little. Not as much as she should have, considering how long we had been apart. She was still scared. As I drove downtown she remained silent. Maybe she felt guilty for staying away from me. For myself, I was a little bit pissed. We were still not talking much when we climbed from the truck and waited for the bus.

The bus is new but little. It is like the buses you used to see hauling kids to camp. The big bus line rents it to the Strouds. Janice was driving because Jill had been sick off and on all winter.

Julie and I watched it swing around the block and then point into our only bus stop. I tried not to be sore at her, to forgive her for her fear. Because of Barrows's inaction we were all sitting like big, fat, quack-happy ducks on a pond with shotguns pointed at us.

"He may be fat and not have any hair." I had not seen Max in a long, long time.

"There's only six people on the bus. Four are women." Julie's face was pale, like on the day of the funeral. Maybe she figured that Max was just one more threat. Julie seemed frail. I know her well enough to know that she would stay that way for a while, and then she would decide on a course of action. She would drive at it with a full intensity that exhausted her. Some people get drunk and have visions. Julie works.

The streets were nearly deserted. It was still cold and windy. One or two ghoulish types had visited town to gawk at the mass burial, but even they were gone.

And Barrows was sitting and suffering because of the blackmail killings in Nighthawk, Montana. In spite of all the deaths, he still thought that a quiet and reasonable approach was the only one that would work.

When Max came from the bus he looked no different than he has ever looked. Max has that definite Semitic face that is the despair of anthropologists. Even Julie. Anthropology can never decide where the Jews belong in its dingdong hierarchy of peoples. Ethnic? Religious? All I knew is it was awful good to see him. Max is a big guy, as tall as Barrows and Jim, but built more muscular. Wearing an ex-army shirt like usual. Smiling easy like usual. Max is so quiet. He grabbed me around the shoulders, squeezed, and it was like fifteen years had not passed.

"Uglier than I remember."

"Just real glad you're here." Then I introduced Julie to Max. They took it well.

I got his luggage to the truck. We drove the main drag, hung a left up the hill, and Max leaned back and watched. His face was still smooth, but it was like he had wrinkles beneath the skin. Age. He watched the quiet main street, the ornate Victorian houses, the surrounding water and mountains.

"Seems quiet."

"Hell to pay a week ago."

"But quiet now?"

"We were raided," Julie said.

"Quiet on the face of it," I told him. "A bunch of people got shot up. Now our dead are buried and everybody is back to chicken stuff."

"Not true," Julie told him. "A lot of people are afraid and crying."

"What a town," I said. "We had some federal oinkers come in, and some army jocks. They waved the flag three times, bowed toward the Pentagon, and then all us sheep went back to pasture."

"I'll get out here," Julie said. Her voice was small and tight, the way it gets when she is truly pissed. "It's nice to meet you," she said to Max.

"I'm sorry. I really am." I kept driving.

"Your diction has improved. All that really matters." Max had Julie's number. She almost, but not quite, smiled.

"I really am sorry," I told Julie.

Maybe she's right, but with thirty-seven people dead and Mike about to go on a vendetta, did she expect me to be singin'?

I pulled up to the house, tried to ignore the tumbling side porch that has to get fixed and helped Max. Julie stood around. She was balancing her interest in Max with her need to dump on me for being bitter. I know her. She would come inside, but she would do a silent number.

While Max was getting settled I went to the living room and started a fire. Julie put water on the stove, then took a couple of licks at the mantel with a dust rag. She was finding quiet ways to tell me I was a slob. Her place is no cleaner than mine.

"Ready to fill me in?" He walked into the room with more grace than he was finding, and more friendliness as well. The fire was beginning to catch. I made a bet with myself that Julie would pull a freeze for twenty minutes. In twenty minutes things would be sailing. I even checked the clock.

"Do you know about the hit over your way?" Nighthawk is not far from Billings.

"Yes."

"The same outfit hit here."

"How do you know?"

"It takes explaining some other things."

"Do that. Over five thousand people were killed in Nighthawk."

"Five thousand and twelve people. At least fifteen hundred dogs, dozens of cats and the wildlife. The insects weren't out yet, and won't be. A few botanic materials, mostly seeds, survived. The old scorched earth policy."

"Why?"

"Blackmail. It was a pressure play to force Barrows into joining up with this outfit."

"It was done with sound waves," Max said.

How had he known that? I did not figure that even the cops knew that. "Every destructive range was used," I told him. "The distortion on faces indicated incredible pain." I watched Julie. The words were hurting her. I revised my estimate. Thirty minutes.

Max just accepted the facts about Barrows. Max is intuitive. I feel a situation, then deny it by applying rules that do not work. Then the situation builds to the point where I go back and make new assumptions. Max just stays open and allows the situation to develop. Then he asks if his knowledge fits. In spite of the differences, we used to be a whale of a team.

"Go further back," he said.

He had to do that. He had to listen and determine if we were sane. He wanted to know the whole situation. Since the work of a man named William Isaac Thomas, no social thinker can safely ignore the concept of "situation." It was almost like having Thomas there, except he died in the 1940s.

"I was one of twenty-seven children . . ."

"An only child," said Julie.

"The youngest and most innocent." Max was smiling, and he really did have Julie's number. Even Julie smiled a little.

"Where do you want me to start," I asked.

"Start with when we last saw each other."

"Okay," I said, "you came to the hospital to see me. You were bewildered and sad. You were leaving for Montana and you almost got busted for asking if I wanted to go along. There was a bug in that hospital room, and some jive-ass fed cop on the other end of the bug."

"Those were strange days," Max said. "Worse in their way than these."

"No one was considered innocent," I said. "If the military had not believed that Nixon was a clown, Nixon would have pulled a coup on his own government. The poor fuck could not even handle his own military."

"Very likely."

"I healed up after a while," I told Max. "Went to Oregon. Drifted around for a while, went south and nothing worked. By then the feds just hated me like they hated everybody. They no longer counted me as much of an enemy."

"You were indicted. I remember." Max's voice was as concerned as if the whole thing had just happened.

"Who wasn't?"

I remember how useless it all seemed. L.A., Frisco, Seattle, the hatred was everywhere. Each morning in some city, traffic started to blaze at seven o'clock. Sound clanged as the confusion and hatred of the day built and spilled into the streets. More fists were raised, more yelling; and the heavy traffic crashed like imitation thunder in a third-rate German opera.

In the spring the government murdered some people on the Kent State campus for the crime of being young. Idaho enjoyed a severe paranoid high. The news came across my face like another slap against reason and divinity. I drifted around the truly seamy city of Boise, while the traffic cracked and even the lousy winos drifting beside me were delirious with joy because of death. I was not old, except inside, and I was not young. For a while it was possible to act invisible. I had money. A co-authored textbook was selling well, plus one little book of theory. I was one with the mob, distinguished only because there was no longer any joy left in either hatred or indignation.

"I picked up a map of the country," I said. "Traced the whole outline with my finger, could not get a passport. I said to me, 'Find the farthest place you can from Washington, D.C. Go there.'"

"But you didn't come here, then," Julie said. "I had already come here by then."

She had, too, on a visit with her folks. She had not come back until a few years later.

"To Anchorage," I said. "I went to Anchorage. Worse than Boise, but not as bad as Salt Lake. Came back here and drove around weekends finding a place."

The first person I met was Dolores. She was not much more than a kid, but we lived together off and on for years. Julie arrived and hung around Dolores. We were all friends and meshed as we got older. Then Dolores kind of pulled out.

Dolores had good sense even in her twenties. Her answer to confusion was direct, with no overtone of possessiveness or obligation. I loved her for it then, love her for it now, and still do not understand.

It is nice to be able to say such stuff in front of someone you love. Julie and Dolores are as good friends with each other as they are with me. The difference is only sex. I watched Julie, checked the clock, and by God, my twenty-minute estimate had not needed to be revised.

Julie was looking at Max in a new way. It was blatantly sexual. Dumbass Max had not picked up. I did not know if Julie was thinking of herself or Dolores, but Max was clearly going to get laid. That made me stumble.

"What do you do in Montana?" I swear she was purring. It was bullshit and we both knew it. It was coming across like—how much money do you make and what are your prospects for supporting a wife? Julie pulls this phoney stuff just often enough to keep a man awake.

"C'mon," I told her.

"Seriously," she said. "We only hear that Montana is a wasteland."

"Subsistence," Max told her. "Billings and Missoula are capable of supporting a moderate economy. I worked at what might be called a general store, although it was once a department store."

Worked, Max had said. Past tense. Did that mean that he had come to stay?

Max was catching on to that mama-san stuff that Julie was spreading. Max did not know about my current dealings with Dolores, if any, and he did not know much about Julie; but he has seen plenty of college sophomores.

"Barrows came looking for you?" Max grinned. He was passing the buck, getting a receipt. Julie looked like she had just invented the whole idea of seduction.

"Yep," I said. "And we've been friends for years. At least as much as anyone can be friends with Barrows."

"And you started the lumber business?"

"Not right away. At the time I was still actually trying to work."

That was true. At the time I had been writing. That is a traditional occupation among exiles and political prisoners. I felt that if I could prove that group creativity existed, it would be a first step to understanding forces that would oppose any dictator, anywhere. I interviewed musicians and theater people and dancers. The main question: Is there a time when a group knows its members and potential so well that without script or choreography the group will create beyond simple improvisation?

The answers were full and startling. That kind of creativity was old stuff in the arts, even if the social sciences said that it was impossible. "We talked about that subject when we worked together." Max leaned forward. He had always been interested in it.

"What were you doing?" I asked. "I figured you were working on the same thing."

"I began to study. For these years I've been reading."

"Only reading?"

"Mostly history."

"And comic books?"

"I read a bit of theology here and there."

"Discover anything?"

"Of course. Why did Barrows look you up?"

"Peanut butter," Julie said. "We even have some without soybeans. Either that, or beans and cornbread." She stood and headed for the refrigerator.

"You hungry?" I asked Max.

"Why not?"

"And tomato soup." Julie was trotting around in old jeans and shirt with the manner of a lady in a housedress and apron. Either she was doing some kind of elaborate protest, or she was trying an apple pie approach.

"She can spell, too," I said to no one in particular. "Why, she can even read and write."

It went right past. There was nothing to do but feed the fire and slice the homemade bread—and I made the bread, she didn't. It was going to be a pretty weird lunch.

We talked during lunch. Mostly about Barrows's motives. Julie ventured the opinion that Barrows's original intention was to save me from myself. That was a truly dumb thing for Julie to say. I guessed that Barrows sought me out because he was lonesome.

"Tell me about Barrows, now," Max said. "He is going through hell."

"He really is," Julie said. "I don't even know if Jake understands how true that is." Then she began explaining, and it was like seeing a personality shift gears. She became the thoughtful, analytic Julie who is so impressive. From sophomore to intellectual, like turning the page of a book. Hell, I don't care if she plays games, so long as she knows she's doing it.

"He blames himself for all those deaths," she said.

"He should," I told her. "At least he should take the blame for Nighthawk. He was told."

"Told what?" Max was quiet with his question, like he already knew the answer.

"He had a kill situation during the raid on this town." I felt helpless. "I told him at the time that if he let the killers get away with it, he would have to do more killing later."

"You advised murder?" Julie was shocked. She stopped eating, and she moved her chair a little way back from the table. She turned to Max. "Barrows got more than Jake's advice. I have been telling him to remain calm." She seemed nearly smug. "Barrows listens."

I just sat there feeling helpless. Julie was like some kid preacher just out of divinity school, yapping about love curing all troubles. If Julie thought that any decent human move was going to placate Mobilier, then she was just dumb enough to try to feed a cupcake to a wolverine.

"I told you I might have to stop you," she said to me. "I'm sorry, babe, but I'm trying." Now her voice was a little apologetic, and kind of loving. Contradictions. She had been acting strange all day. I wondered if she was going nuts.

Then the logical, analytic Julie took over, and she began to explain about Barrows, and about Mobilier. Barrows had been spending nearly all of his time tracing the lines of control in Mobilier.

What he found made Hitler look like a fat child dabbling in the mud pie of history. A lot of questions about the world began to get answered. Barrows was not only too trusting; Barrows had been little short of a fool.

Roll back the years to the turn of the century. Some forces begin to slowly accumulate. The forces talk between themselves. They are at first inarticulate, then questioning. After a long time a glimmer of understanding touches one element of government, one small center of the military, one discontented businessman with too much time and too much money. You have the origins of Mobilier.

Mobilier was a monster that straddled the world and had outposts in space. It was of no nationality, or rather, it was of every nationality. It had no creed, or rather, a thousand creeds. It was incoherent, but it could learn. It learned slow and did not learn some things at all, but with broad strokes of power it learned to be a champ.

Add the rise of totalitarian governments and all that was learned by them about social control. Add instant communication and computer banks. Add the ruthlessness which the twentieth century witnessed from killer politicians who for the first time in history had a technology to support their dreams. Do not forget sheet metal pussycats like Hitler and Nixon, or expert heavies like Lenin and Stalin; but think beyond their lessons.

The product had crawled out of history, and it made no difference what it called itself. Mobilier was as good a name as any. It moved, had direction, and it was corporately insane.

When Barrows looked, Mobilier was headless. Blind. It existed through vast delegation, the autonomy of delegation, and because of the long lines of branches and sub-branches and twiglets which represented parts of itself warring against other parts. It was a juggernaut in motion on crude principles of power that generated its own energy and could not be stopped.

Mobilier was a logical extension of what the corporation could become. A normal corporation has a president and vice presidents and interlocking directorships with other corporate boards. These became secondary as Mobilier grew. It had second boards, third boards, which represented former interlocks with other corporations. It was like a game of musical chairs, except that chairs were added instead of being taken away. A cacophony of size and complexity.

Mobilier was a corporation interlocked with, or owning as subsidiaries, every other corporation in the world except the black market. All of the wars and fighting going on through the world were the results of a headless monster that chewed at its own heart.

At some time in the past Mobilier had entered government. Theoretically, there must have been a point when it might still have been stopped. When Mobilier captured the government bureaucracy, the situation was beyond control. Government became just one of the many corporations that clawed and chewed at its own heart. The line between government and the corporation no longer existed.

That explained why the president of the U.S. was a figurehead, and why the courts existed in shadow. That explained why, more than ever before in history, Congress existed on the level of a spectacle or sideshow.

Mobilier was an economic and social structure that was out of control. Mobilier did not, could not, even conceive what it was.

Coupled with this was its wealth, and what the wealth had bought. Mobilier commanded technology. It used light and sound, lasers and delivery systems that were the culmination of weapons development on earth.

It was shocking. As Julie sketched it together, my earlier premonition came back. It was not that something was going to happen. Something already had happened, and we were standing right where the storm would break.

"If that's what we know," I said, "then we also know that there will be another strike here, and soon."

"We don't," Julie said. "You only say you know it."

"Why do you say it?" At least Max was willing to listen.

"Because we are designated an enemy. Every military doctrine I know calls for a strike."

"The military is not in control," Julie said.

"That's the point. No one is in control. Whenever that has happened in history, the military tries to step forward." I felt so helpless. "Barrows sure as hell is not in control."

The aggravating thing was that Barrows could eventually stop the whole outfit. If nothing else, he could destroy Mobilier's weaponry. The aggravating thing was that Barrows would not act. He was afraid to put more pressure on Mobilier, and thus cause more killing.

"Why doesn't Mobilier just kill Barrows?" Max asked the reasonable question.

"I doubt if they can, now. Up until now, they have wanted the secret of his power. It would give them power in the universe."

"It's an awfully big place, the universe."

"It's an awful lot of power, too."

"Have you thought of killing Barrows?"

"Goddamn." Max had hit one of those secret places where the mind never wants to admit that it goes.

"I'm afraid." Julie's voice was small, thin, her interest suddenly shocked.

"And why doesn't Barrows commit suicide?" Max was not going to allow the situation to remain unexplored.

"Morals," I said. "He's a completely moral man."

"That appears to be your main problem." Max stretched, yawned, blinked at me like some damned wise old owl. "Mobilier is not a problem if Barrows acts. Mobilier is a paper tiger."

Dolores had said that. Those same words. "But he won't act."

"Then Mobilier is a problem. There is some reason to be frightened."

"I'm afraid of me," Julie said. "I could never kill anybody, but I thought of it. With Barrows gone, Mobilier would leave us alone."

There's courage. Having Max there helped. Julie rarely admitted to dark things of the mind. Dolores would do it, and I would not be surprised. With Julie the act was heroic.

"What are we supposed to do?" Max asked.

"The rescue squad, if Barrows will listen. That's us."

"The world has managed some pretty hard times without a rescue squad."

"Yes," I told him, "it has, and look what happened every time. Don't start pulling some kind of eternity crap on me."

He grinned. Max and a grin are pretty nice. He had a wide mouth, and the way it works makes you think he is laughing instead of grinning. "The world can go daddle itself," I told him. "I'm trying to take care of my own, even if all of them do have their heads up . . . even if they don't understand."

"Meanwhile," Max said, "I have no affection for buses and the ride was long. I'm going to get some sleep."

"Barrows will be by later."

"Later, I'll be awake." Max headed for his room and left Julie and me together like we had never been together before. As we held each other, we did not know that to the east a general named Butterfield was methodically telephoning every high military contact he knew in order to understand the problems he might face in reducing our town. He cursed beneath his breath as he phoned.

Julie and I really felt that there was nothing more to say to each other. We just held each other quietly in the creaking and echoing of my old house. This house was built on a foundation of illusion. It cannot stand without illusions—mine, Julie's, society's—but for a while it just creaked and rattled on its own while we held each other.

Chapter 17

Notes of Max Klein: April 21, 1991:

The attack on Land's End will occur on the eighth of May unless orders are countermanded or events dictate some other decision. It seemed to me that because of my peculiar position here, I should seek this information out. The range of my own power is far wider than any power of which Barrows may have dreamed, but unlike Barrows, I have not trained myself to use power. Instead, I shun it. However, in this case, it was easy enough to read the information from the urgent thoughts in Barrows's mind. He knows of the planned attack, of course, and tries to forestall it by remaining passive. He hopes for a change in the situation.

I will not divulge the information. My task is that of the observer. If Barrows has scruples against interfering in human affairs, he holds those scruples largely (I suspect) because every time he interferes he ends up feeling guilty. I do not interfere through other, and I hope as respectful, motives.

It will be of absolute interest to see how all of us react, assuming that any of us continue to live.

Meanwhile, if I am to be of any use to these people, and to Barrows, it seems well to look at their society. They have built an interesting but vulnerable social structure among themselves. It is a structure that promises a good deal of strength, even if it is vulnerable.

1. There is no evidence of group hysteria or hypnotic presence. No mental disorder is evident in Barrows or Jake. Julie is slightly erratic under the stress of fear. Except for Dolores, who is watchful, the rest of the group seems to have placed the fear of attack from their minds.

2. There is no cult of personality, although Barrows is a powerful figure.

3. Group unity is based on affection. Also on the commonly held belief that Barrows's intentions are excellent. Members of the group do not necessarily trust each other's judgments.

4. No one questions Barrows's claim that he is a hundred and fifty years old. I do not question it, myself, but perhaps I have a bit more information and a bit more knowledge about these matters.

5. Objects do vanish at Barrows's will—this confirmed visually. Such power is certainly not unknown, but it is shocking to find such power contained in a frail vessel like Barrows.

6. Locale is approximately as Jake has described it in letters.

7. The group appears as a substitute for the extended family, with two variations. Jake, not Barrows, is the patriarch. Julie, Penny and Dolores alternate a mother role, with the mantle most often falling on Penny. Julie would like to be the matriarch, but she has no chance because of the irreverence of Penny and the realism of Dolores. Julie walks so many secret paths of the mind that she cannot even articulate to herself in which direction they lead.

Jim seems a trusted younger brother, or, in Mike's case, older brother. Mike is the object of much parental concern from all members, which is surely wearing on the young man.

Without realizing it, these people have set up a society which looks more like a tribe than an extended family.

Barrows is the living myth, elemental, the bringer of fire. Dolores represents symbol.

Much is made by the group of Dolores's sexual prowess. All but Barrows cultivate the illusion that Dolores engages in a large number of sexual conquests.

Even before I came to know some of her more private thoughts, her actions did not match the illusion. She could be reached at nearly any time of day or night at her lab. She had few friends beyond the primary group, and only occasional sexual contacts. Dolores lived rather conventionally, was given to normal loneliness, and was acknowledged by the group as their most intelligent member.

But she functions as a symbol. She is a symbol of freedom and liberalism to people who are fundamentally conservative and fearful. Now it is later. The notes are at hand and I will continue to transcribe them, give order, attempt some analysis, assuming that I am alive after the eighth of May. These are not new seas on which we sail, but they certainly are deep. We have agreed between us that if some do not survive the attack predicted by Jake, one or more of the others will collect all writings and attempt to preserve them.

I feel even more strongly the sense of personal change that enveloped me when I left Montana. I shall soon not be myself, at least not the Max Klein whom I have lived with for so long. This sense of change may mean that I will die, or it may mean an alteration in my being that is every bit as interesting. Well, if this is to be the end of human society on this planet, then I am glad to be alive and observant, although I would rather it did not happen.

=

Even later. I have long suspected that the male and female principles so easily observed among the beasts are not valid among humans in a high civilized state. Dolores's actions seem neither male nor female, but unique to her. Difficult to be objective. Remain observant, Max. You are going to learn a lot.

=

Jake is sometimes heavily fatigued. The mental discipline which Barrows has assigned Jake resuscitates him. Coupled with this is Jake's improving disposition. He is feeling better about himself, and I fancy that one reason is that I am here. Jake had no peer in this town. He had forgotten his worth, which in the past was great, and which I hope is not damaged beyond repair. Because I am here, sharing ideas and validating them, he values himself more than he has for years. Jake evidences some optimism, but he still believes that Barrows is making a serious mistake. I do not know whether Barrows is making a mistake or not, although I do know that the attack will be on May eighth.

The discussion of attack, and my present relationship with Barrows, opened during the time I met Barrows on the evening of my arrival.

The wind had picked up through the afternoon, and with the sun low in the west, the wind rattled Jake's house Around here, as in Montana, it seems that one always remembers the wind. Weather moves around the mountains here in explainable but peculiar patterns. A funneling effect makes high clouds race one way while a stiff surface wind may blow from the opposite direction.

As we waited for Barrows to arrive, I could not help feeling that we were engaged in a trifling matter. The very sense of history in Jake's house was enough to remind me that few situations are unique. Other people in other places and times have had even greater powers than Barrows. I suppose, in fact, that mine would be considered greater. History has shown more formidable enemies than Mobilier. Our danger lay not in power, but in error, which is what I thought when I met Barrows.

The wind slapped, the fire popped in the fireplace, and a water kettle bubbled on the wood stove. Barrows entered, was introduced, but did not volunteer so much as a smile. I have seen such timidity before in introspective men. For a man of one hundred and fifty years, Barrows is remarkably naive.

In addition, the situation was artificial. Jake caused it. He was with two of his best friends, and yet he was self-conscious.

"I thought Julie would be here," I said.

"She'll be back," Jake told me. "Right now she's over at Penny's. Nice little clash going on over there."

"What?" Barrows was abstracted as well as timid.

"Jim is getting set to go back to the woods," Jake told him.

"He is a logger, after all." Barrows seemed nearly confused.

"You know why Penny doesn't want him to go. She's afraid he'll get killed."

"He's no more of an occupation for me in the woods than he is in town," Barrows said. "I have everyone under observation." He seemed awfully unhappy as he said those words.

"Except, of course," and Jake winked at me, "when they're fuckin'."

"Jake. Please."

"Does it ever get warm here?" I asked. It seemed time to assume some convention so that the situation would ease.

"It never gets real cold." Jake was acting like a Cub Scout introducing his father to the rest of the boys. I thought of other days, of Jake's great compassion and basic decency—which ended broken in a hospital from a nonviolent demonstration.

Barrows pushed a chair closer to the fireplace. "I'm a little put out by having to interfere with people by keeping track of them."

Barrows was clearly not a social scientist, which is to say that he was not a compulsive snoop. It is a characteristic of the trade that we who work in it must come to terms with it.

"I have some work for you," he told Jake. "I want you to begin studying an approach to controlling mental energy."

"You want Jake to learn how to make things vanish?" I asked.

"I wish there was some predictability," Barrows said. "There is none."

"But the work is productive?" I knew it was, but asked to see if Barrows knew.

"Something comes of it, if only in personal terms."

I did not relish the implications of Barrows's statement. I did not like the words "if only." They denoted that Barrows was still a man who could think in terms of profit and loss. For that reason it seemed to me that Barrows may once have been a mystic, but he was no longer a mystic.

"I confess that I am suspicious," I told him.

"You would not be a scientist otherwise."

"Social philosophy is not a science."

"It's a way of looking," Jake said. "It is one approach to the world that is not totally fucked."

"My process is easy to describe," Barrows said. "I suppose I would not even mind telling Mobilier, for what good it could get from the information."

The method was simple, one used often by many sorts of mystics. The frontal lobes were not involved. One learned to let the weight of consciousness shift to the back of the skull. Then, instead of aggressively projecting the mind, it was necessary to become complacent. Physical presences rushed into the gulf of complacency and the genius of identifying them became the largest task.

"To make them vanish?"

"Not easily described," Barrows said. "Roughly what happens is that you allow matter to rush at you, and at its approach you conceptualize space."

"At the risk of offending, will you demonstrate?"

"I'm not offended," he said. "We can rebuild it."

The fire vanished.

I pretended surprise, then leaned forward to feel the heat that remained in the fire brick. Then I withdrew my hand.

The reason Mobilier could not use the knowledge was because of the passive technique. The measure of passivity required would be impossible to achieve by any diplomat, leave alone a military or business man. The power could not be chased into a corner. Unless a person cultivated complete reverence for life and matter, then it was impossible to reach the required level of complacency.

In other words, the technique had its own catch. By the time you were tranquil enough to use it, you were wise enough not to use it.

Yet Barrows was not tranquil. My feeling of imminent change was strong. This man Barrows was not serene, and that spelled the possibility for catastrophic changes.

There was obviously a catch to the catch. Obviously, after Barrows had once mastered the technique, life or circumstance or history had so affected him that he was not tranquil. I actually shuddered. The man had lived beyond his time. Now he was a desperate man, and he still had this power.

"If you wish Jake to study this," I said, "then you have a singularly likely candidate." For a moment it seemed to me that such study would take Jake into realms of the mind that would offer him understanding. I doubted that Jake, having an aggressive mind, would ever completely master the power.

"Jake is a good man," Barrows said.

"I don't know it," Jake said. "Half the time I want to pop somebody, and the other half I feel ashamed of wanting to."

"You just explained it," I told Jake. "Most people never consider any alternative but conflict."

"Most people would piss green if they got in a mile of the violence they promote every day." Jake turned to Barrows. "Which is why you have to get off your ass. We are going to take another hit."

"Julie seems to be headed this way," Barrows said.

"Be right back." The Cub Scout eagerness returned and then gave over to a small sense of urgency. "You guys get acquainted." Jake nearly sprinted from the room.

"We'll be alone for about twenty minutes," Barrows said. "I hope that is long enough to clear your resentment."

"Is it that obvious?"

"Your affection for Jake is obvious."

"So that you infer the other." I stood to go to the kitchen and feed the stove. It smoked. When Jake fed it the thing did not smoke.

"What puzzles me," I told Barrows, "is why this situation was allowed to enter into these people's lives."

"It isn't puzzling. I was stupid." He replied so readily that I trusted his honesty. "I am not natively an analytic man."

"You know that the word 'victory' is a comparative term."

"I'm not looking for victory," he said. "I'm looking for a way out."

"And mysticism?"

"How much do you know?" He asked the question as if afraid. At the same time his face seemed almost young, eager and hopeful. "A man gets tired," he said, "and the beliefs become relative. But if you know something . . ." He broke off and waited, expectant.

"I am not exactly Hassidic and I have limitations." Mystics need not explain much to each other, although there are as many varieties of mysticism as there are mystics.

"I would like to learn." He was sincere. A man still looking for answers.

"Learning is our profession," I told him, "but it would be a poor thing if we learned at the expense of the present reality."

"Meaning?"

"You have made the fundamental mistake of the pacifist," I told Barrows. "You have waited to do something until after the action has been joined. Now you must act."

"I have no right to do that."

"You have no right to refuse. Since you started this situation, can you sit silently by and watch these people destroyed?"

"Yours is a hard kindness," he said. "I have seen millions destroyed."

Of course he had. Hundreds of millions. With his great age and his ability, he might have seen death camps across the globe in no less than a dozen major wars. He had seen disease, starvation, genocide. At least he had seen such things if he had looked. I did not believe, watching him, that Barrows had looked much. No man could bear to see all that he might have seen and still remain vulnerable to human suffering.

He was certainly vulnerable to his own suffering. He sat before me like a child who has accidentally done some shameful thing. Barrows's face was somewhat like Julie's face. He had no protective mask. What he felt showed darkly.

"I have one more burden for you," I told Barrows.

"I know Jake and I love him. Because of that I have always feared for him. He is his own enemy through generosity. Jake does not simply behave like a nice guy so that people will like him. He has worked harder than nearly any other man, has accepted responsibility for others, and when he has failed—as was often inevitable—he has remembered the failure and forgotten the many successes.

"Promise if the situation deteriorates beyond reasonable hope of success you will kill Jake quickly. He merits better treatment than to be a pawn."

"I must have a plan." Barrows was nearly desperate.

"I have accepted your promise although you have not made it." I turned from him, walked to the window and looked to see if Julie and Jake were approaching. They were just in sight, two blocks away.

"What are your impressions of the people close to Jake?" I might have questions about Barrows, but trusted his observation.

"We'll speak at length soon," he said. "They will be here in a few minutes."

"At least some key to Julie, since we deal with her this evening."

"Brilliant, self-centered to the point of occasional selfishness, also generous. All kinds of contradictory emotions."

"Her relation to Jake?"

"She more or less runs his feelings," Barrows said. "She often runs his actions. When the time comes she will leave him, and she will be sad but hardly distraught."

"She will leave?"

"Julie is at present a dependent person, but a time will come when she feels self-sufficient."

"Jake was always a dreamer."

"I hope Jake always will be."

"Still, this makes it difficult."

"Yes," Barrows said, "doesn't it?"

=

They entered laughing over some private joke and, seeing them together, it was difficult to believe that there were ever any difficulties between them. I wondered at my solitary life. The life of Max Klein, shirt and paint salesman, scholar, sometime theologian. A man who could count his own losses in these affections between the sexes. Max Klein, alone because he chose the reality before the illusion. Nonetheless, the man Max hungered after those illusions on too many nights when the ancient voices of forgotten authors no longer gave consolation.

The evening darkness, which had been growing, seemed to gather rapidly. It was like a force above the small group. The ceaseless wind was a low whisper in the huge, budding tree beyond the windows, while surrounding the town were the black hulks of mountains, the stunted third growth forests, and the deep, urgently flowing water of the strait.

"We ought to be talking business." In a tone that cared nothing for business, Jake and his sense of responsibility carried us to present concerns.

"I do not know what we must do," Barrows said. "Max?"

"I've not had time to absorb the situation," I told him. "If something must be done, then it should be limited to an effort likely to succeed."

"Mobilier is killing people." The laughter was gone from Julie's face.

"Life is killing people," I told her. "Nature is killing people. People are killing people." I spoke to her in that manner because it was the truth, but also because I wanted her to quickly move past any illusions about the importance of Mobilier.

"I've only just met you," she said. "I don't know you."

"That does not have much to do with the question." Barrows leaned forward. He replied so quickly there was an uneasy sense in the group that he knew her thought before she spoke.

"You have to quit pooting around and act." Jake looked at us like we were quarrelsome children. His thin nose and high forehead gave him the look of a party intellectual of Russia, circa 1917. "You guys have seen what this outfit will do and you still don't believe it."

"I believe it," Barrows said. "What I don't believe is that we need more of the same."

"Then why in the world are we here?" Julie was already withdrawing.

"We are here," Jake told her, "because by bad luck we have been pushed into defense. We're here to see if moral clout is of any use to pacifists."

Good for Jake. He is better at definition than he has ever believed. "Then I feel superfluous." Julie turned to Jake, and it was curious to see how both the complaint and the plain need for defense combined and centered on him.

"You are not superfluous," Barrows said. "I would like your opinion."

Julie changed. She became thoughtful, although it seemed that she was still indignant. "Negotiate. Balance one power against the other."

"Like what was once known as the arms race?"

"This is different," Julie said. "On one side is tremendous power. On the other side is absolute power. You have the stronger negotiating hand."

Julie had an extremely able mind and was making the essential distinction. If Barrows chose to act, Mobilier was helpless.

"I do not pretend to like that," Barrows said. "It means that I will have to destroy some things as a display of the power. Finally, all it does is perpetuate the problem."

"Then blow it all to hell, sweetie." Now Julie was once more indignant, and swinging into offense.

"Of course not."

"Then set up a benevolent dictatorship."

"That is offensive."

"I've been doing your thinking for you," she said. "There are limited possibilities, and the last one is to bow out."

"Mobilier will then destroy all of you."

"I'm surrounded by doomsayers." Julie turned to Jake. "Drive me home."

"Whenever you're ready," he said, "but I wish you would stay."

"But don't rush me."

"I'm not rushing you," Jake told her. "Take as long as you want. Just when you're ready."

"You rushed me last time, too," she said.

It was too funny. I began to laugh, then Barrows laughed, and although we were laughing into offended silence, it seemed that we could not stop. Barrows's hands shook from laughter as he lit a cigarette. Jake and Julie looked at us as if we were two strange creatures in a zoo. It was obvious they had not heard their own words.

"What the hell's so funny?"

"Sit down," Barrows said. "Before I really do blow it all to smash." His voice was laughing, but his words were not. An edge of threat was in his voice.

"Give me some other alternatives," Barrows said.

A monster had risen. It was a soft-spoken and seemingly inoffensive monster, but monster just the same. Power never needs a loud voice.

"I would like a new system," Barrows said. "I would like it to be a self-perpetuating system of thoughtful or spiritual force that will render weapons obsolete."

"Move to another world," Julie said. "This one is too big and nasty for you."

"It has been for years," he said. "Still, I know what I want."

"What will you settle for?" I asked.

"A sincere attempt."

"You must make your own commitment," I told him. "You are the weakest man here because you are uncommitted. Find an affirming cause, find a person to love, and look for a goal greater than yourself or your present knowledge. Right now you find time to waste feeling tired and complaining of the burden of being ancient."

It rattled all three of them.

"You have lived alone in the woods for too long," I said. "Having done so, your mistake was that you did not stay in the woods."

They still said nothing.

"A man who can hardly wait for someone else to take the reins so he can depart just loads the situation with defensiveness."

"Don't," Julie said.

"You detest intellectual contempt," I told Barrows, "yet you have removed yourself from humanity as surely as any dictator."

"You are harsh." His eyes now showed interest. They showed him capable of intelligent engagement.

"I am your closest cousin," I told him. "Because in my own way I have done the same. I too have lived alone." I nodded to Jake and Julie. "Look at them."

"I understand," Barrows said.

"I have, like you, feared additional pain."

"And I fear your insights."

"What in the hell are you two talking about?" Jake was missing the subtlety, and Jake has his own problems, for as sure as those windows rattle in the wind, he is going to get spiritually bruised through his love. He was always willing to put his life on the line for great matters—and he is getting bruised now—as I bring some of these papers into a coherent narrative.

At the time he still had hope that he could move Barrows to action. He extracted a promise from Barrows that amounted to very little.

"I'll think seriously about taking action," Barrows said on that first night. "I will decide in only a few days. Meanwhile, Jake must immediately get to work."

"Meanwhile," Jake told him. "Do you know the old Anderson house?" He looked at both Barrows and Julie.

"It has been abandoned for years."

"It has a bricked-in root cellar. When the shit comes down, because it will come down because you won't do anything, I want everyone to head for that cellar." Jake's voice was a command, the voice of a military officer. "You got that?"

"Yes," Julie said, and her voice was timid.

"Now about the work," Barrows said.

"What about the work?" I did not give Jake a chance to answer.

"It should be done quickly. I will help Jake. I may be a strong man, but I really do not know how strong I am," Barrows said.

"So you are going to pass the entire responsibility to Jake?" I asked.

"To a man I trust."

"Although he differs from your wisdom by at least a century?"

"I am not more moral," Barrows said. "Perhaps I am more Victorian."

"A difficult condition."

"Will you help?"

"I'll not hinder at this point. I will give you my views."

=

More later. These notes could become voluminous, and Jake's entry, which follows, explains much that I would otherwise end up duplicating.

And I took my own advice, for I have been cloistered too long. I have spent too many years in reading and meditation, while failing to find someone to love. Now Dolores and I seem to be turning toward each other. She is so straightforward that I find myself nearly shy.

Dolores's generation, that generation of the sixties, is only now privileged to think in terms of constancy. There were so many of them, and life shifted fast as people came and went like shadows cast before a light show. They formed attachments, dropped them, formed new ones. Dolores has paid the price of freedom, which in that generation was attended by the denial of constancy. While I, of a slightly older but hardly wiser time, have sought freedom within the constant. I wonder what we will learn?

Chapter 18

I TRIED TO FIGURE OUT HOW MOBILIER WOULD STRIKE, WHILE trusting Max to talk to Barrows. Mobilier was acting screwy. I thought about all that had happened, and all that I knew.

Then, I finally understood. Mobilier was engaged in a probe operation, which meant that Mobilier did not know how much power it was up against. Barrows had taken no action for years. After so many years, the original information on him could no longer be trusted.

Somebody out there was doing a truly professional job. Instead of Barrows hitting Mobilier's weaponry to introduce psychological shock and defeatism, Mobilier had done it to Barrows according to the textbook. Psychologically, Barrows was not bowled over, but he was at an awful disadvantage.

So, Mobilier had the edge. Almost anything it tried was going to partly work. That is the way I would be figuring if I were running their show. I tried to put myself in their place.

There are four basic ways to attack, not counting infiltration, which would no longer work here. Anything on land, sea or air, or even in space, is going to be a spinoff from one of them.

A frontal attack I don't like, because it allows the enemy to mass its fire. Even a weak defense can smear that kind of offense, if the offense gets sandwiched in by the geography. That stopped the Persians at Thermopylae, and it was the fundamental weakness at the Battle of the Bulge, where the krauts could not maintain their hard shoulders for their tanks.

Penetration of a line is a second way, especially if you get the enemy to commit its reserve. You throw all your firepower at one point of the enemy line. Then, when you bust through, you swing left and right and roll up the line. The third way is to flank the line. The fourth way is double envelopment, if you have the men and tools and terrain.

I figured we were going to get full encirclement—an extension of double envelopment—and it would be a hard, shocking attack, with enough reserve to mount a second major attack if needed. Mobilier had been probing, but it still did not know our capacity. I would not screw around, and I did not think Mobilier would, either.

So I figured all this out. Then I took it to Barrows. He was kind, and vague, and started to make me mad because he was acting like forty kinds of fool. He looked terrible, like something that all you could use it for would be a bar rag. He sat in his living room; beyond the front window was forest, but it was sparse this close to the water. The strait tumbled gray and oily-looking in the mist. Barrows's house was small and well ordered, a little too neat. It was like the house had been cleaned up before its owner left on a trip.

"Have you talked about this with Max?" Barrows asked. His eyes were not exactly glazed, but they sure didn't have any springtime sparkle.

"Why talk to another damned fool?" I was pissed. Max would ask questions, and maybe would agree, but it was still up to me to convince Barrows. I know Max. He would not bust his scientific detachment by getting all hot and bothered.

"Talk to Dolores," I told Barrows.

"She agrees with you?"

"Dolores knows that there will be another attack."

"That may make a difference." He stood, stretched like he was trying to unkink wet knots, and walked to the window to look onto the strait. "Max was right. I chose to live in the woods, and I made a mistake by leaving them."

"You got lonesome."

"Yes." He turned to me, and there was a kind of affection—no, love—in his eyes. The affection was shy, but easy to read. "Perhaps I really should have searched for someone else, but my wife, she was a very great woman, and so greatly missed. She was a saint . . ." He stopped, knowing that I was not going to like that word, saint.

"Listen, Barrows, I don't mean to be tough."

He waved it away. "Years of inaction. You don't get such convictions and live a long time with them and then change. At least you don't change until you know what you are doing."

"Disable Mobilier's weapons," I told him. "That's all you have to do. Bust up anything big that you find sitting and unmanned."

"That is aggressive."

"C'mon," I told him. "Gandhi was aggressive. Martin King was aggressive. Aggressive nonviolence."

"And it is provocative." He still had Nighthawk on his mind.

In one way I was ahead of Barrows. He had never killed anybody, or done much else until lately that should cause guilt. When it came to guilt I knew what I was talking about. Society runs on the stuff. From kids stealing pennies to congressmen wearing pink panties, guilt is a main form of social control.

He straightened a little. "I have not been inactive. I've been making an assessment of Mobilier."

"And found what?"

"In weapons, anything you name. In organization? It is immense. Top-heavy. One thing I count on is that by the time all those organizations and administrations and power groups get done talking, the situation will be forgotten or changed."

"Someone pushed the button," I told him.

"Yes," he said, "an oilman named Chester. He spoke to me on the phone this morning."

Oh, shit; oh, no; and oh, well, well. "What did he want?" I asked.

"He is willing to deal," Barrows said. "He has a grand notion. He wants me to use my power to uncover resources, mostly oil and uranium. Having located the resource, he would want me to remove the inconvenient parts of the geologic structure so that he could get the resource easily."

"In return?"

"He leaves us alone."

"And you told him to rub it up his ass?"

"I told him it was an interference in human affairs." Barrows still stood and looked at the strait. "At least I can solve some mysteries for you. The way Mobilier knew about that tree was from our conversation. These people have sound equipment that can pick up conversations through a brick wall two miles distant."

I thought about what he said. The sound equipment must have been operated by the informer in our town.

"Who?"

"One was Les Godwin, when he was not at sea."

"Well, that sumbitch had quite a little time for himself."

"He's paying for it."

Barrows had that one nailed and clenched. Les was not going to go berserk or kill himself. Ol' Les was living inside a booze bottle and hitting the speed.

"There was a mike, a bug, under the fender of our truck. Covered with dirt."

"The other one, the other informer?"

"The mayor."

"Well, hot shit." That two-bit punk. It made me lose some respect for Mobilier. When the dust from this mess settled, his honor was going to get a conversational visit from me that would scare the wine dregs from his toes.

"You could save Les," I said. "Les is just dumb. You could clean the booze out of his system, keep it clean until he comes to his senses."

"That brings us right to the whole point of this." Barrows was suddenly firm, even commanding. If I wanted him to listen to my case, I knew I would have to listen to his case. "Max and I have discussed this," Barrows said, "and you must understand the issue even if you don't understand the decision. When does a man have a right to interfere with another man?"

"You should know, since you've already done it once. You saved Jim."

"And the only reason it may have been proper interference is because the trees were falling wrong." His eyes were momentarily interested. "You know, that is the only real mystery in all of the things that have happened. Why, on that day, which was no different from a hundred other days, were the trees falling wrong?"

"It happens sometimes," I said. I knew exactly why those goddamn trees had fallen wrong, but was sure not going to explain it to Barrows. The explanation would cause him to get into another round of belly button searching.

"But why?"

"It isn't my line. Trees fall wrong, but at least the damn things always fall. What about Les?"

Barrows smiled, but it was faint. He began to lay out a situation in ethics. "Suppose Les came to you and asked to borrow a gun in order to kill himself? Would you lend him the gun?"

"I wouldn't lend him the sweat off my balls."

"Suppose," said Barrows, "that he already had a gun. Would you try to talk him out of killing himself?"

"Sure. Of course . . ." Then I thought about it. Patty and Joan were dead. Les had to have it figured that he was at least partly to blame. "No. I would not lend him a gun, but I would not try to talk him out of it." After all, with the kind of stuff old Les was living with, suicide was the most sensible thing to do.

"Abstract it," said Barrows. "If we're not talking about Les, but about a lot of people, then you can see why I can't interfere unless it is certain that my actions are correct."

I saw his point, and I thought Barrows was just plain nuts. No one in this town had provoked that attack. Barrows was placing his weird conscience ahead of the town's situation. The town was in a war.

When you are in a war, people die. No matter how much you want to stay out of the war, directly or indirectly, you are going to kill someone. The pacifist who sits proudly on his tail and suffers death while gently forgiving his enemy may look like Jesus's little sweetie pie, but he is a killer. He has killed himself—which I don't argue with, since it's his own business—but he kills others because he has been sitting on his ass.

I know them. I know their round-bottomed and gentle voices, and I even know that some of them have it together for themselves. But, like Barrows, they do nothing beyond themselves. When the shit comes down, no pacifist can die in honest silence unless he or she has been vigorously trying to stop the shit before it starts.

Most pacifists are as full of crap as any senator. Makes no difference how many burned orphans you adopt, how much food and clothing you send to torn up parts of the world, or how humble and lovely and soft-spoken you are. The minute you settle for only that, you are a killer.

Thinking about it made me so angry that I said a quick good-bye to Barrows and headed out to see Julie.

A rainy spring. I walked through the forest, up the trail to the road, and the forest was red. Rusty red, the way it gets in dark weather when there is a bunch of cedar coloring the gloom.

I don't see why I have to get so mad. Maybe because no one else does. They just poop along. I thought maybe Julie and I might spend the evening together, nice and quiet, but most of all I wanted to explain to her what to do when the attack arrived. She would try not to listen. Julie doesn't like to think about stuff like that. She likes to poop along with the majority. Julie is still enough of a child to believe that some numb-nutted deity will interfere and the weapons stockpiled all around the world will not be used.

Chapter 19

MAY SIXTH WAS THE LAST HAPPY DAY I WILL EVER SEE. THE SHIT CAME down on May eighth.

Got to get this written down. Got to keep my control, hold up my share for as long as I can. Going to go crazy in a little while. Only thing that makes sense, maybe, is to go crazy. We got total encirclement, just the way I predicted.

Thinking about that last happy day helps. It's almost like I can get beyond my grief, or like the grief is separate because life is split in two, the way my mind is split. I'm like an actor who is engrossed in a happy scene upon a stage. I know that I act in a tragic play, but the tragedy is not until the next act, and this scene is so pleasant and happy and real that the coming tragedy is forgotten.

What happened for a couple of weeks is that I went right to work on the mental discipline that Barrows assigned. Worked hard. Got up at four o'clock each morning, worked, and then at daylight went with Jim and Mike to the woods. During those dark morning hours, I did not know what kind of mind forces I was frigging with, but from the very first I could feel Barrows's mind close to mine. From the very first, my mind was picking up impressions and shapes and forms it had never known before. It was like the whole discipline was being handed to me. Sure I worked hard. I worked like hell, but the results came so fast it was alarming.

Besides, I had the work in the woods with Jim and Mike. The woods kept me in balance.

Max helped. He told me that Barrows was dealing with matter and forces that shaped content without limits. A painter had to use paint, a writer had to use words, but Barrows just threw out the paint and the words and looked to see what was happening. Max had been splitting firewood when he told me all this. He was wool shirted and healthy looking and manly. Well, Julie had introduced him to Dolores. Got to keep my control. Got to get this written down. If I go mad pretty soon, I'm not going to go all that mad. I got good reason.

Barrows. I'm going to get him, going to get that son of a bitch.

That last happy day exists like it is almost hypnotic. In fact, I've been messing with this mental energy business long enough that I can throw myself into hypnotic states without fear. Maybe this is written in a hypnotic state. Maybe, with Barrows's help, I've accomplished ten years of work in less than a month.

As Max saw him, Barrows is a maverick. There are mystics and psychics. Both deal in force, but differently. Psychics—whether they talk about spiritualism, ESP or witchcraft—are dealing in the use of power.

Mystics are different. Whether they are religious or not, mystics are concerned with experiencing power but not using it. Barrows called himself a mystic, but he had used power like a psychic.

"Or it may be," Max said, "that the incident of the tree called up an automatic response. He saved Jim automatically."

"Uh, uh," I told Max. "Barrows has planned to use the power. He has been hanging around the scene for the whole twentieth century waiting to save the world. Now, when push comes to shove, he can't even save the town."

"I want to think about that. Barrows obviously has other pressures that he is undergoing, although they may be subconscious."

"So Barrows has some other reason for hanging around, in spite of claiming to hate it?"

"I fear that is so."

"What reason?"

"While you work that is what I will attempt to uncover." Max is so kind. "For Barrows's sake," he said. "If it can be of any use to him."

I was suddenly grabbed by the hope that the combination of Dolores's tough-mindedness and Max's detachment would come up with a new definition of the situation. Meanwhile, Barrows's strike potential was my problem.

So I worked hard at the discipline. During the days I loved the work in the woods more than ever before.

Jim and Mike were finishing the last, ugly show. Reports filed, fines paid, and the job reopened and finished before the wimps from the state had time to stop us for some other reason. We trucked with the old KW, dozed and burned the slash, then moved to the next job.

The boys were not talking about Mobilier. It was like they had forgotten the whole thing in the concentration of work. Mike has always been quiet. I did not know what he was thinking, and did not think to ask. Two weeks had passed and he did not try to get instructions on how to build bombs.

The evening of the sixth we stopped for a beer after work. Everybody was pretty high and happy because of the new job. We had a plan for the weekend. We were going to fix the upstairs of my house into an apartment. I don't know how lady Dolores got through to old sobersides Max so fast, but Max was walking around with a silly look, like an ox that has been hammered in the forehead. Yep, we were feeling pretty good.

Jim rolled the truck to the outskirts of town and we stopped at the redneck bar for a beer to settle the dust.

It is a dark, seamy bar at all times, and we just shoved Mike into a booth and brought suds to him. After a while we rolled on down the hill and stopped for a couple at the old folks' joint. Anyone who comes in the doorway of that place is automatically assumed to be over ninety or a banker.

Jim was happy. The new show looked just fine. His face was easy. It was not haunted anymore.

"Want to come up to the house?" he asked.

"Want to go home and clean up first," I said. "Then sure."

Down the bar a couple of lush type old gents were arguing the baseball plays made during a game in the forties. Maybe they were the only people in the whole world who remembered that particular ballgame. They argued in passionate voices, eternally damned each other, and then one bought the other another beer.

"Got a date?" Jim asked Mike.

"In this town?" Mike's voice was quiet. In a way I wished Jim had not asked that.

"Come on over."

"I'll bring some ready-mix," Mike said. "Just bring dago red. I got plenty of beer."

In the streets, waves of tourists were not exactly enjoying the first week of the season. There had been sun, but the evening was going to be chilly. They made a show of being tourists, though. Bellies hung free over tops of golfer-type pants. Young girls wearing V-neck shirts that barely covered the rise of their pointy tits chattered to each other and pretended they were not cold.

"I got a bunch of canned stuff," I said.

"Penny will feed us."

"I'll call her and ask. You aren't any help."

"Of course," Jim said, in a voice like a schoolteacher, "you ain't spozed to be drinkin'."

It was true. That mental energy business did not combine with booze very well. Minds don't combine with booze, except occasionally when you drink a lot. The psychologist William James spotted that one back in the nineteenth century, and I suppose other people did it even before. Alcohol takes off the mental edge. All that the mind usually comes up with are a few pretty good aphorisms.

"Just this once," I said. "You got to have some fun."

"And you ain't having any?" Mike dipped a finger in his beer, rubbed behind each of his ears like he was a lady putting on perfume. The kid has never clowned much. I like it when he does.

"Grow up."

"Be like you?"

"Be somebody."

"I be a mechanic."

"Work on Lincolns?"

"Drive Lincolns. Work on diesels. Make a heap of money working on diesels." Mike did not quite get the bitterness from his voice, but Jim did not notice.

"Both of you are nuts."

"Drop us home," I told Jim. "I got to wash."

The back door was standing open when we arrived, which is unusual but not alarming. When I bought the house the real estate guy gave me a ring of keys but they got lost. The neighbors sometimes drop in to borrow a tool. They forget to close the door. Then one of the neighborhood cats comes in and makes itself at home.

Or maybe it was Julie who had come in and forgotten to close the door. She does that sometimes, and it is always a nice surprise to find her there.

Or maybe it was Barrows. He would do that just to be sure I was not surprised.

It was Barrows. He sat in the front living room and seemed in deep meditation, but he came out of it right away.

"Do you have some time?" he asked.

"Sure. Gotta clean up." I felt the side of the hot water heater with my hand. The heater is hooked to a coil in the wood stove. I had left a good fire banked. The hot water heater was still way up. Because I had some madrona, that's why. You can really bank a fire with madrona, because it burns almost like coal.

I walked to the west bathroom and turned the water on into the tub, then returned. "C'mon in while I wash. Sweating like a pig. Hot today."

"It really did get warm," he said. "It was sixty-five degrees at three o'clock."

"Thought so."

"How is the work going," Barrows said.

"Got the equipment moved. The new show is okay. Not much junk, very little cedar, pretty brushy in spots."

"I mean the other."

"Come on in." I headed for the bathroom and was bare-ass by the time I got there. The ability to dress and undress on the run can save you time.

Barrows followed and was uneasy. He glanced around and found no chair, so he lowered the lid on the john. Barrows on the john was not a sight anyone was going to see too often. He was at a disadvantage.

"You look almost cute," I told him. The water was good and hot. I eased into the tub and began to pour it over my head. Even my bald spot felt sweaty. Wash what's left of the hair, run more hot water.

"Is anything happening?"

He has never lied to me. Why did I suddenly want to lie to him?

"You ought to know," I said. "I don't know how you're doing it, but the capacity is tuning up fast."

"You are doing most of it. It is your mind, not mine."

"You're doing something," I told him. "For the last two mornings it has been like another consciousness is just outside my own consciousness. *Just* outside." I didn't really want to talk about it. What I really wanted was to get the day's work rubbed off. Soap is a really nice thing when you are sticky dirty. It probably doesn't do much more than plain water, but it feels nice. More damned training. Ever since the Phoenicians invented money, somebody has been selling soap.

"It's hard to describe," Barrows said. "The best and fastest way is to say that when I am present, you have antennae."

"It worked in the woods without you. I can tell the difference between a tree and a bulldozer."

"Wonderful." He was pleased. "It is coming along fast."

"Have you thought more about what I said?" He was constantly trying to get off the hook of action.

"They are quiet," Barrows said. "It would be wrong to provoke them." Now he seemed timid, and it was more than just sitting on the john. "We need your abilities. Mine are great but not infinite."

"I thought they were."

"Perhaps. I could reduce Mobilier's weaponry in two weeks."

"You may not have that much time. Have you been talking to Max?"

Barrows looked like a man betting his last buck on long odds. "Not for the last two days. Max has been occupied."

"Couldn't happen to nicer folks."

"At least that is true of Dolores."

"Max is a good man and a good friend."

"Ruthless in his expression."

Then it came out. It was not like my memories of sitting fat-assed in a college department while listening to the woes of a freshman, but there were similarities. It never occurred to me that Barrows needed a confessor.

His problem was that he could not bring himself to any good emotional sense. His passions were dead. After years of self-imposed isolation, loneliness and mystical involvement, he felt like a diseased fish. He felt squeezed like an old grapefruit rind.

"Still," I said, "you feel enough to feel awful lonely."

I kind of wished I hadn't said that. The raw, new pain was back on his face. Thinking of his wife.

"I'm sorry," I told him. "Only, usually people come to terms with loss after years have passed."

"Her name was Esther . . . I've told you that. It is not just the loss of her."

"Then what?"

"There never were many women as wise and moral. As the years pass there are none. Women are different now."

It was not the first time I ever guessed at his prudery. Now he stopped me. I did not know what he remembered, and while I'd read a lot about the times he had seen, I had not really been there. He *was* different. I was pretty sure that his Esther would not have given me houseroom, as grandma used to say.

"I'm going to be as ruthless as Max," I told him. "You can't repeal history. You are alive now, and not all women are wanton if that's what you think."

"I have no right to judge." He stood up, kind of unwrapping himself from the crapper.

"Bull. You do judge. Apparently you judge every day. And the only answer for you is to get laid. If you can't feel anything good at first, at least you can feel fear."

"You make it sound deadly simple."

"It can be deadly, especially for people who try to solve every problem in the world by thinking about it. That's you." I knew my man. It was better to have Barrows's problem than to have the problem of most people, which is to say that most people don't think about nothin'. This man Barrows was okay, but he sure was narrow. Maybe when he was a kid, his old man had once caught him jacking off.

"You can think yourself to death," I told him. "How long since you been laid?"

"What does that have to do with any of this?"

"Listen, you either have to be a saint—and maybe you should be—goddammit, you do not even hate Mobilier."

"I hate what it does. And I have extended myself to you, which was a mark of trust. And I have been celibate."

"Yes, you did extend yourself to me."

"Even that was a fearful thing to do."

"And you have been sober," I said. "Come on over to Jim's house. We are going to get tight and happy and maybe throw things."

"With my power I dare not drink."

"A little."

"Think of the power of alcohol on the imagination."

He had a point. After the first few drinks some actions seem reasonable that would take some explaining to yourself later on.

"Then find a lady."

"At my age."

"Come off it. You are physically a young man. If you were not so starchy . . ."

". . . would not even look at me."

"The average American woman is so fed up with the average American jock that she will look at anyone who has his head sewed on halfway straight."

"I'll think about it."

"Quit—thinking—for once."

"I'll trail along for one beer," He grinned. "Must start somewhere."

"You can vanish it from your system."

"And yours as well, if you feel terrible in the morning."

"Friends in high places." I began to whistle, kind of shoved him ahead of me, and we walked.

The temp was down to about ten celsius, and the camellias were beginning to bloom. I know the cycle and love it. Next would be the rhododendrons. After that the town would glow with peonies, the deep reds and startling rose-marked whites massed beneath open sun.

Along with them, raspberries would hang over garden fences and you could cop a few as you walked. Then, next, it would be black-berries. The whole town would take a small vacation. Around here blackberries grow like weeds.

The strait was lighted with the afterglow of the sun. Here, on the back of the hill, people were moving around the early evening, and they followed the tasks and small patterns of centuries. In six weeks there would be ladders all over town leaning into cherry trees. There would be the picking of fruits, the pitting, and then bringing the day's work into the victory of a pie. Yes, what people commonly do at their best is worth understanding and cherishing. What they do at their worst—well to hell with it—but I like it when they pick cherries and make pies.

"I'm remembering something," I told Barrows.

"From the way you look it must be nice."

"Important, too."

What I was remembering was once in Madrid, where time is always on your mind. I was in a huge square at sunset. It had been built in maybe the sixteenth century. Old, old brick, and the square was enclosed by buildings that had shops on the ground floor, while people lived in the upper floors. The sky was orange behind the buildings, and it was filled with swallows that dipped in the early evening, flying high and then diving around people who strolled here and there, or who sat at cafes sipping drinks and watching the approaching night.

I looked up and saw a woman leaning on one elbow at a windowsill. She sat looking out into the square. She was not especially pretty, but to me, then, she was beautiful. I thought of how many generations of women had sat at that window in the evenings over the hundreds of years. Somehow she seemed to me like all the women who ever lived. Then she stood and disappeared back into her rooms to face her chores or problems.

Barrows was purely happy with the tale. It was the first time I have ever seen him that unreserved.

"As Max remarked, you are an extremely likely subject." His happiness was as quiet and firm as the tranquil evening.

I had forgotten to call Penny and see if she needed anything. Well, if she did, I could always get the truck from Jim and come back.

How to get Barrows laid? I walked beside him in the warm evening and felt like it was always me who was engineering things, and it was my fault. Daddy Jake. The pimp.

But with Barrows it could not be a temporary, happy fuck. With Barrows it would be commitment or not at all.

"Ask Ann for a date."

"I thought of it last year."

"Well, for chrissake." Ann is probably fifty but does not look it, and even if she did look it, she would still be a warm and attractive woman. Class tells.

"A year is not much."

There it was. We were dealing with an enemy that could make us all dead in ten minutes, and Barrows was saying that a year was not much.

We walked along with the conversation pretty well dead after that. Past the library, turned down Jim's street, and for a few minutes my anticipation kind of cooled. Then we got to Jim's, and it all came back. Mike's heap was parked in front. The company truck was sitting there. They were getting a head start.

Penny opened the door. She was happy. Dressed in an old work shirt of Jim's that she had cut down. Plus sloppy jeans.

We got inside and dinner was going to be spaghetti, and she did not need no damned canned stuff, thank you, and get into the living room and don't spill nothing.

We went.

"Long time no see." Mike opened a beer and shoved it in Barrows's hand before he had a chance to refuse. Barrows did not look as uncomfortable with the beer as he had looked sitting on the john, but he did look like a preacher caught leaving a cathouse. Then he sort of shrugged, slugged hard at the beer, looked like he was going to lose it, and then smiled. Everyone pretended that nothing was happening.

"To absent friends." Jim said it like a joke, but Barrows winced.

"Julie's working, " I said.

"And Julie don't drink and gets on my wheels about drinking." Mike looked in pretty good shape.

"Max and Dolores are up north," Barrows said. "A visit to Victoria."

Victoria is the last Canadian town where Americans are welcome, and then only the tourist money.

"What a name for a town."

"Who's she?" Mike was feeling the beer a little after all.

"An English lady who would not be fascinated with Max and Dolores," I told him.

"I never met no English ladies," Mike said. "Met a Boston, once. Talked like she had a cob . . ."

Barrows slugged at his beer. This time he did not have any trouble holding it.

"Get done with this job and you go back to school." Jim really did have a head start. He can usually handle it unless he gets mad. Then the booze seems to turn to adrenaline.

"For why?"

"For to learn about iron pants Victoria, that's for why. Living like you do in this town."

Penny called from the kitchen and told him to have another. When you come from a family of cowboys, you know about booze. Penny would have seen this hundreds of times. She would know how good it could be. She would know how to keep it from going sour.

"An English queen—Queen Victoria," Barrows told Mike. "She had an extremely rigid sense of style."

"She was prolly a dyke," Jim said. "Bull dyke."

"You're thinking about a king named James," I told him. "Victoria had nine kids."

"She was saving the monarchy," Barrows said. "Had it not been for Victoria there might have been no English monarchy after World War I."

"Nothin' wrong with that," Jim said. "Topping good, rather." He winked at Mike, opened another beer and shoved it at Barrows.

"Not done with this one."

"Hurry up, coach. Did you know her?"

It didn't stop Barrows and it didn't stop Mike, but it sure stopped me. Barrows and Victoria had been alive in the world at the same time.

"She was the drummer. I did the fiddling."

He does not joke, if that was a joke. Usually he is just amused. Did two-thirds of a beer do that? No, he had finished the first one and reached for the second. For a moment I was scared, until I remembered his innate good sense.

"And Disraeli, too. And Gladstone, too. A lot of drumming and fiddling."

That couldn't be. One beer does not make you milk a joke. Especially when no one laughed the first time.

"But I actually did know Wilson. That is, I met him. And William James and Mary Baker Eddy." There was just a touch of bullshit in his voice, the kind you hear when the VFW starts telling hero stories about itself. I headed for the kitchen.

"Beat it," Penny said. I shushed at her.

"What is it?" She was alert, quick.

"Did you ever know anyone to get buzzed on one beer?"

"Me."

"And Barrows," I told her. "No damn wonder he doesn't drink."

She seemed relieved. She had been nearly terrified. "After the third one," she said, "he'll be okay."

"How do you know?"

"Jake, babe, he's that type." She was happy again. "Get out of here or starve."

I got.

The funny thing is that Penny was right. Barrows kept being extravagant through the first two, then on the third settled down and acted like he had drunk nothing. It seemed okay if I went ahead and caught up. By the end of that third beer, dinner was ready. No one had to force that on me. When you work in the woods the last thing you worry about is appetite. It was a good thing Penny was used to cooking for cowboys and loggers. You deal everything triple.

We switched to dago red. Barrows was quiet, but then everyone was quiet. The man had good sense. Why had I been worried? After all, I promoted this in the first place.

"You comin' back to the job?" Jim asked Barrows. Jim is usually about as subtle as a broken leg.

"I don't think so," Barrows said. "A lot depends on some personal decisions, and I have no clear idea how to make them." He was bound to be talking about what we had discussed earlier, about feeling squeezed out and dry and having no genuine emotions.

"Max was the one who presented me with the problem."

In a way I could understand why he was doing it. These people were a part of the jam that we were in. They should maybe be told about anything that affected Barrows. Still, it was not something to parade before the whole town. Booze.

Barrows explained and Penny understood almost right away, but not even as fast as old Mike. Mike caught it right off the top.

"Feeling the same thing," Mike said.

"No, you ain't, punk. You can't. Ain't dry behind the ears." Jim sounded as positive as the dumbest kind of cop.

"Maybe he can," Penny said. "There was a time when I felt that way, but not lately."

"Do you really?" Barrows asked Mike. Barrows was doing his second glass of dago red. Sneaky stuff.

"I been in a holding pattern," Mike said. "Did I have something to do besides work, or somebody to go with . . ." He broke off, and turned toward Jim. "I'm going to get outta town pretty soon. San Francisco. I'll be back, probably."

"You can't."

"I got a little money saved."

"You wouldn't last ten minutes on the streets." Now Jim was acting tough to keep his hurt feelings from showing. He did not want Mike to leave. I did not want Mike to leave. What is more, I guessed why Mike was going. There was probably one more resistance movement starting in San Francisco. Mike would be closer to the grapevine than I would ever be again.

The drinking was not going to help on this one. The world seemed changed into about forty acres of dried mud, and this dago grape juice was a downer unless someone did something quick. The small house seemed to have lost some of its shine. Bad stuff does that to you.

Penny saved it.

"There's girls in town," she said. "It isn't girls. It's not knowing anything." She turned to Barrows. "And you're just as bad."

"How?" He was shocked. He is used to being argued with, but not attacked.

"Sometime or other you quit taking chances. You stop learning when you quit taking chances."

"It isn't different, is it?"

Penny is sometimes so smart. "It isn't fucking," she said. "No amount of that helps. It isn't sitting around being cool and smart, either."

I wondered how she knew.

"How about yourself?" Mike asked.

"Are you kidding?" She pointed at Jim. "Look at that big, drunken dumbass."

Mike understood that one. Even Jim understood that one.

I watched Barrows and Mike, and decided to push it a little. "Penny is saying you can't drift. Either you are in or out."

=

"I don't get it." Mike was missing stuff again.

"You can't go off without a plan, and you can 't sit around all the time planning."

"Gotcha." Mike suddenly looked even more confident than he had on the day we talked. Sure as hell there was a resistance movement, and sure as hell I had just talked him into joining it. Bigmouth. Legendary figure of the Pacific Northwest.

Maybe I could talk him out of it when we were all sober.

"Think about it," Jim said to Barrows, "and have another little sniff." Jim was drinking serious now, but it felt okay. For some reason the situation felt almost hopeful. It also looked like the pace of the evening was going to be quick.

It was. I nursed a beer and then another, and we talked about lumber.

I watched Barrows. He was not out of control, but a little bit snockered. "Going home while I can still drive," Mike said. He got up and hugged Penny. "You're a nice lady."

"You ain't bad for a punk."

I went along with Mike for the ride. It was not that far to walk, but the booze and dinner had me pretty swelled up. I was awfully tired.

If there was a resistance movement, then Mike had to be talked out of joining. I turned to him. "What's in San Francisco?" The dash lights on his junker had a poor contact. They sort of blinked on and off. It was like seeing his face in slow frames, like a movie being reeled at one-third speed.

"I won't know until I get there."

"You know something, dammit. Tell me."

"Bunch of guys."

"Listen to me. Really listen close. If it's a shit storm you want, then go alone. Plan careful before you make any move. Leave margins of time, in case something messes up. Think of what constitutes evidence. Remember the shock value of surprise . . ." I trailed off. Next, I would be giving him details on how to blow up a bank.

"I'll remember." That was all he would say. The next day Mike was gone. He had dropped me at home, went to his place to pick up his bucks and then split. Jim and I never did get back to the woods.

But that was the next day. That night, that last happy night, I went into my house, stripped by the still warm cookstove, then went to the can to get rid of some beer. Looked in the mirror at my balding, incompetent head.

The funny thing is that I thought of Dolores. The thoughts were not sex thoughts, just warm. Dolores. Not Julie.

We are all of us alone. That's true, but most people don't handle it very well. We speak to each other across space and vacuum. Like in Thomas Hardy's poetry.

Thinking of Dolores. Why was I not thinking of Julie?

Because Julie makes me afraid sometimes. Julie does it because she kids herself. Dolores does not kid herself very much. When Dolores tells you a thing is true, then it is true. When Julie says something is true, her words are tinged with illusion.

It was a buzzy night. How did Penny get so smart? Knowing that it is yourself, and illusion, with which you must come to terms.

Go to bed. Sack out alone. That is real. Ghosts upstairs, haunts. And in myself shades of a mind now buzzed from rapid but not heavy drinking.

Old mind-washer booze. This was not a heavy drunk. This was a coming-to-terms-with-reality drunk. Maybe that is why I thought of Dolores.

Somewhere between thought and sleep a presence began to gather. It was elusive and hesitant. At first I did not feel it much more than you feel an echo. Then it began to grow. It was over in the dark corner of the bedroom, where moonlight never reaches. A presence that might enter sleep and become nightmare.

My mind began to press back toward awareness, but it did not do well because of the fatigue. The presence was not threatening.

Then it expanded. Not fast but inexorable. It began to move toward me. I recognized it now. It was Barrows, or rather, it was the mind that had hovered next to mine for the past couple of days.

There was a different feeling now. The mind was sad and it was apologetic.

It seemed ready to speak. So much living, and in my case some killing as well. I let it come. If it wanted to talk, then let it talk.

But it did not. It rested alongside my head like a corresponding measure of my own fatigue, like a dark sympathy that told of eons. I loved it for a minute because it seemed to understand lost hopes, lost dreams.

Then it came nearer and it was still not frightening. It sort of pressed against me, and I knew that I could let it inside my head. The mind was lonesome, like I have never been so lonesome. It takes years and decades to be that alone. At the same time the mind was apologetic and humble. Barrows was afraid of commitment. He had come to the one person to whom he had not been able to make a commitment.

"Not now," I said, and I said it kind and easy. "Not now, Barrows. I don't know enough. Besides, you won't take action and you make me afraid." I really tried to be nice about it. It was the booze, of course. When you are lonely, booze sends you searching, and Barrows was no exception. He had drunk enough to at least allow him to take this much action.

Lonely streets, arc lamps, jukes playing from long ago: the lonely streets of searching for love.

The mind withdrew, and the next morning it was beside my mind the way it had been before.

But it comes to me, writing this, that I was nearly one with Barrows then. Either I nearly received his mind, or he nearly took mine. And, when he gets troubled enough or lonely, he'll try it again. I'm waiting for the son of a bitch—because the next time he tries, I'm going to capture him.

Chapter 20

NOTES BY MAX KLEIN:

In my life I have seen two massacres. The first was long ago, the second was this eighth of May. Strange, how I remember the first one every bit as clearly as the one that has just happened.

The first massacre still remembers the surrounding summer fields, with the hot nights interrupted occasionally by thunderstorms that swept across the land bringing a scent of crops, of ozone and magnolia and animal stink from hog lots and barns. I was five years old.

The main street of that small farm town continued from the town square to the outskirts, where it disappeared ambiguously into dirt roads and fields. There were two blocks on that street of large old brick houses. They were in decay, but they had once been the center for wealthy residents. The rest of the town was clapboard.

Along the street was an arch of large trees, and during that summer they became the roosting place for tens of thousands of starlings. The birds had never been there in such numbers. I remember the incredulity of old people who Biblically held that the birds were a first plague, like God and Moses inflicted on Egypt. We had no local pharaoh, or rather, none with power. There were hardly any Jews to scourge. Our family composed all of the Jews in town.

The birds swarmed from the fields each evening. As the sun moved toward the edge of the distant fields and woodlots, it seemed that a black hive ejected into the sky. Five years old is young, yet I remember with awful clarity.

In the lingering summer light the trees would be solid and branch-bending with birds. There were birds to a number as there are screams in history. It was then that the shooting began.

The remarkable part is that this was a massacre by children. I remember only one rifle present on one evening, carried by a boy who seemed as old and wise as King David. I suppose he was not more than fifteen. Each time he fired, the swarm bunched in the trees like the heaving of a vast, dark sigh. Then the birds would settle, and the killing would resume.

Droppings piled up and killed the grass. Bodies sprinkled like a constant light shower under the directed fire of BB guns and slingshots. I suppose that as many as two thousand birds might be killed on any evening, for I sincerely believe that every child in a town of ten thousand was present. What I recall more than any other thing is the blood lust, but there are also pictures of gasping, dying birds, of birds hanging upside down from branches. A bird's foot is constructed so that it grasps as pressure is put on the center. In some cases the foot stayed clasped after the bird toppled. They hung like dark pendants from the branches, with bloody beaks open and yellowish in the twilight.

I had no gun because I was too little, and because of my father. Had he known I was there I would have been forbidden the summer evenings, but Jews in small towns live in a particular isolation. My father had not even heard about what was happening.

I had the blood lust, although I had no gun. I wanted to be one with the directed fire, to join the babbling older boys and the excited shouts that sailed like banshee wails in the hot summer evening. The blood lust had a price. Each night I would be sick while on the way home.

When a boy had BBs but no gun he could trade for shots. Two or three or four BBs for one shot. It was the first time in my life I ever stole, and the last.

A boy dropped a tube of BBs. I helped pick them up and restored them to him. I withheld three. I traded for a shot and missed. I was bewildered. Guilty. Sad. After that I did not go back to the trees, although the killing lasted all through the summer.

The saucers rose from the deserts, from secret hangars in high mountains, from beneath polar ice and from the back side of the moon.

The driving was simple. It has been since 1955 and '56, with the anti gravity experiments carried on at Harvard. The drive only partly suspended gravity, while projecting a high magnetic field. The saucer literally pulled itself here and there by directing the field. It was like having an electromagnet that you could beam back at yourself. On a small scale, using magnetics, it is possible to make a piece of metal dance, jump through the air, or slide back and forth.

The control units had variable flow on the power. It was like a rheostat. They could start slow and gain speed. The slave units were not sophisticated. Since they were unmanned, they could be jerked through space and the atmosphere like so many tin pie plates. Because of the enormous speed, they had to carry refrigeration machinery to ice them so that the friction of the atmosphere would not burn them to cinders. The manned craft were far more sophisticated.

It reconstructs this way. He, Jake, was engaged in the mental discipline Barrows had assigned. Barrows, who obviously knew Mobilier's plans, was waiting and watching, in the hope of deferring action. Jim was at home, his job closed down because of Mike's departure. I had spoken to Jake that morning, then walked downtown to Ann's restaurant for a late breakfast.

Looking back, one can almost imagine that nature itself had conspired to illuminate the horror that was forming around us.

Sunshine spread across the town like a wand of benevolence. Varieties of hawthorn bloomed in a glow of rust and white along the streets, where hand-carved, red cedar business signs were silvered by weather and the sheen of the sun. Shadows of buildings lay like a child's tumbled blocks in the streets, and people traveled the walks from shadow to sun in a myriad shifting of colored and shaded patterns. Young girls chattered, flirted, walked with the quick confidence of youthful ignorance and the visceral knowledge of spring, while, waiting to direct traffic at an intersection, a policeman who was little more than a boy rubbed his sleeve on the buttons of his new coat and made them shine in the sun.

Old men in musty clothes moved from seedy rooms of decaying apartments to sit by the now dry but still flower-ornamented fountains of the small, downtown park. They gossiped in the sun. Dark-suited businessmen strolled to morning coffee, and a young boy in worn jeans and flapping tennis shoes ran through the crowd. Farther down the street, a heavy, white-haired woman dressed in a purple and red housedress stared, apparently at the behest of the child beside her, high above the strait where sunlight glanced from the polished and icy sides of a dozen shining discs.

We now know the commander's name. If Butterfield made a tactical error, it was then. The military mind is sometimes godlike in its joy, and, like some Olympian god, Butterfield allowed those saucers to hover. If he had used them immediately, there would have been even more destruction. No doubt Butterfield was searching for a first reaction. He had been warned about the quality of his enemy, but knew nothing about the nature of that quality.

Another group of a dozen saucers appeared, traveling at low speed and low altitude above the strait to the north. Because of the dark water, and the deeper colors of gray and dusted blue from shadowing mountains, the saucers looked icy and dark. They were close enough that it was easy to judge their size. Eleven of them appeared to be about a hundred and fifty feet in diameter. The remaining saucer was at least twice that size. The large control saucer looked more than icy. It seemed frosted, like snow clung to its surface.

This group hovered only a few yards off the water and looked like a line of crouching, armored cavalry. Along the western range of mountains three more squadrons appeared.

I was not as helpless as the rest of the people in the streets, yet knew that I must remain as helpless. If my powers are great, that does not mean that they are to be used. For, I reminded myself, this particular frame of history belonged to Barrows and Mobilier.

I stood and stared. If the attack was to be an attack with sound, then safety lay in the water, shallow, where a person might raise his head to breathe. The water here is cold. A healthy adult might live twenty or thirty minutes in that water.

In the south and east sectors the sky began to fill. Sunlight danced and flashed from the curve of hulls. It was horrible and not horrible. My mind could not accept the meaning of what was happening. There was an orderly and lethal beauty to the situation. It was like watching a caged, poisonous snake. The mind could not accept that the snake was not caged.

The squadrons appeared, line after line, flank after flank, until the horizon was covered by a band of flashing steel. The people in the streets were still watching. I thought, with a first sense of terror, that this must have been the way the massed horsemen of Genghis Khan had looked with drawn swords twisting in the sun. The machines continued to appear and fill the sky, rank after rank, glistening. They hovered like metallic beasts chained by command, but ready to pounce and destroy at a word.

That force actually seemed proud. There is no other way to describe it. Most of that force was mechanical. Only one in every twelve of those ships was manned. The rest were slaves or drones. Collectivity of nothing more than objects is still a creative force as long as there is one mind to think about it. Explain that one, Max Klein . . .

The people in the streets remained silent. Images came and went across the mind. The people looked like crowds of flowers from seed randomly scattered. Some stood alone. Others clustered. Plaid-shirted flowers, green dresses, blue-jeaned forked stems above the pavement. The people stood staring into the sun and the clear air at an icy, regulated doom which they could not understand belonged to them.

Then the crowd, which had not really been a unit, became a unit. Before the massing of forces each person had been intent on his or her individual goal. An errand, perhaps: a visit to grocery or pharmacy to pick up some item routine in sustaining life.

Now the people reacted collectively. The group took its pattern of behavior from itself. People looked into each other's eyes to see question and uncertainty and fear. What they saw was reflected back, and their feelings were increased because their own actions were reinforcing the signals. The crowd shuffled, murmured and was momentarily imprecise. It was confused.

"You must take your people into the water," I said to a group close to me. "The water is the only safe place." The group look, the group stare, said that they believed me mad.

The first saucers had been a shocking curiosity. As the numbers increased beyond imagination, what had been curious became an awful and impending threat. A beginning sense of fatality started to overtake the crowd. It was the sort of sense that one might expect in a people who had felt the first shock of a volcanic eruption, but who still lived in a world that had yet to exhibit sound and flame.

Then the crowd arrived at consensus. I have seen such things before, and they are strange and wonderful each time. Not a word had been spoken except my own, yet everyone moved at once. The people began to ebb from the streets, to businesses, storerooms and nearby houses. The silence maintained. Women and men pushed children ahead of them. They moved deliberately. Even the children understood. The men watched each other, testing and checking their perceptions and resolve. A few men walked quickly to old trucks where they pulled illegal pistols and rifles from beneath seats. In the rapidly emptying streets only one man broke the consensus. Whether through fear or determination of other action, he sprinted to his truck and left the curb in a burst of engine noise and scorching tires. The truck looked like a tattered, red leaded spotted antique, but it ran fast. It was like a derelict being chased by the police. It caused the first sound in the streets.

A few people stopped and watched, and when the truck disappeared around the right-hand bend a quarter of a mile down the road, they saw the smoke at the same time they heard the explosion. The truck was destroyed by a laser beam so brief that many who were watching did not even see it. From the low bluff around which the truck had spun from sight, smoke and flame boiled, and a piece of glass rose unshattered into the air. It twisted and sparkled in the sun.

That was the catalyst. The few people who remained in the street ran yelling or screaming to the illusory sanctuary of buildings.

It was then that Barrows reluctantly began to take action.

Above the strait eleven of the saucers seemed to hesitate, to stumble in midair, and then they tumbled. They fell flat at first, then heeled over on edge and entered the water to slip under with little more splash than if they had been lids cut from giant cans. The twelfth saucer began to move higher and sideways at a slow rate. Above the mountains the brilliant sides of the saucers began winking out in the sunlight as if someone were shooting out a string of mirrors. Barrows was destroying the unmanned craft.

. . . Funny how the mind can go cold, and how the trained mind can go professionally cold. I was convinced that within moments we would all be dead . . . and I record this because I want the assurance of this.

After the first sensation of terror I became calm. It is the product of years of thinking about it, and expecting it, this singular adventure which is death. I have long accepted the fact that I am a dead man. We all are, from the moment we draw our first breath, but you can play with philosophy and history and theology for a long time without really believing you are dead.

I was not afraid. I was not unhappy. It seemed like there was a time for this, as there is a time for all things, and now the time had arrived. It is almost amusing that my only real sorrow was that it would happen fast. I would not have time to fully test the experience.

Above the mountains the brilliant sides of the saucers continued to wink out like candles being snuffed. The dark forms on the strait sat down on the water like plates, toppled and rocked with the current, eased with small splashes beneath the waves as the second command saucer rose from darkness to light. It was a gleaming, speeding machine, grasping altitude to join the other command unit.

To the east, where the long, chainlike command of saucers was rapidly beginning to close, they as rapidly disappeared. Some fell off and coasted like leaves toward the water. No saucers over land were dropped. Those simply vanished. Over the water, Barrows was disabling them. They coasted in like gigantic skipping stones. In fact, at least two did skip, turned edgeways, were spun into the water. In less than two minutes the huge force was cut down to its command units. The screaming had stopped as the people disappeared from the streets. Now the only sound was the cry of an infant, the squawking of gulls about the boat moorings, and the splash of water against pilings. The infant's cry was indignant but not fearful. It mingled with the other small sounds, like a question in the silence. The people could not know what was happening. Few of them could have a good vantage point from the buildings. A grim, silent war was being waged above their heads, and they could know nothing, do nothing, until the first shock.

What had been an attack force of three hundred and sixty machines was decimated to a force of thirty. Those were widely separated by sector and altitude. Hovering behind them, but now growing larger as it closed from great distance, the central command vehicle loomed like a mountain suspended in air by magic. It was gray. No sunshine glanced from its tubular, or Zeppelin-shaped sides. Instead, the sun seemed absorbed into its mass.

We would later discover that the attack plan had been to saturate the town with sound. It was to be a heavy, total strike that would immobilize all, and destroy most of the population. Low hovering saucers were then to surround the area. They would serve as cover for airborne troops landed to secure the area. Once secured, which meant once every living creature was dead, the ground troops would withdraw to a then approaching submarine. After withdrawal, low-level bombers using conventional explosives would reduce the buildings. The area would be further reduced after the bombing by demolition crews from the sub. The intent was to leave not one brick mortared to another. This was to be total destruction. It would not be another Nighthawk, where silent buildings stood above contorted corpses.

Now, with the sudden decimation of their forces, the command units fled. Their crews must be going through heavy physical torment, for the acceleration was incredible. They disappeared beyond the far range of mountains, leaving empty streets in a silent town. From back on the hill I heard the rapidly winding roar of an engine, and then at the end of the main street Jake's truck appeared broad-sliding the comer. It recovered, fishtailed back and forth, and he accelerated for the first three blocks. He braked, the truck fishtailed again, and he got it stopped about fifty feet beyond me.

"Run. Jump, goddammit." His face was tense, tough, and his eyes were slitted, cold, and they gave no sign of friendliness or recognition. His voice was low. It held tones that you felt would shatter you if you did not obey. I ran to the truck, and it was screaming its tires in the street before I had the door closed.

"How did you know?"

"I sensed the goddamn things." He was winding the truck hard, pouring it toward the bend in the road around which the first truck had gone and then burst into flame.

"There's a wreck ahead of you."

"I know it." He ran up on the curve at seventy, punched the brake hard twice, downshifted, and we went into a delicate, four-wheel drift that I did not believe could be accomplished in a pickup. The rear end started to break, and Jake nudged the gas, jogged the wheel twice, and the truck came on around. The still-burning wreck straddled the center of the road, and the biggest shock was not the sight but the smell of burned flesh. Jake drove to the right of the wreck, still working on the skid. The rear end broke again. He bounced it off the wreck. The truck staggered, he jogged the wheel and accelerated. Metal peeled from the side of his pickup and flapped hard as we pulled away and drove for the turnoff. Jake hit the brakes, the tires squalling, and we skidded into the intersection. He twisted the wheel and we were away and up the hill pointed toward Jim's house.

"They've gone," I said. "Barrows knocked out most of them. Why the rush?"

"They've shit gone, too," he told me. "They have like hell."

"You're sure?"

"When will you bastards learn to listen?" He turned to me. "When we get there you handle the rest of them. Jim, Penny. Take the truck to Julie's house and get her. Take cover. I'll handle Barrows." By the time he had said it we were there. He skidded to a stop and was running before motion was entirely off the vehicle. I reached over, set the brake, cut the engine and climbed out. By the time I was inside, Jake had Barrows literally backed against a wall. Jim and Penny were standing by looking helpless. They could not decide whether Jake was sane.

"Knock them out. Now." Jake was talking to Barrows in that same cold, command voice.

Barrows said nothing.

"Where are they?"

"North," Barrows said. "They are clustered at about forty thousand feet, in the northern part of the Bering Sea."

"All of them?"

"The command vehicle is above the Gulf of Alaska."

"Knock them out."

Barrow's voice was calm. It was even gentle. "Jake, those craft are manned."

I thought Jake was going to kill him. I began to move forward and Jim came with me. Jake caught himself. He must have realized that he could not destroy Barrows because Barrows was his only weapon.

"Do it," he said. "If you don't do it, we're dead."

"They are high and over water."

"They are going to attack."

"After that kind of defeat?"

I thought Jake would have a stroke. He stood, mouth open, disbelieving.

"They have no weapons," Barrows said. "I have knocked out their sound equipment. There is not a weapon left to them."

"Goddammit . . ."

"And I have knocked out the weapons carried by soldiers on some approaching aircraft. They have turned back. I have destroyed all guns and explosives on a submarine. They have nothing. "

"Get out of here," Jake said to all of us except Barrows. "Take cover. Get to Julie's. Take her with you."

It was Jim who got us moving. Of all of us he had the best sense. Jim did not understand what was happening, but he was trusting Jake, not Barrows.

"The deeper the hole the better," Jake said. "Make it to that root cellar."

As we left, he turned back to Barrows. "Now, you goddamned bastard . . ." We went through the doorway and to the truck.

The saucers, stripped of all but essential flight equipment, gave us a fifteen-minute respite. By then Jim had lodged Penny and myself in the root cellar beside an abandoned and decaying Victorian house. Penny was angry and worried but she trusted Jim.

"I don't even know why I'm doing this," he told her.

"Stay here with us."

"Got to get Julie. Where's Dolores?"

"Collecting on a low tide up north," I said.

"There ain't a hell of a lot I can do about that."

There was nothing to say. He was a brave man making decisions. The soundlessness that surrounded us seemed complete. The sunshine that swept the town lay outside the entrance to the root cellar like lights on a stage. Not even a bird was calling out there.

Downtown, as we would learn later, the people began to emerge from the buildings and stood talking in the streets. Excited. Speculative. That saved some of them from dying.

Far to the north the saucers flamed back into action. Barrows could not understand that instead of fighting an organization, he was now fighting a general officer. It was one on one. Tactics were dictating events. Jake could only stand helplessly by.

With his forces badly crippled, and weaponless, General of Air/Space George Butterfield was forced to innovate. The first thing that would naturally engage his interest was that he had lost no men. When his support forces reported the same thing, that they were weaponless but without personal loss, one can imagine his first hypothesis.

It must have seemed for an instant that he was up against a weapon that could not destroy flesh. That would have been immediately rejected.

Yet the weapon was clearly selective. He would have been forced to one of two conclusions. Either he had received a warning, or the weapon opposing him was limited by some set of rules. What kind of rules made no difference.

It is a nice question that asks what he would have done if there had been a substantial time lag. Would he have committed his remaining forces, or reconnoitered first at the hazard of giving his enemy a breathing spell to get even better prepared. Because of the speed of his arms, he was not troubled with the question. The machines had hardly gotten grouped above the Bering Sea before three of them were dispatched at different altitudes to come across the town at varying speeds. The fly-by suffered no attack. By that time Butterfield was getting readouts from his computer.

A man uses best the weapons he knows best. In this case there was a general who dealt in sound and frequencies with all the dexterity of an old-time infantryman field-stripping his rifle. The town of Land's End was two-thirds destroyed by sonic boom and the resulting fires.

It was not a succession of booms, which the town could have partially survived even if they were perfectly placed. It was a boom generated by absolutely precise flight patterns at various speeds and trajectories. The computer combined these with every possible bit of atmospheric information as well as the height above sea level. Twenty saucers dispersed to various locations on the globe. They converged with pinpoint timing, with the accuracy of professional dancers.

The result was a series of sonic booms lapping into each other and reinforcing each other to combine into a boom as heavy as any earthquake, greater by far than any hurricane. It was a new genius in killing, unique at that time on earth. The airquake struck and the town literally flew apart.

In the root cellar it was difficult to even guess what was happening when the ground shook. The sensation, even underground, was that an enormous hand pressed against the earth to flatten and destroy. In the sunshine beyond the root cellar, the air changed to a rush of dust and debris. I found myself choking as the air in the cellar was pulled out with a suction that nearly carried us through the entry.

The sound, when it did come, did not crack or split as might be expected. Instead, the sound welled, and it was deep and full-throated and seemed to roll and thunder like the surrounding mountains were collapsing into the sea. In the brilliant sun, the air was dark and then light: whirled, tossed and filled with trash.

It was like the end of the world was going on out there. Penny moved toward the entry and I caught her arm. Whatever had happened was already a fact. A fatality. There was nothing that could be done to alter whatever already was. She stood trembling as the shock subsided.

"I will," I told her. I walked to the entry and looked out. What was left of Jim's truck was tumbled into the wreckage of what had been a house across the street. That house was already burning from short-circuited electricity. Behind me the old Victorian house had passed from decay into nothing. Bare foundations marked where it once stood. I turned back. There was nothing that could be said that would offer comfort or hope. "It is as bad as your worst fear," I told her.

She nodded. Unspeaking. She walked to the entry almost placidly, paused, and then she ran screaming.

We found him fifty yards beyond the wrecked house and truck. The head injury he sustained might have killed him. The piece of knifelike cedar debris from the exploding Victorian house that had entered his chest and fragmented like a grenade had been sufficient. There was absolutely no sign of Julie. From a hundred locations black smoke was already rising into the sunshine from the sites of fires; and madness began to overwhelm Jake. He searched for Julie, and as his hope faltered in the days that followed, his madness increased, as shown in his tragic entry, which is next included.

Counterattack

Chapter 21

THERE ARE ONLY DAYS OF HELL AND MADNESS, BUT I WILL SAY THIS: Madness is like most things in life. You can do it better if you've had some experience. Sometimes I think I am older than Barrows. He has seen more seasons, but he has tried to avoid life.

This man who is me, this peculiar creature named Jake, walking upright on two highly developed and disproportionately heavy legs that are one specialized feature of Homo sapiens; eyes staring at night skies, stars, meteors, comets in their season. Why, I have seen frost lying like frozen breath across the ground. I have known the easy ways and days of that love that is an emotional style of my breed, those days confident and singular. I have known trust, which is another concept of my breed. When the sun has risen between layered beneficence of clouds, I have been there.

The sea has crashed and tumbled, thrown wild spume like ghostly white devils fathered by wind, and my face has been wet and salty. When I was a kid I drove the roads or hitched along them. The land unfolded before me. I sang wild songs into the sunrise. Jake is not a casual passer-through, one who picks at life with the corner of his eye.

Madness and grief. The grief lies centered in my mind like the coldness of history that is littered with millions of violently dead, the hideously sprawled members of our breed. The coldness of the dead. I do not know what has happened to Julie.

Barrows never lied to me before. Is he lying now?

The madness comes and goes. I can tell about it, because now my mind is frozen and pure. I range the world, searching, testing, looking at weapons emplacements and all the grim paraphernalia of war. I am at home with these things. I am now.

Your governments told you that you were making your nations strong, but those governments would not have needed those weapons if your nations were not riddled with cowardice and fear.

And weapons get used. All through history, when a weapon was developed it has been used.

You are not exempt, you businessman, you bureaucrat, you pablum-brained housewife chatting banalities of Johnny's first and soon to be his last word. You senators pompous and grave, you presidents and judges and spellbinding preachers who will look to the sky or hear deadly and quick the last sounds of this planet squalling.

You have my curse. I curse you with thirty seconds of extra life. Thirty seconds of exquisite suffering as you look at what you have done.

Oh, creatures of smoke. Do not say that you love your children.

You hate your children. The smile on your face as you bend over the crib is a murderer's smile.

There is only a piece of meat loaf in that crib. Maybe it, the meat loaf, raised by someone who is not a murderer, might become a human being. It might discover theologic or scientific or artistic truth.

This crib child, beautiful, potentially capable of your salvation, is already dedicated to murder. You kill and teach killing, and it will kill and teach killing—while you speak in meat loaf language and say that your senators are honorable men.

. . . thoughts and impressions and moods. I see Julie walking toward me laughing. I think of the decency and form of her, and of her trust. I see her timid, afraid, resolute, working, see her walking the stormy beach. Now she is gone and I don't know where. Mostly, I think she is dead and Barrows vanished the body. My strength increases. I can sense things and distinguish faces fifty miles away. Some other part of my senses, a part which I don't understand, spends time on other continents examining planes and bombs. My time is spent searching, and searching makes the power grow.

I think we tell things, write them down, record them, because we are not smart enough to accept futility. I think we know we are temporary voices in an enormous silence, a silence so pervading that we are impressed with our ability to squeak.

. . . I nearly had Barrows once. As I get stronger and he gets more confused and guilty, I think he will approach me again. It is my job to fool him, to get him to try it again, because if I capture him I will be able to find Julie. And if Julie is dead, there is going to be a rain of hell and it will flood he world.

=

. . . things are timeless now. People walk through this town, around this house, daily passing through a little more life toward a little more death. I pay no attention, and when change comes I think to myself, why, time has passed and I did not notice.

She appeared beside me in the darkness, Penny, small, chaste, purified by grief. Penny had not come because she was afraid.

On this side of the house, the dark side, shaded by old trees, there is still enough of a structure left that you can live in it. The upper floors are gone, shattered and twisted away; the glass all over the house is a rainbow of shrapnel and colored dust. The water system is out, the electricity out. This dark side of the house, fire-smelling, acrid, stinking of a hundred years of disturbed dust and plaster, is habitable until the heavy winter rains.

"It's you, huh." Penny had caught me in the trance to which I retreat. It is a substitute for sleep, and is more productive than sleep. "Move over, Jake, babe." In the darkness, her voice gave shape to the rest of her. Penny has always shaped life with that voice. I followed the lines of her face with my mind, her hands, her movement. My way of seeing is as good as any other. It is like being able to see without eyes.

Never look underground. Underground is where we bury dreams.

The dark, shallow closet of the earth. It is all one graveyard down there, sprinkled with bones and the putridly running sap of the newly dead. It is beneath the soil that we conceal our choices.

I was sitting on a salvaged mattress and leaning against the wall. The room was not busted up too much. Barrows had vanished the plaster and crap. I was sitting in the same way I had been sitting for most of the last two weeks.

Penny eased down beside me and shut up. Both of us had traveled on our mouths for so long that when mouths no longer worked we were helpless.

"You keeping it together?"

She said nothing. Just sat beside me. I said nothing more. We were going to have more time than we needed, or either of us wanted.

I brought my mind back from the places it had been searching, routinely running it across the town. We were going to take another shot from Mobilier, and I watched to figure out where it would come from and how.

A few people were still awake and moving through their houses. No one was in the streets. A few of the smaller houses were more or less intact. Sections of the town still stood where they had been protected by hills or cuts in the terrain.

The humandamned human race.

Here and there a few people were fucking. Bedsprings bouncing in a squeaking protest against eternity.

Penny's house stood like a small, intact piece of gilt crap like you used to win at carnivals. A small log house can take a pretty good blow.

Barrows's house was up the beach and surrounded by second growth. It had not even been badly shaken. Barrows was sitting in front of a mirror. He had been doing that a lot lately.

Julie's house . . .

Max and Dolores were snugged up together and asleep. Max was touching her lightly. His hand sort of rested on her hand. That was nice, I guess.

Julie's house was empty. The raw salt wind poured all around it, through it, flapping the helter-skelter of tossed books. At least Max had gathered her papers. Her work was not lost.

Twelve hundred miles east, a general named Butterfield slept. He was above ground, but his hangars were below ground and masked by fields. The quarters looked like an old farmhouse. I understood the son of a bitch. He had been doing a job, impersonally, and he did it well. In fact, he did it superb, when you stop to think that he had only his own innovation. I was going to kill him pretty soon, but for now he lay sleeping with a soft wind in the open windows, a wind that would be carrying the scent of new growth from the fields. Below him, in cavernous hangars, ranks of men slept near various kinds of air and spacecraft. I was going to tumble those fields down on the whole shitting mess pretty soon.

I understood a lot of other things. In Seattle, Cincinnati, St. Louis, Chicago, Newport News, New York, the houses were filled with people asleep, some of them soon to wake as the sun hit the East Coast. They were snoring and secure in their certainty of tomorrow. They would rise, blink maybe, curse maybe, and go about the business of trying to keep life together in a subsistence economy. They were as happy as the mass of people had ever been. Looking at them caused me to understand something about the humandamned human race.

I always figured that people wanted to be free. Hah.

They deserved to live in a totalitarian state because they wanted, more than anything else, to be secure. In other times they had called freedom the opportunity to amass wealth. They did not care for thought, speech, even the ability to move from one town to another. Totalitarianism was easy for them to take. They loved it.

They had never wanted to be free, and if I hate them, which now makes no difference, then the hardest thing I could do to them would be to make them free.

So much for an ideal society.

When the attack came, old Barrows wouldn't touch a one of those manned ships until the town was already burning. When he finally got it through his thick skull that the fun and games were over, he caused interruptions in the gyros of the ships. All of them got back and landed except two, and now Barrows was sitting and staring at a mirror and telling himself that he was a killer.

He is. Counting Nighthawk the death toll is over seventy-five hundred so far.

On the other hand, seventy-five hundred are not much. A million people are not much. Your wife or husband is not much, you sleeping people who love security. Your kids are nothing. Peel you and your wife and your son and your daughter away from the human race, lay the four of you out with stopped hearts, the meat turning cold and stinking, and it is just nothing.

Because, cookie, you are the one who grooved on overkill.

I have looked everywhere for her. Except underground. If she is dead and somehow in the ground, then that is one that even I cannot bear.

Maybe Penny was sane.

"What do you want?" I asked her.

"Nothing." Her voice was as hard as mine.

"The time of day? You're here for some reason."

"Where else would I be?"

"I don't know," I told her. "Where else have you been?"

I could see her better with my eyes closed. Impossible for Penny to lose weight, because she didn't weigh hardly anything to begin with. Now, running over her body, I saw that it had happened. She was in refinement. Her body was like a perfectly balanced weapon. She had the directness and completeness of a well-cared-for knife.

"You come to kill me?"

"Barrows," she said. "You're just a sucker like the rest."

"It's a great idea. Don't do it yet."

"Why not?" Her voice seemed to just rise from the lethal presence of that refined body.

"You must have some sense left. You came and asked before you did it."

"If there ain't a good reason, I don't care what you say."

She could do it. If she walked up to Barrows that minute with a knife, he would be glad. It would take one more decision out of his hands.

"There's a reason." I explained how I was waiting until his guilt got deep enough that he had to turn for help. Max would not help him. Max would just turn him loose on the problem and let him figure it out for himself. Barrows would have to come to me, and I would get a trade off. Once I had the power, then to hell with Barrows.

"Okay." She sat silent like a tomb. I drifted back into the searching, trance state that comes so easily now. Barrows warned me not to rest in it. He was afraid that if I did not take care of my body, the state would cause me to self-destruct.

Mike was crashed in a dump in San Francisco. There was a bunch of hangnail-looking freaks in the same room. The only good part was that there were no bottles or drugs. Mike had found his resistance. A laugh. A bunch of punk anarchists who would pull one job, get away with it because of the surprise, pull a second job and get caught. I told that fool not to go except alone.

The rubber stamp murderer who pushed the button on us was a dildo named Chester, a fat-faced little guy in Louisiana who stood at the head of a list of fuel corporations that would make any Rotarian cream through his polyester sport pants right into his naugahyde lounger. Chester was English, by way of the Middle East, then by way of them good old Australian coalfields. He collected Renoirs, and everything about him looked like the reason that God invented kitty litter.

"Jake, babe." Penny's voice was toneless. It took me a little while to come back. She actually probably said it two or three times.

"Huh?"

"I can't stand much more."

"Sure you can. I'm standing it."

"You got hope. You can still do something." She sat with her arms around her knees, kind of mooshed into a tiny, upright ball. Her narrow face was nearly hollow, her small breasts shrunk until her chest was like a boy's. It was almost as if she were a live spirit that was capable of living inside a wire.

"What would make you feel good?" I honestly tried to feel something. Some compassion. Some sympathy. It was dangerous to let myself feel, but it was satisfying to know that even when I tried, nothing happened.

I actually grinned. All my life I wanted to see things perfect. If not for me, at least for others. I searched for perfection and found it. Perfect hatred.

"I don't know what would make me feel good."

"You can have Barrows when I'm done with him."

"I still don't know." Penny was not as emotionless as I thought. Her voice was full of tears. It was interesting. Of course, Penny is not theoretical.

"You just want to hit, right?"

"Not just. I want it to mean something."

"Then hang up. None of it means anything." I thought of Noah and the Flood, except now everyone was a criminal and there was no Noah.

She didn't believe me. That meant in spite of what she was saying she still had hope.

So what was I going to tell her? Life goes on. Accept and adjust, sweetie. Smooch the humandamned human race and pretend that love will return. Let her take her t. s. ticket to a preacher.

"I'm not going to do much," I told her. "The spectacular clowns only make up about five percent of the population."

It would take some time, but I could get whole bunches of them all at once in big population centers. When I got hold of Barrows's power, then a lot of people would disappear like smoke. No trace. Just empty spaces. Then we'd see just how much fun it was to be top cat. Anyone wearing a business suit would not be discriminated against . . . one of my fantasies, vanish all business suits . . . then uniforms. Disappear their cesspool of flags, a plague of cleanliness to sweep the planet.

"I'm not like you. I'm glad I came, though." She stood and looked down on me and seemed as passionless as before, but somehow her body seemed more alive. She actually seemed a little bit relaxed. Maybe I had turned her against me. Well, hoo hah. It might make her boobs grow back. If she blew my plan to Barrows, then I deserved it. The first time I trusted anyone since the attack, and look what happened.

"You going to Barrows?"

"Nope." She tried to sound tough, but now there really were tears in her voice. It sounded like the tears were not all because of Jim. I almost felt an emotion, pushed it down.

"Don't do it, babe." She kind of gathered herself, made like she was going to touch me, then turned and left. I followed her with my mind for a while. She wandered sort of aimless in the direction of her house. Another cowboy mentality. Cut and shoot, drink and yell. Don't ever, ever think. At least Mike was trying to hit back.

Odysseus was a cowboy. *The Odyssey* is no more than a tale of a cattle drive by a bunch of crazy Greek cowboys.

So add one more odyssey to the world. Penny was wandering, looking for the home that would never be, and strictly speaking, never had been. Even I had once called this dump where I sat home. Home. There is none. None. None. None. None none none none none noned nonednoen nonnone non non no None ever at no none at all at all Never . . . Never . . .

But there are police, their billies swinging alongside their mace pipes, walking toward you looking glad . . . yes.

Chapter 22

Now it is fully my tale, or rather, it is the tale of many, but I have accepted the task of completing it. Max Klein, this man who is me, placing papers in chronological order and writing bridging material between them.

Two writings shortly after the attack should be included here. The first is a random notation by Dolores Cosa.

"Nothing is real. I sit writing and that is not real because it is changing, so it is only happening. Things we call real about people are by far the least real because the change is so quick. Material things are changing. The principle of entropy is no joke. Someday is not real. It will only be real when it happens. All is shadow. Physics are no more concrete than metaphysics."

The second is a fragment by Julia Martin:

"Alone, alone I am all alone. I am like Barrows, I am like Ophelia washing down a wild and incoherent and angry river that bears me up only enough to breathe, and I do not have the strength to put my face under the water. I am so afraid. Where are you, Jake, and I remember where you are and if there weren't so many spirits all around and chasing me, I would come to you and you would hold my head with both your hands and that would make me not all by myself and my head hurts.

"It was the spirits of the wind that came after us and then all over the place the fires burned and there were dead people and they looked at me and laughed because I was so afraid and alone.

"And so I ran, of course, and did not even look to see where Jim was because he was out of the truck and just picked right up and flew through the air like a wizard and vanished and the truck rolled over and I got out and ran and hid in the woods where there is a place I know, which is all mine and no one not even you ever got to know about it because I could always come here when things got scary or bad. I think it was a trapper's cabin once, but there is lots of storage space for things, like it could be another home and so maybe it was a homestead except no well and no outbuildings but a good root cellar beneath the floor and no one at all can get in because even the spirits do not know about it. So when it is light outside mostly I can come out, and when it is dark or the sky is too gray I stay in and feel like I am Ophelia in the river. I am hungry too, but not so much. There are plants this time of year and there are berries too and I live like a bear but bears live don't they?"

To resume. When Butterfield's attack with the saucers ended, dark columns of smoke rose in the clear sky and turned blacker, then faded to gray as Barrows extinguished the fires. The sun spread across the wreckage that was alive with screams, but the wreckage was also death-filled with the stench of burnt flesh. The majority of the dead were downtown, but there were dead everywhere.

In the center of town brick buildings of three stories exploded like grenades. People in the streets were cut apart by flying fragments of splintered brick as effective as steel shrapnel. Had the people been in the buildings, even more would have died. As it is: 983 dead in the initial attack, over 1,200 injured, of whom nearly 300 sustained violent, dangerous injury. To date, 43 of these have died. Total deaths from the first and second attacks: 1,063. Other deaths are recorded separately.

Fire mains knocked out, water pressure gone, so that the blood dried in the streets and turned black on the saturated clothing of corpses; electricity shorting, wires falling to hit an unlucky few who danced beneath them like thrashing puppets. All over town the streets were choked by rubble, overturned vehicles and the panting bodies of the injured. The dying hid in comers. They were searched out the next day by parties combing the town as if in one gigantic Easter egg hunt.

=

I am not going to dwell on this. My days of dwelling with words are past. The language no longer has the lovely texture it once had.

The town owned two dump trucks. There are three backhoes. The best I could do for Penny was to dig a grave and get Jim in it fast. It is no consolation to me, but it may be to Penny. At least she knows that Jim's body is not a part of that hideous, hastily covered tangle.

So we tried to impart dignity to a corpse. While we spent time doing that, other people we might have helped were dying. I have reconciled my understanding to this. I say we. I mean me. Penny was no help, and I see no reason to record her actions in the center of grief.

Barrows was monitoring for another attack. Jake ran around like a madman searching for Julie. Dolores was up the coast collecting marine specimens. As she returned she was delayed by people fleeing along the roads, her truck taken, but she was not physically harmed. It is just as well that she literally had to sneak back into town, for by then Mobilier was killing anyone who moved on the roads.

We did not know how soon the attack might resume. Any moment some new weapon might be thrown against the town. It was less than an hour before we received the follow-up attack, but there was no effective attack for three weeks.

The attack was by long-wave sound that trembled the earth and would have spilled the mountains on top of us if Barrows had not traced and destroyed the transmitters. The object was to make the town the center of the conflicting meeting of sound waves. The waves worked in the substrata. They dislodged the structure of rock. The tool being used would not simply have destroyed the town. It would have dropped the entire peninsula, mountains and all, into the sea. The technology for such a doomsday machine has been in existence since the 1960s.

Structures in the town were approximately fifty-five-percent destroyed. Small one-story structures came through intact except for roofs and windows. There is not a two-story house in the town proper that survived major damage. A few were protected by dense forest and the contour of the land.

Barrows worked in less than subtle ways. The population was so shocked that even now no comment is made. Barrows cleared rubble in the streets and houses, mostly at night, so that when the stricken population began to move in the morning light, it discovered miraculously clean streets. Plaster, splinters, trash and glass were gone from the remains of still usable houses. I think it seemed no more wonderful to the survivors than any of the other events. Barrows did not dispose of the bodies. That had the practical effect of giving the population something to do. Because of the directness and shock of the attack, and because of the aftermath, the population was slow to grasp its continuing disastrous position.

There were four major reactions:

Part of the population fled. A large number fled inwardly. They got drunk and stayed drunk until the alcohol ran out. That took three days. Then they fled again, I expect not only from fear, but to a new supply of liquor. These temporarily survived, for by then Barrows had knocked out more of Mobilier's attack equipment. The first wave of refugees died on the roads. When Barrows stopped that killing, Mobilier was reduced to assassination.

Militarily, it makes sense. Mobilier has to assume that any one of those fleeing people might know at least something about Barrows's power and how to use it. In all, nearly a thousand people fled and by now most are dead. Barrows can protect dozens, even hundreds, but he cannot protect a thousand as they disperse and get lost in the general population. To flee was tantamount to suicide, but of course the refugees could not know that.

A second reaction was to rebuild. One of the most bold and pathetic and insane sights I have ever seen was a woman named McKenzie, aged, white-haired, apparently feeble, standing in sunshine among the screams of the dying while she swept rubble from her front walk. The broom moved yellowly back and forth and threw dust with the sure strokes of a lifetime's practice. In twenty-four hours the McKenzie house was not only habitable but enough repaired to afford comfort. There was no glass in the windows, but, because Mrs. McKenzie was among the first to loot, her windows were cased in plastic.

A third reaction was action itself. There were strangely few murders. No more than three or four people were actually killed by others. In the retreat, a few people fled into suicide but, again, the number was small. There were so many dead, and they continued to be discovered for two days, that inquiries into cause of death were foolish.

Most action was direct. It involved aiding the injured, or looting. Rape was minimal at first. The values of a small town served as a conceptual check. Most men capable of the act did not think of it at the time. While rape is almost universally a political act perpetrated by men who feel powerless, one might guess that in this situation it would also be a survival reaction. This suggests that the value system of a small town is even more controlling than has been believed.

Emergency medical aid killed several, mostly from overdose of morphine. This would have been worse except that several experienced drug users took the responsibility for prescribing amounts. Most first aid was done rather well. Medical supplies ran out on the second day. Several cases of gangrene set in at about that time, and all but one person with gangrene died. A man with gangrene in his foot had his lower leg severed by a friend who used a double bitt ax, then cauterized with boiling tar, and wrapped the wound in a whiskey-soaked rag. Both were terribly drunk at the time, but at this writing the amputee is still alive. One local doctor was killed in the attack and the other two fled. Medical services depended largely on one RN, two practicals and volunteers.

The fourth reaction was to wander. In some cases shock actually saved lives because it prevented action.

There is a normal progress in these affairs. If Jake had not been so single-mindedly occupied in trying to find Julie during those first two weeks, more people might have survived. By then Barrows trusted Jake's experience, and he might have listened to Jake. Barrows did not listen to me, although as a social theorist I could predict exactly what was going to happen.

Barrows, for example, did not anticipate the wave of assaults on the third day. When people understood that the town was sealed, that no supplies were arriving, they turned on one another. Looters had accounted for most of the food supplies in the wrecked stores. For a terrible thirty hours all movable property became a target. Individual natures of the looters were revealed. Some people were assaulted in their homes, as looters removed televisions, jewelry and trifles while leaving food supplies intact. Judgmental looters were after basic food supplies. One woman was shot and seriously wounded while trying to steal twenty pounds of flour from her neighbor. Barrows's antipathy to violence was still strong and his imagination weak. The looting resulted in seven deaths, of whom two were under age twelve.

When the rapes began, Barrows finally acted. He devised a technique to cause space to appear in front of the rapist's face. The vacuum left the rapist breathless. This did not alter the fear of the victim or her emotional damage, or, for that matter, the fear and trauma of the attacker. Of these, one died of a heart attack. The local population fell upon itself. Looters from beyond the community did not survive. The town was sealed. Mobilier destroyed the few outside looters before they reached the town.

It was then that I realized what was wrong with Barrows. How could one be so obtuse? Without knowing it, Barrows was a creature of incredible ego and pride. No wonder he was so self-conscious and almost pitiably scrupulous in following his strict moral code. The code was all he had left.

Reviewing these pages, I see that much has been said to be due to mysticism. Nothing has been said about its reality or variety. Since misunderstanding of mysticism is the main reason why all but 693 people in this community are now destroyed, it should be explained.

As to its reality: most people, I believe, know on some level that mysticism exists. It has for all of human history, and mystics occur in every society. In some societies they are revered, but in most they are ridiculed. It is strange how civilized people will accept the fact that Indian shamans and medicine men actually have predicted events or controlled the weather—and then—those same people will deny that mystical knowledge can exist in their own civilized state.

Yet, the mystic has existed all through history, and sometimes has access to awesome power. As this is written there are a few mystics on this planet, including myself, who own power so great that Barrows's ill-used power is paltry in comparison. The fact that mystics limit the use of their power demonstrates the true extent of their power. Perhaps that statement, which seems unclear, will become clearer as the tale unfolds.

As to the variety: most mystics in our western culture are Christian, as is Barrows. We Jews have produced mystics, and there are many mystics in the Eastern world.

I thought of all this and decided that I must talk to Barrows. By this time life in the town had settled into an urgent but less desperate pattern and the population was clearly split. On one side were those who had not engaged in looting, murder or rape. On the other side was a minority who had. Neighbors recalled to neighbors the events they had witnessed. Since there was no government, containment of those regarded as criminal was impossible. The town grouped into small sects that were based on mutual trust. Most people traveled about town in small, protective groups, if they traveled at all.

The townspeople, unable to defend against Mobilier, tried to bring sense and reason into their lives by learning how to defend against each other.

And this had all happened because Barrows, a one-time mystic, had run into a trap. The trap was built-in. Barrows and his peculiar theology had been doomed from the beginning.

The Christian mystic, John Barrows, had to account for the peculiar notion of original sin. That meant that he could never really become one with the forces of the universe that he experienced. While an Eastern mystic could feel that he joined that force as a drop of water slipping into an ocean, John Barrows had to feel that he was separate. He coexisted, like sunlight shining through air.

For a long time I could not understand why Barrows was a prude. You cannot be a mystic and a prude. Then I understood. Barrows was raised in an evangelical time, during the decline of the Victorian period. He is a flawed creature. To that extent, his belief in original sin is nearly accurate. His mystical experiences have been great. There is no question about that.

Here was the crux of his problem, and the hideous crux of ours:

The Christian mystic feels that he must be reduced to his true nature in order to get to that state of helplessness that brings him to universal power. He has to arrive at a condition of complete abasement.

So he works for tens of thousands of hours and succeeds. The experience opens his goodness to him.

In experiencing his goodness, there is deterioration of his abasement. His humility becomes a variety of pride. That pride stands between him and the abasement that he once more seeks to achieve. The Western mystic has certainly woven a most amazing net in which to entangle himself. Barrows was in a trap. He had to consider himself so good that he had to work at being abased. When he considered himself in that state, he engaged in a variety of pride. Because of pride he had to believe that what he did made a difference in human affairs, and perhaps in the universe.

Eastern mystics and Jewish mystics do not have this trouble, of course.

The answer to Barrows's problems, and to the problems of this dying town, was for Barrows to abandon himself and thus abandon pride. That is a terribly hard answer for a man who had only learned what he knew through the abasement of himself.

I went to speak to Barrows about all this.

At the time it was earlier in the tragic game than Jake or Barrows knew. A thousand people were dead. Another thousand had fled. That still left about three thousand in the town. After the wave of rapes the population became defensive and quiet. Anarchy existed, but the memory of order existed as well. There was considerable patching of buildings with material gleaned from abandoned structures. Property was still somewhat respected. A few people commandeered the houses of older, weaker people. There were two revenge killings because of killings during the looting.

The town is sprinkled with gardens, and already this early in the season the peas, spinach and lettuce were up. It appeared that no one would starve.

It is a long walk from Dolores's house to Barrows's place. I left while Dolores slept, for I wanted to return by noon. Dolores's house is not large, but it stood near the blast and was badly shaken. We spent half of each day at our work, the other half on repair.

Dawn was approaching. Thin clouds broken with strips of sky were muddy, a brown and dingy color. Night mist lingered in the streets. Broken houses lined the streets, and here and there was the sour scent of ashes. In the first light the town seemed spectral and abandoned.

It was safe to walk in the town. Because of the revenge killings, Barrows had cleared the town of small arms. That seemed unwise. When winter came it would be necessary to hunt. At present most protein came from dry stores and from fish handlined from the strait. Several men were repairing boats and rigging for sail.

I passed Jake's house. The trees on the side away from the blast had set a lot of fruit. As that fruit matured it would be needed. Inside that wrecked house my friend was sitting and coping with nearly ungovernable pain.

It was a pleasant walk in the early morning. Some big change was about to take place in my life. I had known that it was going to happen for a long time. In fact, I had known it since that night in Montana when I waited for Jake's call. It is not difficult to sense these changes. The road of the mystic does not offer surprises. It offers new shapes. At any rate, I walked slowly and enjoyed the morning. Today or tomorrow or soon, I would change. At the time I simply celebrated the eye and heart of the man who was me.

On the outskirts of town the mist thinned and pastures lay across the rolling terrain broken by patches of forest. By August the road would be enclosed with a tangle of wild rose and blackberry, a narrow path which would point to the forest and the strait.

The smell of putrification was light with the first rotting taste on the tongue, a taste more than a scent. There was no wind. A body, animal or human, was somewhere in the area. Surely it must be an animal. If Julie were not missing, I would not have searched.

The smell remained light as I pressed through a tangle of brush into the equally brushy field. I recalled having told Barrows that he might be obligated to kill Jake.

The stench in the brush seemed held in pockets of mist. I traced a narrowing circle and did not understand why the smell did not get worse. Then I leaned down to free a snagged pant leg. The smell hit me like a physical blow. The smell had been held down by the mist. It was like diving into an ocean of smell, like swallowing tarnished copper, like being immersed in liquid putridity. I stood and for a moment was held by a strange sense of terror. Then I took several steps forward and saw him.

The body lay spread-eagled, face down in the mist. The skull was gray, stripped by crows. The hands were the same. I could see his boots. One had a large, heavy sole and heel while the other was conventional. This could only be the man, Gimp Sam, who had sometimes worked with Jake's crew. I backed away, looked for the wreckage of his truck and found none.

Thus his neighbors had left him.

Sam had clearly been killed for his truck, in which his murderer fled. I trudged back to the road, through the thick brush and mist.

When a human dies I mourn not only the person but the lost possibilities. Behind me, face down in the wet, misted field, a man lay dead. By all accounts Gimp Sam did not amount to much in everyday terms. He drank when he could afford it. He was a mooch. When he drank too much he was capable of breaking furniture or starting fights which he had no hope of winning. Yet, my mourning was real. With so much death around, though, it seemed foolish to become emotional. When I arrived at Barrows's house it became clear that I would not return to Dolores by noon. Barrows sat in stupor. At first I assumed he was heavily fatigued. Then I saw that the problem was elsewhere. Barrows sat slumped, his beard pressed against his chest. His hair was now completely white and not simply cut with streaks of gray. The hair was thin on top, and the pink skull seemed shocking when seen through the light web of hair. His face, what could be seen, sagged in folds. His neck, thin, seemed too weak to hold his head upright.

I took a chair and waited. Barrows was deep in mystical state. I knew that he would soon communicate with me, and that the whole affair would take considerable time. No matter his deserts, the man must be offered my kindness, and unfortunately, my pity as well. Barrows was a failure, but he was a magnificent failure. There was nothing common about him, and he could not be judged in common terms.

Because it was going to take some time, I emptied my own mind, became receptive and felt serene. No doubt we were doomed, but the serenity made that fact unimportant.

So, for the moment, I simply sat beside Barrows and waited.

Chapter 23

I DO NOT KNOW HOW LONG BARROWS AND I SAT TOGETHER BEFORE there was communication. There are many forms of meditation, and through long practice several were available to us.

On this day I allowed my mind to become a limitless field.

In this state the entire mental being may be suddenly rocked. At other times truth is revealed like a thin, pure song heard from far away. During most times all that is revealed is that there is to be more waiting. Silence is an ally. Time is an ally.

The first flicker of communication came and went. It disappeared like a spark of light diving into the depths of a well. It was engulfed like a meteor instantly swallowed by the night sky.

Then, as suddenly as the appearance and vanishment, Barrows and I were talking, although we spoke beyond any ordinarily describable framework.

Yet, I mistrust writers who say that a thing is indescribable; thus, I'll describe it.

Think of a completely dark and empty theater which holds the possibility of a play. You are in that theater, waiting.

Now the theater does not actually have a floor. It has no stage or walls or roof, yet it is not simply a void. The stage is represented by planes of possibility, like geometry. There are just as many planes of changing dimensions. Time exists, but not linear time.

In such a theater it is possible to hear a chuckle, a belch, and the slap of a hand against a face. You discover in that part of the play that Falstaff has just been slapped for pinching the leg of a bar girl in twentieth-century New Orleans. All of history and all of the present are mixed together. The fictional Falstaff and the very real bar girl both exist beyond ordinary time.

In this theater everyone is both actor and audience. From Falstaff the play might move to a lone World War I plane that is shot up and limping home. Or, it may move to an English farmer discovering an ancient Roman gorget while plowing his field. He is standing, holding the gorget and wondering what it is.

One knows that Falstaff, the bar girl, the pilot of the limping plane, the farmer (and the ancient Roman who is also present on one plane of possibility) all understand the meaning of each event, and of all events in combination.

This is the level on which Barrows and I conversed. So it is apt to say that the lights went up and the play began.

Barrows was mourning before the casket of his wife. He was also watching himself mourn as he talked to Jake, and he was watching himself talk to Jake while he stood alone in a forest of virgin timber and prayed. His wife was beside him during each occurrence. He was unable to take her hand. Barrows, it seemed, could not understand that the death of dreams does not mean that one should feel guilty for having dreams.

Julie appeared, crouching and hidden, her face a mask of dirt that was streaked with tears. Her clothing was tattered, filthy, and her eyes were glazed as they dwelt inwardly on some hideous madness. Her mind seemed to be producing demons. She was thin, her fingers like fragile sticks. Surrounding her was a cacophony of voices that was both ancient and contemporary, a mixture of shrieks and accusations and moans, a spectrum of both living and dead languages. Mike appeared, bruised, dazed, his right leg swollen and clearly broken and untreated.

Then crowds appeared. Former townspeople, those who had fled, hurried here and there. A familiar face was seen in an otherwise unnamed crowd. The man was bumped by another man. A knife flashed. The townsman fell gasping with a stab wound. A presence like smoke glowered, took animal shape, clawed at Julie's face and then vanished.

Barrows's ego was all encompassing. These scenes were attributable only to him. At least he thought that was true. Barrows's warped ego caused his conscience to accept responsibility for every trouble. Because of that he lived in a world of screams.

His wife touched his arm, a gesture of love and admonition. She was a tall and splendid woman, lithe and with graying hair braided and pulled from her face to display the wide form of her face. Her mouth was wide in the manner of compassion and generosity.

A thin line of fire wound from a concentrated center of darkness. It unreeled like linear time, and the line began to knit and turn and build and spark, producing a rippling fabric within a fabric surrounded by a fabric: the whole a smell and mixture of World War I mustard gas, of decay, combined with shadows of hairless heads gasping as they died in extermination camps of a later war.

Barrows had not dared touch these historic catastrophes with his power, knowing that he would make them worse. Yet they had become part of his guilt.

No defender of any fortification has ever been more surrounded. A bell tolled through otherwise perfect silence, while at the same time Jim shrieked and fell and Penny tore open her shirt to hold him against her. An old policeman wept, and the sobs joined the boom of the bell, throbbing, pulsing, as birds fought over carrion and Jake sat, apparently dispassionate.

The statements from Barrows's conscience had turned to questions. He asked help from me.

My answer was silence.

Silence took the shape of a green field. It stretched far but moved close. It yearned toward Barrows and Barrows toward it. His wife touched him gently. She was granting permission, encouraging, endorsing silence.

It was all right for him to leave. Did he not see that he had overstayed his time and usefulness?

A mist appeared above the field, independent of the green, and from the mist a black-suited proctor rose, stem, its eyes like talons of scorn. Barrows shuddered.

The proctor had risen neither from Barrows's question or my answer.

It was not simply the shape of Barrows's conscience, but also the history of the shape of that conscience.

A flying saucer lay shattered, colored inside with blood. Blood ran like the layering streaks of sunset, threatened the green silence and moved above the silence like a bizarre wash of watercolor.

Barrows's thoughts and emotions ran back and forth like frightened children, although Barrows was curiously unafraid. His wife moved away from him, granting the dignity of his own space and decisions. Her face was tranquil.

The proctor was nearly a man, or formed like a man, and its emotions were inhuman rather than alien. If a small boy pinned living flies to a collecting board, then this might describe the proctor's emotions. With the difference that the proctor had no self-involvement with sadistic joy. The contempt of the proctor, while being one of the strongest emotions I have ever felt or observed, was as important to the proctor as the knowledge would be to a usual man that it was necessary to clean the dirt from beneath one fingernail.

Barrows trembled and visibly shrank in the face of the contempt. His mind fluttered, darted, projected clouds and legions and webs of alternatives.

What bound him here? Why could he not leave?

Few Victorians, early or late, would have denied the overwhelming importance of duty. Duty gave strength, and it was the source of honor. At the same time duty limited alternatives. Barrows's myriad alternatives dealt with only one concept of duty. He would not leave his friends defenseless for as long as he held power.

The proctor stood firm, its torso bent slightly forward above rigidly straight legs, the position of the eighteenth-century attitude of ministry or public address. This proctor, this conscience of Barrows's, was a creature of many centuries.

Intricate machines throbbed sound through all ranges, hums, moans: shrill electronic pulses sparking blue, green or dull-toned as sound became color. Weapons both familiar and strange appeared, and from Barrows's past sounded the curiously flat report of muzzle-loading cannon, the presence of a long sweep of river, of deep forest, of a young man walking, stumbling from a battlefield with smoke staining the air and men falling behind him.

The proctor may well have met its match. Barrows was apologetic, shamed, filled with pain and the anguish of guilt, but Barrows remained unafraid. That was his victory. His wife smiled with pride. I did the same.

The green spread like a springtime field washed with rain. Barrows ached to become one with its oblivion, but no part of his longing dealt with fear. Barrows was in a physical pain of longing. He wanted to depart the scene, to become one with history.

Alternatives flew and sparked, suggestions made to me. Barrows offered his power, immediate and intact and without reservation. Such was the measure of this good man's trust.

There could be no kind answer. Barrows's power was impressive but narrowly limited. I needed his power no more than he. Barrows sensed this as I gave no answer, then he turned partly away in shame, partly in question. I still did not reply. He questioned. Insistent.

I answered. A blade of grass grew yellow, then green in the middle of the air. It seeded, faded, grayed, died and went to dust. The proctor disappeared.

Yet, Barrows's poorly understood ability to manipulate matters was not to be undervalued. While I denied accepting his power, I still valued it as a tribute to the curiosity and sincerity and fundamental decency of the man. In the balance of what constitutes power in the universe, the power of Barrows was negligible. Transubstantiation is greater. Creation is greater.

Even with my refusal to accept his power, Barrows remained unafraid. He was ready to depart. It was momentarily possible that he could leave. Then the guilt returned. The ego of the man verged on the insane.

He wanted a promise. Were I to protect his friends, he could go. With what he knew, with his mystic and mental ability, to ask for such a promise was an indication of his madness. There was no protection he could offer that his friends needed. There was none that I would offer. The town was doomed, had been doomed since the first timber was raised a century before: doomed to one or another conclusion as all things have conclusions. Doomed to history, as was Mobilier, as were the mountains themselves. Surely Barrows, conversing as we conversed, understood something of history. Here, at least, could be a kind of answer.

His friends appeared, a multitude, of which Jake, Julie, Jim, Penny, Mike and Dolores moved as certainly as the rest. They did not appear as illusion or spirit. They were not sad.

He understood. They did not need him. The man's intellect was good, it was his strictness and sense of personal responsibility that inhibited him.

It was all right to depart. His wife moved toward him. The field of grass touched him, rose slowly about him. His wife now faded rapidly. Barrows stood, accepting the silence, his mind rested, grateful, momentarily at peace. The field enclosed him lightly, the green not more vivid but more alive.

Then startled, suddenly volitional, he moved from repose to tension. His eyes were awake, bright, and then they were clean and free of guilt.

It was startling. Shocking. It was surely a catastrophe that would destroy another good man. Oh, clearly. The last stroke of ego had been greater than Barrows. Now his eyes dimmed to repose, the field became dense, thick, and Barrows faded into it as a sinking object disappears in a deep fall into the sea.

And from the dense field a new form appeared, rising toward light.

Jake stood suddenly erect. His eyes were wide and exuberant. His shoulders were high, his hands clenched, and he trembled with the sudden knowledge that Barrows's power had been passed to him.

And so it was to continue.

I stood alone and thought. There are branching paths in the life of the trained mind which require decisions and which only promise change. I was on the threshold of that change in Max which for so long had been coming. In the great depth of the meditative state, in the empty theater, it seemed that there were two paths.

One path led back to the temporal world, a world in which Jake had power and Julie would soon be found.

The greatest power in the universe is to deny the use of power.

The other path led deeper into the planes of the possible. One would be required to be a swimmer, like a diver with expanded lungs fighting downward, or like the passage of sperm toward the ovum. One might disappear into darkness, or emerge squalling.

Max dove into darkness, into possibility. Max, who is Me, as I am him, felt the possibility of distant illumination. Traveling into the vast depths of consciousness, his mind accepting that he was on the most delicate and fragile edge of control, Max gently drifted to the bottom of that sea of darkness. He lay there and was washed in the sea, the planes of possibility shifting like networks of warmth and illumination. There was a delicate unknitting of his being, a new knitting of the self-being that is us. Together.

And then we began the rise toward consciousness. The temporal world where Max remains, while I, who am Max in transfiguration, am the source of his power which is constant and limitless.

He ascended to find that he still sat by Barrows in the tidy, well--cared-for room into which the brilliant rays of a setting sun were for a few minutes free as the sun passed under cloud cover before dropping below the horizon. Max turned to Barrows.

Barrows had suffered greatly. With his will gone, his body now existed as little more than a husk. Max felt the cooling corpse and estimated the passage of time in his long trip back from the meditative state. He felt the chill that lay in the cooling body, then returned to his chair and sat beside Barrows for the time it took to complete the sunset.

Shadows seemed to gather benevolently about Barrows's feet. Then the shadows moved upward, finally engulfing him like a shroud. Barrows was still seated. The passage had been without violence. Max watched the shadows hide the pink scalp, the indented creases of the dead face, and saw that the shadows gave substance to the thin hair.

Then came a further change in the planes of the possible. Max, who now knew that he could refuse the use of all power, was finally able to take action.

Max told himself that there need be no sorrow for Barrows. The potential of Barrows was filled, exhausted, fully used, and Max argued about this with himself as he searched the house for a hammer and nails. He thought of it as he nailed down the window casements and as he boarded up the door against the incursion of animals.

The day's sun was by then a memory. The dark forest pressed close. Max finished his work, cast the hammer clattering onto the porch and turned onto the path through the forest. He left Barrows sitting before the window that looked onto the strait, as Barrows had doubtless sat so many times over the long and tedious years. And, as he walked along the dark path that was like a narrow river running through jungle, Max wept.

Chapter 24

As he once strove to set aside ego, Max now began to balance the newly discovered world in which he worked, ate, slept, transcribed the preceding pages and what follows; and with Dolores, investigated the smooth and time-worn words of love. He was self and self. In the days that followed he was troubled with the knowledge that Jake was hurrying toward some hideous conclusion. Yet, when he sat beside Jake he found that Jake's mind refused to be joined. In the completeness of power, Max found that his power at first weighed heavily. Max did not yet fully realize who he was.

Jake, shifting from helplessness with the passing of Barrows's power, became a monster.

Jake's last entry follows :

Chester the button pusher died hard. I had to admire the little twitch. His fear was so great that he just hung on and on, long after he should have been dead. I bled him pretty good, busting up his small veins. I had that little cocksucker wiping blood every other minute, and maybe I bled him too fast.

But he was hurt and he was scared. I liked it best when the pain was so bad he got glassy-eyed. I got him that way four times before he died. For a while his doctor shot him with morphine and I took the morphine away just as it was beginning to take hold.

That was a good doctor, though. I admired the rich little hog. He had good hands, and he was right in the middle of unexplainable stuff, but he kept doing everything he knew. I halfway regret making his heart disappear.

A few hours before old Chester died, I made everybody go away. I caused anyone who came close to him to start bleeding themselves. I made a new kind of leper out of Chester.

There was nothing else new about the little prick. His tasteless, bland and self-justifying rot is a form of leprosy so common that nothing new has been said about it since Pontius Pilate. After old Chester got his little self all dead, I lasered the body up the middle so that he fell in two halves like a beef. There wasn't much blood left, but there were a lot of guts and fat that peeled back from the rib cage. His brains looked like a dog's breakfast being eaten for the second time.

It makes good memories. He sweated a lot. All of his terrible stuff was happening to him right in his safe, vulgar surroundings, where the rugs were deep and the vases were crystal and the walls were hung with Renoirs. He would sit in the middle of all that stuff that he had accumulated, and sweat. He would just get dripping with it. Every once in a while his eyes would go crazy. I did not want him crazy and I did a masterpiece job because I kept him just in touch with sanity. The fucker prayed a lot. I used to soothe him while he was praying, and give him a good burn when he said amen. Never in his lousy, misconceived life had he ever done a single decent thing. How could he? He was a businessman.

Which means he was no better or worse than the people he did business with. He just happened to be the Judas goat.

But I paid them all. Before dumb Barrows passed the power, and before I overcame the controls that were implanted in the power, I charted Chester's whole organization. I knew every one of them, and I got every single one.

A few lucky ones disappeared like smoke. The punks, the kids, the least offensive. Also, a couple who were extra brave. I took that into account.

With those smoked ones I tried to get psychological mileage. I would wait until they were talking to one of their kind, and then I would take them from inside their clothes. It was funny. Two guys gassing at each other, and suddenly one guy would see space and a business suit crumpling to the floor. I thrived on it. Terrorism like those terrorists never dreamed of.

It was their game. Theirs. They did not like to see it being played by an expert.

You trained me, nose picks. This was your idea.

It was an orgy. I loved it. Some was sexual. One of the last things that happened to old Chester is his balls got sliced.

I was enough of a prude to just smoke the women.

With the bodyguards and hired killers it was more fun. I did a lot of routine arm or leg chopping to watch them make frantic, chicken-like movements to get a belt or tourniquet on—but one was different and especially nice. He was leaning against a wall on the twentieth floor of a building, and I just took a big chunk of the wall. He screamed all the way down.

Murder. For sale or rent. I wondered if he still believed in it by the time he got to the third floor.

Violence. There was not a thing I did that could match what those bastards teach their children.

And that goes for everybody. I do not love the poor. I do truly hate the rich.

Any orgy has to end. By the time this one slowed down, I was pretty depleted and could think objectively about my hatred. I had to think about what I was going to do next. No part of me was dumb enough to think that I could help poor suffering humankind.

It felt good to knock off a bunch of international oilmen, but it did not mean much. You could kill every oilman in the world and all you would have done was tidy up an inordinately large pile of nonfunctional shit. If you boiled them down for fertilizer, the stuff would sterilize the earth.

Then there were a bunch of politicians. They were kind of like dessert. There is nothing nicer than to get yourself a politician and take his tongue out so that he is all red and hollow-mouthed and finally almost quiet.

I'm insane. The reason I am insane is not because I do anything unusual. The difference is that I am not making a profit.

Years ago, two million people in Biafra starved because some oil companies were dickering between some political parties for offshore drilling rights. The political parties were in a scrap for power. The oil companies fed the situation while blaming the politicians. The politicians blamed the oil companies. Two million people. Dead.

So I am insane because I only commit murder but do not have a profit motive. I only kill Decent Folk, instead of a bunch of homeless niggers who have no money.

Because this is a world in which puke is salable. No wonder Max is a mystic, and asshole Barrows was a mystic. They both lived through a time when plastic was invented.

They lived in a world that derided art until the painter was safely dead. A world that denied philosophy, theology, pure scientific research, history. A world that took human studies like psychology and sociology and turned them into a-human statistical constructs.

A world that feared youth, ideas, beauty, music. A world that taught mediocrity, that celebrated mediocrity. A world where the writers could not write, the critics were uneducated, and the humorists sold straight slapstick. Where presidents were pardoned to wander rich and fat and free while burned children wandered starving and homeless.

A world that had it coming, the same way that Jim and Mike and Barrows and I had it coming when we made those trees fall wrong. Numb-nuts Barrows never did figure that one out. He did not understand that we had spent too many days on a shit show and everyone was sick of it. We pulled those trees into wrong falls because we subconsciously wanted to go home. We demonstrated the creative power of the group.

I set out to get Mobilier, its whole organization, and then this lousy compassion hit. I reamed the world of executives and did pretty good. Then I got to the army and I didn't do so good. There was still enough army left in me that I could not take those guys. I zapped Butterfield and a bunch of general officers, mostly out of a sense of obligation. When it came to the rest I couldn't do it. Most of the enlisted men were just in so they could have a steady job.

So I rampaged across the planet taking executives and knocking out military hardware, and Mobilier exploded like a busted light bulb. Now, to be honest, I do not know what to do. I try to decide whether to ease up and get my killing instinct back, or to kill myself, which would be easy and kind of funny, too. But you have to laugh in advance.

Chapter 25

It would be autumn when Julie appeared. I, Max, watched with sorrow, and Max transcribed all of what follows. His mind and perceptions followed Jake's actions as Jake flared his hatred across the world. Max knew that Julie was alive, and that Jake knew where she was. Yet, it seemed that Jake had abandoned her. As summer progressed, Jake more and more abandoned the town.

His efforts were like a monumental tribute to chaos and rust. Some were exquisitely planned, most were nearly formless. To an already suffering world he became not nemesis, but mindless, unexplainable, irrational pain.

Weaponry lay in piles of broken junk. Governments and police forces and armies, some inadequate and corrupt, were picked apart in diabolic slaughter. He overcame his reluctance against attacking armies. Gradually he overcame his reluctance to attack anything beyond the town. The town became the center of the world for Jake. While he abandoned it physically, he was attached to it as if it were a symbol. It was where sense and form had once lived. Jake judged, acted, and his hatred burned bright. With his hatred he believed that he protected the town. The hatred was a hot star in the mist of that haunted summer.

Townspeople walked wide of Jake's house, sensing the hatred and power without knowing what was happening. The town was isolated. First Mobilier, then Jake.

Old Roza McKenzie, dressed in colorful and scavenged rags as she had dressed for years, muttered curses when her business forced her within blocks of Jake's shattered house. She breathed thin and protective prayers, certain shields to protect her. Muttering in the streets so that people might overhear, but Roza did not care. Her mind, she knew, was clear and pure.

—There wan't so many people now. Something had happened to a bunch during the storm and that was good. Them who was left was snivelers and whined about they didn't get no nice stuff to eat and worried too and that showed they din't know what was what. There was lots to eat, just lots, and you din't have to pay for it no more. Times was not good like back in them girl days a-hers when her old evilman husband wan't even a husband yet but only Henry a-courtin'. And then ol' evilman went off to a war and din't get killed, neither. And then the war got over and he din't keer to come back home, neither . . . and everybody knew and talked but she stayed proud because she was entitled and raised two good boys which married white trash which is why they din't come to visit no more hardly. A course boys were dumb, sometimes, even hers, and a course they had old evilman's blood which was garbagey because he was one of them what old folks used to talk about like witches and spirits and killer animals bred outta Indians, and if it was all changed now and eats were easier to get, it still din't make anything any good—

Roza did not know who to blame, but she thought it was Jake and Roosevelt and Churchill. When she prayed she cursed all three, and those were the times when she felt she had her best prayers. Roza fought heroically against madness and death, and she had made that same fight for fifty-three of her eighty-two years.

It was a wet summer. The colors of flowers were subdued among glossy leaves, or beaten against the ground. With the heavy rains the days were sometimes chill. Wood fires smoked a layer of smudge above rooftops to mark which houses were still alive.

Jake's closest neighbors had business best performed beneath the umbrella of his care:

Les Godwin and the mayor realized on an alcoholic level that they were creatures of Jake's pleasure and worked at systematic self-destruction over that haunted summer. They did not know of Jake's power, but they knew that they feared him.

Their atonement was to distill a raw, crude liquor from potatoes.

When Les belted it sharp, it choked him and he spat and hawked and pain churned in his belly. Vomit rose in his throat. Les thought during times of alcohol-inflamed emotion that he would kill Jake, who had caused him to lose everything—a purty good wife, a good boat, a nice kid. In a few more years he would of had it all, yes, and then this sonovabitchin' college professor goddamn timber jock with his smart ideas—

And then Les would turn from it. The world was lost and lonesome.

Les would watch the mayor talking to himself, and sometimes the mayor acted like a preacher. The mayor would preach and Les would not listen, just watch the mayor's fat, drawn mouth go on and on and on like the quack, quack, quack of a duck. The mayor sipped his liquor and was turning yellow. He was losing his memory about how to distill it right, and that was going to cause him to make a bad mistake some day. Les watched the distilling part careful.

They moved dully together, isolated like the fated creatures they felt themselves to be, and on their rare appearances in the streets they repelled people by their smell of filth and decay, by the sour odor of bitter mash.

=

I, Max, watched and mourned and studied. The mind of Max and the Man who was Max sometimes felt separated. The mind continued to open to Jake. Jake refused to open his own mind. Jake was a rush of self-destruction and outward destruction, of flashing hatred that slashed across the world. Occasionally Jake was morbid, compelled by the romance of death in the way that the Victorians had substituted death for the culmination of sex in a variety of gymnastic, mental poetry.

Jake was a monster. The man he had been, the idealist, dreamer, romantic, was overlaid with violence. Jake had once been one of the great consciences of his day. His decay was spectacular and worth mourning. He was like a hurricane or airquake. He rushed at destroying institutions, but in his rush he guaranteed that the constant blows would fade his winds. He would soon depart the scene. Jake ate nothing, drank nothing, did not sleep. He remained constantly in trance, his body's processes nearly stilled. Max sought communication, but refused to force it on Jake. Max was invincible now, but he did not yet understand his complete nature. His journey to the very depths of mysticism had so transfigured Max that he had to learn to accept who He was.

At first Max was dependent in a way that had never happened before. He was especially dependent on Dolores, and he suffered for it. It made no difference to him that Dolores sustained everyone who knew her, or that in some way Penny sustained Dolores.

The final round of death came as Mobilier cast a last, desperate attack two days after Barrows passed the power to Jake. The timing was excellent.

Max had experienced the event, coming from sleep as a throat-contracting spasm of airlessness pulled on his chest, and confusedly awake, he accepted the incrushing explosion of a heart attack. Then he knew he was not having a heart attack. Dolores woke beside him, open-mouthed and breathless. In the frame of window the moon hung in the clear night like a monster star, and the room was cut with black shadow and the brilliant moon rays. Max rolled toward Dolores, not knowing whether he was trying to protect her or be protected, and felt air return with the rush of a wind that tore at the already badly broken house. There was a boom and a crushing press of air. He felt the house bow and resist exploding, the way a man shouldering a surprising load throws extra tension into his legs.

He gasped, sought Dolores's hand, and they sat in the moon-cut room and waited. Somewhere on the block a man's voice rose in a scream of pain, and the scream was a hot, dark thing flying upward in moonlight.

Dolores moved quickly. She was dressed and waiting as he still fumbled his shoelaces. She stood, a slim, dark figure silhouetted in the frame of the open doorway. He would see her so for the rest of his life, as he would see her in countless other ways of genius or passion; or of accurate movement with competent hands over lab equipment; or kneeling, as would soon be the case, over a man with a shattered leg who was trapped in debris.

As Max fumbled his shoelaces and observed his fumbling mind, he watched Dolores and felt the loneliness of their still separate beings.

They were not yet the single being that they might become. He tested the loneliness of that thought. Then he told himself that he had a lot more to learn. He grinned, thinking that whether one did well or badly, at least it was possible to deal with a heart attack.

Then he told himself that his wryness was out of place in a world of moonlit terror. He followed Dolores through the luminous night. In the end all that was necessary was to free the man from the wreckage of his house, and splint his leg while gritting teeth against his pain.

"Do you know what has happened?" Dolores was now getting used to asking him such questions.

"I do now."

"Do you know what will happen?" She was not used to asking that question. This was new. She was trying to understand the change in him.

"I know what is possible. A terrible thing has happened, but all that is possible is weighted heavily on the side that says this was the last attack. Poor Jake. Poor friend."

Jake was the source of the explosion that rocked the town and destroyed the downtown. Concussion killed Ann, Al the fisherman and hundreds of others before they were thrown into the strait along with the exploding remains of buildings. Jake was in defensive combat, and his defenses were barely adequate.

When Barrows's power was passed to Jake it came with controls that Barrows had scrupulously built in over years. Jake had the power, but he had to learn how to wield it and subdue the controls. His opening attempts were clumsy. The power would not be under precise control until after he destroyed Chester. At the time of Mobilier's attack, Jake was like a man wielding a sledgehammer when the tool he needed was a scalpel.

The attack was an attack with nerve gas. The gas killed instantly.

Sitting alone, his conscious mind exhausted from exaltation, Jake's awareness had run across the world, prying, opening dark and secret corners. He neglected to overview the town and the strait. Later, he remembered the shock of near hysteria when a flicker of his searching consciousness picked up one corner of the town and found a dead man in the street.

Jake was beneath the ocean with his mind when that happened. He was feeling something akin to savage love as he dwelt with the sight and presence of a submarine. The long shape was like a piston in the dark cylinder of a course that ran deep through the lightless ocean.

The inside of the sub was a well-lighted and nearly independent world. The vessel was five hundred and fifty feet long, a giant machine compared to the underwater craft of Jake's youth. This submarine was like a small city. Highly skilled men performed routine tasks maintaining the atomic drive, monitoring sophisticated electronics, and working precisely with computer systems and sound transmitters. Cooks and storekeepers handled logistics, joked, complained. Men moved easily through clean spaces, nearly unconscious of the liquid-sounding power of distant machinery that supplied light and heat and motion. The working interior of the sub seemed as unspectacular as the purr of a clock in a well-lighted office.

The sailors were like submariners everywhere. They were experts in controlling their imaginations. Most sailors do not allow themselves to think of depth, only of surface. These men, being without imagination, were capable of enduring great stress and reporting only minor incidents to their homes, in dull, interminable letters. There was still enough of the traditional seaman about them that a few loved their weapons and all of them spoke of the ship affectionately as "she" or "this old hooker" or "this pig iron." When Jake was harshly pulled back to Mobilier's attack, he had enough control to shatter plates in the pressure hull and feel the sub implode.

A half mile from where Jake sat, people had died instantly and in silence. The nerve gas came from beneath the strait. It was pumped through an abandoned pipeline, and the gas was a creature of the breeze. A light movement of air pressed it here and there, causing pockets of death, leaving pockets of life. Where it rolled it killed all life, insect, animal, bird and human. By the time Jake understood what was happening, the gas was rising toward the upper town. The gas was a part of the air, and Jake did not have the sophisticated control that would allow him to remove it from the air. He could do only one thing. He removed the air, projected space and caused a vacuum in the lower town. Air rushed into the vacuum and caused the explosion. Without wanting to do so, Jake had caused his own airquake.

When the shocked remnants of the population came from their houses in the early daylight, they would find the lower town missing. In an excess of fury Jake had cleared not only rubble, but even the pavement. The population yielded to a numb hysteria that held it stumbling and inept for several days.

Chapter 26

THROUGH EARLY SUMMER, AS MYSELF, MAX, TRANSCRIBED THESE notes, the rain was fairly constant. Julie was going to reappear in autumn, and Mobilier had made its last attack. The rain filled cisterns and slickened battered roofs. Then, in August, clear days overtook and passed the days of cloud and rain and wind. Steam rose from the scrub forests as the sun lay glistening across the massed, low leaves of salal. Uncut grass, tall and already pocked with high weeds, began to droop and brown. The grass knit and clustered tight against itself to preserve moisture. Weeds gathered around the ruins of buildings where ornate Victorian facades Jay in broken heaps to display carvings of charred roses. Weed seed blew through abandoned houses, rooted in corners of rooms, in sinks where food scraps and blown dirt and plaster were beginning to turn into soil. Dandelions were yellow and green, like new spirits in the rooms of abandoned houses.

Shasta daisies fought to continue their cycle, brushing against the sun while the taller stalks died back. Fence rows disappeared beneath running tangles of blackberries. The berries that August were full and sweet and profuse.

More than any other thing, it was the blackberries that restored equilibrium. The berries were more dramatic than the tides because they were annual. Like the tides they were inexorable. Even at its height of power Mobilier could not have destroyed the blackberries, short of dropping the entire Northwest into the sea. The tangling, weeding bushes seemed to the townspeople like a reaffirming principle. The heavy, drooping bushes brought the survivors to their senses.

The strait might hold enemies. The mountains were too huge to feel companionable. The crowding forest of scrub fir, cedar and alder was as familiar as the tides; but the berries were a principle that was fabulous.

The survivors turned away from thoughts of why so many were dead and thought of why so many were miraculously alive. Les and the mayor retreated further, hid blinking from the sun. Roza McKenzie muttered, warmed her bones, squashed berries into her thin mouth with purpled hands.

Grace McCloud, whom Jake had called the town's bulldog, appeared in the street like a centurion. Her white hair was piled high and washed with the faintest hint of bluing. She walked stately in the sun. She was impeccably dressed and set a standard of appearance for the motley groups of people who picked berries and chattered and sometimes trembled with a chill in the warm light. Grace McCloud had not invented war, but she had lived through five of them and two depressions. She would not demean herself by giving in to hardship. As soap became scarce she hoarded fiercely and saved every rare drop of animal fat. Grace harked back to her grandmother and remembered how to make soap, but no one would ever see her work. The bulldog jaw, the stiffly pressed formal blouses delicately worked on with a modern, useless electric iron heated over a wood stove, the woolen suits, she looked like an anachronism in the broken and weed-grown streets of the town.

Yet, there was substance in Grace's appearance. She had never known anyone who did not either dislike her or toady to her. Now she sometimes received a genuine smile. It was a new experience. Grace knew, without thinking of lonely and wasted years, that her job for as long as she lived was to maintain a standard of dignity for this town where she had spent her life. Her only concession to the present trouble was to lower the large flag from the tall pole beside her house and fly a smaller one from the porch.

Old man Jamison was dead in the second attack, Clete Simpson was missing, old Mrs. Porter was dead in the final attack and Sam Johnson was painfully dead of blasted kidneys.

By then radio batteries were exhausted. No power could be raised, nor would it be that year. People worried about relatives and friends who lived in other places, but the radios were dead. One man, Jim Conklin, built a small, hand-cranked generator, but Jake destroyed it. In his madness Jake isolated the town, as if even radio waves might contaminate the one spot on earth that he tried to protect. During the dreary, rain-filled winter that would follow, a few men would salvage enough material to build a small steam-powered generator fired with wood. During that summer, however, there was no contact with the outside world. No one dared venture on the broken roads. No ships came from seaward, for Jake disabled every vessel. Seattle and Tacoma languished, began to die.

For all that they knew, they were the last people alive in the world. A people without boats, because the boats were destroyed in the crushing winds of the final attack. Their equipment was torn, wrecked, rusting. Their diet was largely vegetarian, although they handlined for fish and built snares for ducks. Dolores, with an eye to the future, turned her attention from the marine biology of the beaches to the biology of the surrounding lakes and ponds. She began to work with the freshwater fish populations, knowing that she could increase them by using careful husbandry. In the absence of game officials and elaborate equipment, she was still able to teach the population how to take shellfish that were safe to eat, for in summer many were not.

Some men and women, uncomfortable with continuing day after day on land, salvaged material and once more began constructing boats. One man, Sol Esten, had been lonely and secluded for years. Now he built a forge. From that time on he found that he was never lonely.

And the blackberries were dark, burnished purple.

=

Penny understood when Dolores told her that so much pain as Penny had was ridiculous. Dolores said it quiet and left it at that. Penny thought it was just the way Dolores always did things.

Or maybe she didn't understand it right away, but by the time she took it home and studied it she understood.

I have been selfish, Penny thought, and I have cried enough to fill the cisterns of this town. I got stiff and silent and drew in close, and that made me mean, or pretty mean.

She sat in her small house and looked into the sunlit street. A young hackberry was tall and elm like in the yard. A breeze moved through its shadow-knitting leaves. Somewhere in the distance someone was chopping wood: blow and echo, blow and echo. Down the block sounded the voice of a small child, subdued, then suddenly shouting happily in the sunshine. Maybe, she thought, the kid was shouting just because of the sunshine. Children had to stay close to home these days. They didn't play and wander the way they used to, but maybe would again someday.

When she was a child . . . she was as full of hunger as the town was full of sunshine. She was almost twenty-four, and that did not seem very old to have come so far and have so much good and bad happen. Her heart was all stirred up with hunger, and not just the hunger of an empty belly.

Sitting there, her emotions that for so long had been held in tight check now began to free themselves like unfolding fists.

In her memory was a growing-up time of dust-filled heat and lathering horses. Men riding, cursing, stringing fence, bouncing four-wheel-drive trucks across wild country in sheer defiance of hunger. The trucks were hot steel, enamel-smelling, gasoline-smelling in the eastern Oregon sun that was so direct it seemed to nail you in place.

The overflooding sun, and the desert sage stretching all the way out to the horizon where ice-capped volcanos towered over an eight-thousand-foot range of mountains that circled the antlike action of the roaring four-wheels. The sex hunger in the men got all mixed up. They turned it into scorching rubber and high whining engines because they did not understand. Shit. She understood that much. Anybody ought to. Those guys wanted to build stuff, so what did they build? Movement, action, wipe-outs, because they didn't know what else to build.

Herself as a girl. Loudmouthed and vulgar and shy. The runt of the family and that made you tough. She helped raise the little kids, took them along to help with the watering, helped repair irrigation pipe and wiped snotty noses at the same time. The whole family was that way, and her very own family just by itself had turned out forty-one people for her high school graduation. Uncles and aunts and cousins. All that stuff. Now that was all good. The winter coats of horses, cattle, the thick tallow wool of sheep. You couldn't knock it, and nobody had better try.

Her first guy. He was a loudmouth too. Another runt, but tough. Drunk a little bit. She would not have tried it with one of them too drunk. She was afraid of them when they were too drunk. But he was just a little drunk and he was strangely rough and strangely apologetic at the same time. She had lain feeling him push in and out of her, trying not to be tense, and not doing good at it so that it hurt some but not much. She was interested. She accepted it that way because it was a job that had to be done. She did not want the first time to mean anything, but it had, sort of. When he was sober, and she was, they were kind of not shy or standoffish with each other, but they never fucked anymore. They almost were friends, might have been.

She had not wanted it to mean anything because she had seen other girls, in high school, who wanted it to mean something. When it did mean something, then those girls married it. When they married it, it changed. Before she was eighteen Penny told herself that she might be dumb enough to someday die for love, but she would be goddamned if she would ever rot for it.

Now she realized that she was rotting. That was what Dolores was telling her. Jim was dead. Dead. In the ground, deep, but not below the reach of the rain. He was rotting, too, and she would not turn from that. She did not examine it, did not imagine how it was happening, but she did not deny it. He was dead, and she was rotting faster than him.

Then the tears came, hot and fast and body-racking. She allowed it to happen and after a while told herself to shut up. She wasn't the only woman in this tank town that had lost a man, and there were men without women, too.

She did not know whether she needed a woman or a man, but she needed someone. And that was only one of the hungers. She could say something like that to Max or Dolores and they wouldn't give a damn. They would just accept it, and maybe be glad she was cleaning up her act. But even Max and Dolores never understood about Jim in the first place. Max and Dolores were smart, but sometimes they were pretty dumb. It balanced everything out, maybe.

Now the kid down the block was bawling. She half rose, then sat back down. He was bawling mad, not hurt. The hackberry was getting dark-leaved out there. Before all this sun it had been light. Those trees threw up so many main branches. Lots of them looked like giant shrubs, and if they grew back in the forest that's how they grew. In the forest they were shrubs; in civilization they became trees. Max and Dolores wouldn't understand that but she did. Max and Dolores would like the idea. They would analyze it and have theories like a cat having a litter of kittens. There'd be striped theories and spotted theories and bobtail theories and boy theories and girl theories; and after it was all done everybody would shake hands and agree that the hackberry was a shrub until it got civilized.

Okay, it's true. Jim had looked like a redneck. Okay. Was a redneck, if the way you described a redneck was: did he only read a magazine once in a while and drink beer and didn't give two whoops in hell for anything but building the house and cutting down trees. Okay.

Jake had liked the woods well enough, but he despised the job and hated the tools. But Jim loved all of it. When he came home smelling of gasoline and pitch and woodchips and fresh sweat, then he was his own kind of man, and all the intellectual stuff in the world wouldn't make up for that. And he loved her and would put up with her crap until it got too much, and then instead of giving her a smack, or going off and getting drunk like guys did, Jim would tell her to get her little ass into bed—and the minute they were there he was with her like that breeze in that hackberry. That breeze could turn into a wind that would blow the rest of this town apart, but it was touching the hackberry the way Jim had always touched her. And when people talked about rednecks, they didn't understand that the hot engines and the squalling chain saws weren't always the only things those guys had going.

And so Max and Dolores thought about philosophy and science and all that, which she didn't knock; but at the end of the talk all they came up with is that everybody is alone and we all ought to try to love each other, and what the fuck was so awful great about that? She had known that the first time she ever had cramps.

Well, there was never going to be another man like Jim. Okay. She had to accept it. Maybe there was some good ones around, and maybe somehow the rest of the people in this hick town were going to live through this. Maybe there was a future. But there was never going to be another one like him, and if the next one was good she would have to make sure she didn't make him second best by comparing him to Jim.

And then there were the other hungers. She'd ought to be doing something for these people who were left. Been sitting and bawling and walking around full of hatred as pus in a boil, and did that do anybody any good? Hell no. So it was time to say good-bye. Wasn't it?

But it wasn't easy. It wasn't.

Penny stood, touched the frame of the window, looked out into the sunlit street and into the young, wind-whispering tree. Then she turned and walked to the bedroom.

Not a very big house. The logs were still shiny with preservative. The bed wasn't even over its new look yet. Goddammit, they had just got started.

She had to get him out of there. Haunts were real. They didn't just live on the night wind like back home when it used to blow around the house off the sage. They lived in places. Maybe he was sad and couldn't go away. Maybe he would just keep coming home every evening to this place for as long as she lived.

But he had always been free, which meant that no matter the bullshit, he had always *thought* free. When he wanted to get married he was really giving something, and she had known it and appreciated it, too. But now he had to be turned loose. Yes.

The room was shadowed, drapes pulled, the gleam of the fresh logs subdued and reflecting light from the living room. It was new, and to her it was pretty and she had to add things and subtract things, for this was where she lived and would live.

"I remember you, kid," she whispered. "I'll not forget you, and I'll not never love you." She paused and listened to the silence in the house. Sounds seemed gone away. The streets of the town were quiet. No movement in the house. Nothing.

"You know that, don't you, kid. Sure." She looked around the small room, felt the silence. "You have to go now," she said. "You just go ahead. Go ahead and then I'll get in and cry the right way, and we'll be all right then."

And for her it seemed that the silence lifted. The air seemed to clear, the house felt empty, and Penny dwelt in the privacy and truth of her sorrow. On the next day she felt stronger. She felt toughlike. If anybody tried to chew on her, they would think they were biting down on a whip handle.

She went to see Jake.

Chapter 27

Max followed Penny with his mind. More and more often his mind followed the power and presence of other minds, and he stood in admiration of the power that lay potential in some people.

She had not seen Jake for a long time. Not since she came here before Barrows croaked, and Jake had been no help and told her his plans for tearing up the world.

It was surprising how fast he had gone down. When she entered the room the smell was like old sweat and beer farts. The sunlight poured through the glassless windows, and, overhead, the lath held pebbles of plaster that had not fallen. One wall buckled inward and the room was bare. It was like he had decided to rid himself of everything and be a monk or hermit or something. The only thing in the room was an old mattress, and Jake sat on it the same way he had sat the first time she came here. He looked spaced. Out of it. Penny wondered if he even knew she was there, and then figured he probably did.

His face was thin, like somebody had tried to make a sculpture of a man but started out with a rock that was too narrow. The face looked like rock. It looked like when the flesh went out of the face the skin just tightened up to take the slack. Jake's bald head was dusty. There was even dust and plaster and crap in his thick eyebrows and in the beard that was all over his face. He had always shaved every day. He claimed it itched. He must really be losing it to have that much hair. He was just living in that body. That's what was happening. He was using it like you used a flophouse when you were broke and on the road. No goddamn wonder he was crazy and wouldn't talk to Max or Dolores. He probably wouldn't talk to her, either, but she was going to try.

She sat in front of him, drew her blue-jeaned knees up to her chin and just watched. Breath was going in and out of his thin nose. The way she could see it happen was there was a little movement of some long nose hairs that sort of hung out toward the mustache. He'd ought to clean himself up.

"You smell pretty bad," she said. "Thin too. Like cancer."

She watched him and he didn't move. He didn't even look like he knew she was there.

"Of course," she said, "there ain't nothing wrong that we can't fix. New coat of paint, put rollers under your ass, and tow you around town to scare little kids."

Still nothing. Except either she was getting used to the smell or else it was gone. It was gone, that's what. The dirt spots on his shirt had disappeared along with the dust and crap.

"Pretty tricky," she said. "For a jerk. You'd ought to eat." She looked around the room. Nothing. Just nothing. She stood and went into the remaining rooms. Nothing. The old stove he'd liked so much was gone. All the dishes and furniture gone from the kitchen. All empty. He wasn't eating. He was living off that body. Must be. How could you do that? Magic, maybe. Some of Barrows's damned foolishness. He really was a jerk. She went back and sat beside him.

"You really are a jerk," she said. "Can you come out of it for a while?"

He could not. He was trapped by the very thing Barrows had warned against. He had stayed in the state for so long, had neglected the requirements of life for so long, that if he had come back and the body started to function normally it would immediately die. He did not care about that. What he cared about was to absolutely cauterize Mobilier.

He had solved a lot of mysteries about Mobilier. The attacks on the town had come from a variety of places, for a variety of reasons. The main attack by Butterfield had been prompted by Chester. Chester had wanted power. The other attacks, either by motorcycle bums or the early attacks with sound or the assassins, had not come from a desire for power. They had come from frightened men who were trying to prove that they had a loyal, rightful place in Mobilier. Even the poor sappy mayor, who hired the motorcycle bums, had been proving his loyalty. Mobilier, headless, heartless and blind, had controlled a world that was every bit as headless, heartless and blind.

He, Jake, was destroying everything. Not simply weapons but all property. For the last two weeks he had been making war on paper, destroying written records and computer banks. He believed there was not a record anywhere in the world that said this town existed. There was not a human being anywhere who thought of this town as an enemy. He had killed them all, even some former neighbors who had fled and who had not been killed by Mobilier. He was ruthless, efficient, as rational and direct in his purpose as Lenin or Beria. He was looking all over the world for little pockets of information, obscure places where he might have missed something. Technically, he could die any time he wanted, but the body was paced slow. He ought to be able to hold out until he was sure the job was absolutely secured. When he was sure, he could wake the body and let it die.

It was a lousy answer, but after where he had been and what he had done, it was the only answer. He was a monster, a snake, a griffin. He was worse than Stalin, worse than Beria; he was a cankered beast that breathed fire across the world and there was no place in history where he belonged. He was already dead, except for guilt and sorrow. Even the hatred that had sustained him was worn out long ago. He did not hate Mobilier. He did not even hate the memory of Chester. There was nothing left except the knowledge that to protect the world he had once loved, and now could not love or hate or even laugh at, he had to destroy that world's destructive capacity. When that was done, and it virtually was done, he could go.

His power was immense. It was stronger than anything Barrows had ever allowed himself to imagine. Barrows had feared and detested the power. But Barrows had not been trained to kill men, and Barrows had never had any appreciation of the clean, knife-edge beauty of a perfectly functioning weapon.

This kid Penny sitting beside him. Back in other days, when everyone was happy, he had loved her for being a smart, savvy, dedicated person. He had thought of her as someone he would always defend, had liked it that she and Jim were together in their crazy, plaster, gilt spangled, carnival world. He had never thought of them separate, had never thought of her sexually. She was sitting there right now thinking that she was still talking to Jake, but Jake was gone and all that was left was a glowering consciousness of destruction and despair.

There was only plague and flood, and he was the first of his kind ever brought to power in America. The Andrew Jacksons, the Nixons, the Mathers and the J. Edgar Hoovers were tinhorns. They were controlled like children by superstitious beliefs that kept them from being anything but two-bit destroyers. They were inside of history, because they were tinhorn and cheap; but he, Jake, was outside of history. There was no place in history where his futility belonged.

That idea came back over and over and he did not exactly understand, but he thought he should care.

The last time Penny was here she went away crying. This time she was not crying at all. The way she was walking he would not be surprised if she were not looking for a stick to smack him with, just to get his attention. He watched her tough, driving little body hurrying down the front walk and pointing toward her house. She wasn't through with him. He knew that because he knew Penny. Keep her in view. Protect her. Protect her.

But you could not protect anyone, and of all men everywhere he was the least able to protect anyone.

He had tried. All his life he had protested and fought and tried to understand the cold butchery of institutions, of greed, of ignorance and opinion. And the blind, mouthy destruction of nationalism. With Barrows's power he had struck here and there, randomly, and then systematically. He had tried to lance the boil, and each time he acted new pus appeared in society. Raw sores drained disease through the streets of society, but it was humanity, not himself, who had caused the sores.

They, humanity, were inept and ignorant. They were dependent and small and vicious. They groaned and wept beneath the hard hand of tyrants, and when the tyrants were removed, they fell on each other's throats and wept to be fed, directed, made to stop their own killing.

When surveillance died in Chicago with the passing of the police, the people rioted and burned. They fled into the countryside taking their fire with them, and they were met by farmers who gunned them down because they intruded. In London, Paris, Athens. In Hong Kong and Leningrad and Honolulu. No dictator anywhere had killed so many, destroyed so much, burned away all hope of ascendancy of the human spirit, as the human spirit itself had done when it was freed.

No. You could not protect anyone.

He touched here and there across the earth with his mind, feeling his saturating despair at the same time he did his self-appointed job. Occasionally a small flicker of anger would rise as he encountered some new blaze of stupidity. When that happened he was like a broom sweeping through cities. By then he thought he must have destroyed a hundred thousand rapists, slaveholders, drug pushers, flicking them off as he passed by on other business. He had destroyed despots, turned back again to destroy their despotic successors. He had rooted out and destroyed thousands of professional killers. He had blown away military installations larger than cities. Still, no matter where his mind looked, there had been weapons, weapons, weapons.

You could protect no one. Not Max, awkwardly perched on the roof of Dolores's house fixing tarpaper patches beneath split and shattered shakes. Or Dolores, weeding in the garden. He could destroy the bombs, submarines, rockets, atomics, sound transmitters, saucers, but he could not destroy the rocks and the clubs.

He could not protect Julie as she crouched and huddled in her madness, or Mike, huddled in a California jail, arm and leg in casts and maybe going to lose an eye no matter if he, Jake, had removed the infection. He could not protect Penny . . .

. . . It was unbearable. It was the last trick and she was taking it, and she was such a sap she did not even know it. She had arrived home and now she was headed back, coming toward him, and by all that was pathetic and all that had once been holy, and no longer was holy, she was bringing him food.

And he was Stalin, Lenin, Beria.

He was not just ferocious. He was ferocity.

He had discovered one thing. Those old feelings of his, how society and wind and water, people and cultures, how somehow they could all fit together if only you could figure them out. Now he knew that they already fitted together, awkwardly, ill-shaped and often core-rotten, but that when you touched one part of it you touched all of it. He figured that he had always almost known that, and that he had added to the almost-knowledge by believing you could touch it and make it better.

Maybe you could. But he would not be there to see it, because he could not bear the process, no matter how pure, that might rise from his deeds. He could not bear it any more than he could bear Penny's brisk movement toward him, and her set look that announced that nobody and nothing, nowhere, had better get in her way.

Stalin destroyed ten million kulaks because a war was coming and he needed industry, and to support the industry he had to commandeer food to feed the cities. Ten million, and that was not even a comma, not a pause in the relentless destruction that Stalin had leveled against his country. It was nothing. It was just nothing.

And what had Stalin bequeathed? A totalitarian system that gradually changed, so that someday, maybe in another fifty years when the resources were thinner yet and the technology of control abandoned through lack of fuel, maybe then there would be a people who could live in moderate freedom and peace: a people, who, like all peoples everywhere, would immediately begin to construct new roles and customs and prohibitions and prejudices and immoral laws. A people who would have weapons powered with compressed air, because wind and windmills did not cease. Carrying intricate devices of destruction powered by solar cells, the people would rise with the cry, "Freedom, I want to be free," and from those same people would also rise the cry, "Kill them. They are not like us."

And now he knew that all of his life he had been in combat with the by-products of means. He, himself, had never really had a dream of what a good world would be like. He had only known what a good world could not be. He had only fought against what should not be.

There was still one thing to do. Mike was a long way from healed, but if he could fight off the pain he could walk in that cast. The very first time out with a bomb run on a bank, and who got hit? Mike, that's who. He, Jake, on his bomb run, had only got concussed. Long ago, a long time. Well, set the kid free. Make the jail walls vanish, maim the guards. Mike was on his own. A long way from home, Mike. Fade into the crowds. Learn to disappear among crowds. Walk as light as that cast will allow and leave no trace.

There was nothing he could do for Julie. He knew Julie and he knew she was all right. She was alive and she was out of this town and for a long time now she had been safe in her hiding place. Now, with the town as safe as it would ever be, she could return. Dolores or Max or both of them could work with her and make her sane.

But what they did not know was that Julie would never be insane for long. He knew Julie. He knew her ego, her self-centeredness, her ability to inflict small cruelties when her expectations were disappointed. Of course. And every fact he knew told him that Julie would be insane for only as long as she felt she could afford it. Julie was very human.

Of course, they would not know the other things about Julie, either.

Julie was form, grace, movement. Julie was possibility, the beautiful and artistic and sensible shape of possibility. Julie was the dreams you had when you were young, the dreams before that first man fell away from the muffled crack of your pistol, blood foam beneath wide-eyed, surprised, hawking and gasping fact that rolled dying into a cruddy, garbage-strewn street.

It was really all for Julie. Cops walking toward you, their mace pipes standing out from their belts, clubs swinging, the thin smile of killers who enjoyed their job. It was for Julie, and always had been, and he would not call it dream or hope or truth or innocence, even if at the time of some of his acts he had not even known her.

There was nothing more to say. There was nothing to hope for, and maybe hope had always been illusion. Penny was near. Penny was a sap, but Penny was right in her sappy truthfulness. Penny was ordained. He did not understand why he thought that word, and he thought that before he left he really ought to understand it. All he understood in a brief light of realization was that it was sappy and decent and clean, that the ordination of Penny was no different from that of Julie.

He felt his body with his mind, caressed it, the space it owned. A good body that had moved him well for a long time, but was pretty much wrecked now. All he had to do—but carefully because this final vanishment must be perfect—was to surround his body exactly with his mind—touching it gentle, like he had once touched Julie's face—but he must do it fast, for Penny was coming up the front walk.

He vanished as he expected, perfectly, instantly, and although he did not believe it, history did not shrug aside to let him pass, for that is not the way that history functions.

Chapter 28

AN OFTEN TOLD AND OFTEN MISUNDERSTOOD TALE OF ZEN CONCERNS a neophyte who approached a master to learn the way. The master slapped him and told him to return. When the neophyte returned, the master slapped him again.

Irrational and inexplicable pain. Jake, the always impatient and sometimes tormented man, wrought possibility he had not wanted. Jake was the possibility of aftermath. Volcanoes offer this, and hurricanes. Tidal waves, floods, fires leaping across prairies or forests. Wars. Where Mobilier dealt chaos, Jake defined the situation with mindless pain.

His departure was no assurance in a world that had not known of him in the first place. The madness of that summer would be explained in many ways. Scientists would ponder. Popular science would speak of creatures from space, or sunspots, or mass hallucination. Religion once more called down an angry and vengeful god with new fires from heaven to wreak destruction on the Sodoms and Gomorrahs of earth.

While they explained and argued and looked to heaven with fear or at the skies with suppressed terror, the people began to rebuild. New leaders rose and confronted the new situation with old customs and bias. Power groups began to form. There was talk of rebuilding the roads.

But here and there men and women picked up tools salvaged from attics, basements, museums. They returned through necessity to the implements of an older time. They did not discover much that was valuable in their thoughts about technology, for they did not think abstractly about tools. They did discover much that was valuable about work, and how work could be direct and with purpose, not simply dishonorable or useless. As they whittled new hoe handles, clumsily learned the fine movements to operate drop or lap spindles, rigged sail, or read, with lips moving, old and formerly worthless books that told how to make useful things like glue, the people realized some truth about work and its worth. Many realized a little and forgot. A few understood a lot and did not forget; and they wondered almost incoherently how to tell this important thing to their children.

For the end, it is said, is in the beginning.

Max, knowing this, now felt his power cease to weigh heavily. Max, in transfiguration with the universe, now stood as quiet witness while he comprehended eons, galaxies, the timeless and eternally sliding planes of the possible, and the liquid hearts of stars. The eternal was not as surprising to him, and not more beautiful, than a rare snowfall or the presence of Dolores in the house.

Some townspeople liked to be with him. One might join him as he walked the rapidly chilling beaches. They were content in his presence, and he in theirs; but most people had more important business.

With Jake's passing the haunted feeling slowly drained from the streets of a town now reduced to a village. Summer passed, and on the second chill night Julie appeared like a specter. She wore her madness like a badge of achievement, and it was this madness that Max and Dolores and Julie defeated over the term of the winter, sewing threads to the fabric of sanity, tightening knots, snipping thread ends to make a compact vision. The town was doing the same. So was the world.

Looking back on it, Dolores understood that while Jake had been a monster, Jake was correct in thinking that order and form could be discovered beyond one's self.

She thought about it. Always before, her work had seemed separate. Chores and sex had been separated. Now all of these things moved in a flow. Even during physical moments, there was union and a sense of timelessness with Max that she first called ineffable, then finally called human. At times she was not distant from him, although at those times she felt more independent and strong. It had nothing to do with sex or role or romance. It had something to do with respect for persons and work.

The world might be mad—was mad—and to be human was to be limited. Always before, she had believed that she could only be free by trusting herself, her work and her own perceptions.

Even science was sometimes mad—blundering conceptually as it puzzled relativity, DNA, the chemistry of life; juggling neutrons, lasers, rocketry, computers and radical psychology—yet, science—still—was or could be as clean-lined and rational and intuitive as the Parthenon. Science was not a temple where you worshiped. It was a temple that you built.

She remembered how she had first learned to be alone.

The chop, chop, chop of the helicopter and the whistle and whir in the chopping as the machine cruised a strangely deserted campus.

She had been little more than a girl in that spring, an undergraduate at the huge university. The spring was close and brilliant. The campus was planted with budding cherry trees and enclosed by tall buildings etched with phrases that began or ended in "veritas." She walked, preoccupied with visualizing the structure of a frog's eye, a slight young woman with dark hair dressed in practical knee-length skirt and short-sleeved blouse that did not tangle with lab equipment. The sun was warm. She pressed books to her chest as she carried them, the flat solidity of the books touching her firmly in a way no lover could ever touch.

It was then that she heard the chop, chop, chopping of the helicopter. For a moment she felt like the only soul in a strange and abandoned land. Then, for a moment, the sound seemed friendly, like the voice of her grandmother calling her from play in evenings long past. Or it was like the voice of a concerned humanity calling one of its members home. Then she realized she had been dreaming while awake. She realized that she should run.

The machine came in low over the roof of the humanities building, growing fast and loud as it sped silver in the sun toward her. It throbbed, pulsed, a metallic locust that lowered fast and pushed toward her fast, like it was homing in on her. Then it hesitated, leveled, dropped easily to the grass twenty-five yards away. The wind from the rotors was like an indifferent blow. The sound seemed unbearable. The rotors cut, whispering, and six men dropped rapidly from the open door to the turf. They were dressed in blue and seemed not to have heads. The riot helmets and masks made them look like mechanical creatures. The guns they carried were not rifles.

The dying rotors chunked to themselves, faded, the silence of the quadrangle returned and the men began to fan out. They headed for the entryways between buildings, corridors to concentrate their fire. The one that walked toward her, machine looking, machine gun hanging from its left hand, walked like a polished insect in the sun, panted and chuckled and with its right hand, black gloved, gently and slowly moved fingers up and down, up and down the polished nightstick at its belt. It crooned, "hippie girl, hippie girl." It walked as exactly and mindlessly as a toy operating from a compressed spring. Dolores learned, and knew while she was learning, the unbridgeable aloneness of being human. She learned the pure beauty of solitude and reason. She clasped the firm, clean-minded and sane books like a shield, holding them to her as she fled.

And because she understood aloneness, and understood flight, she understood why Julie had temporarily gone mad.

=

"Sometimes you play games," Dolores told Julie. "We all do, but with you it's obvious."

The winter rains cloaked the forest as Dolores, Penny and Julie left Julie's house. Wind from the strait wrapped around the tattered house, salt and cold, following them into the forest gloom and pressing around them. Somber red tones cast by cedar illuminated the forest floor. Moldering deadwood turned to soil. Seedling trees grew on the backs of nurse longs; long rows of young trees rooted in the decaying trunks of the past. The women looked for freshly downed wood that was not yet penetrated by rain. The summer had been good for game. The sea ducks were fat, and even the freshwater ducks yielded grease for working leather to preserve their old bow saw from rust.

"I understand it, though," Penny said. "About games. You got to quit it, but I understand how you got to have it, too."

Even to Julie, Penny seemed more easy in her mind these days. The small wrinkles and lines of tension that had once shaped her face were no longer invisible. Penny was tougher now, but different. The small, etched face that had once seemed pretty to Julie now looked wise and beautiful.

"We'll free this one up and drag it back," Dolores said. "We'd better get out of this rain." She pulled sideways at the butt of a young alder broken by one of the blasts. The tree moved and then stopped. It occurred to Julie that Dolores was not all that much taller or heavier than Penny. Penny grabbed the butt from the other side and pushed as Dolores pulled. The tree slid sideways. It was little bigger than a sapling. Twigs snapped and rustled and flew away as the tree was dragged from the undergrowth.

"If you know you are playing games," Dolores said, "you can also know when to quit." She said it kind and quiet, but definite.

It seemed unfair to Julie. Julie knew she had not been playing games. Madness was a glowering dark, a primitive and unholy lightlessness where guilts were like torches seen distantly flickering and pressing toward you as from the depths of a cave. Torches of ragged flame edged with smoking, ebony lines; and the torch that was Jake burned bright. It waved and waggled before her like the red eyes of some hideous beast.

If she had not run away, Jake would have remained in control. She had told Jake that she would fight back, that she would oppose him. And then, when the time came to fight, she had actually fought by running away. That was a crazy way to fight back. If she had not hid, not dived into fear, then Jake would not have killed all those people. Jake would be here right now. Right now. Helping with the wood and going back to the house. It was such a nice house, but now the windows were boarded against the wind, rags stuffed around casements, and the door was skewed and might never fit just right. The trash and filth were gone before the vanishing wind of either Barrows or Jake.

But, Julie told herself, she had to say everything right. Because if he were here, right now, they would not be going back to the house where he had been so happy. Because she would be inside the house with a big fire, instead of a niggling little one that almost heated one room. He would be outside bringing in the wood, glad to love her, glad to show he loved her, and not the least aware that he was making her dependent and obligated and afraid.

Because Jake had made her afraid. When you got right down to it, fear of Jake was the whole reason she had done what she had done. She was afraid of being made dependent. She had not wanted to be loved like that. That kind of love made you little. She had loved Jake more than she had ever loved anyone else, but she had feared him in a way that was as bad as the way she had feared Mobilier.

"You don't understand," she said to Dolores. Her voice was low and she liked how it sounded, because it did not sound apologetic.

"I probably don't," Dolores told her. "That still doesn't mean that you aren't playing games." The tree slid easily across the forest floor. They were making good time with it, hauled in close together, faces close.

Dolores would never understand. Julie could see that. Why, Dolores was almost old enough to be her mother, like Penny was almost young enough to be her daughter.

"And guilt too," Dolores said. "You can't hang on to that, either."

"But I am guilty." Julie's voice was still unapologetic. She liked its sound.

"You ain't a kid," Penny told her. "You did what you had to do at the time you had to do it. So let it go."

Penny's words made a little sense. She looked at Dolores. At Penny. At the lines in their faces and their eyes that told her they would give respect, even love, but they would give no quarter. Julie reached almost timidly to touch Penny's hand, the tree slewing sideways until she recovered the balance, and Julie realized suddenly that she had always been in a game.

Even her work had been a game. She had called herself an anthropologist, and she had spoken like an expert. But she had only studied peoples. She knew their customs, their values, their totems and dogmas and rites. She knew all that, but she had missed one big thing. She had never studied their hearts. It was that kind of study, that kind of feeling toward people, that would finally turn her into a real anthropologist.

Julie saw that she must have a plan. By winter's end the village would start to reorganize. Some kind of government would form, and strong members would rise and take control.

Winter passed and Julie's plan grew. As April opened with low skies and wind, the village met for the first time as a group. They met according to Julie's plan.

That plan was to form them into a tribe. It was not a plan for the perfection of society which Jake had once pondered. A tribe was only the least flawed kind of society of the many several ways that an ambitious race had devised to govern itself.

Some people came because they were afraid or lonely. Some came for the novelty, and some because of self-importance or hunger to obtain power. And Max, knowing they were one more breath in the eternally sliding frames of history, loved them.

A few people came in support of Julie's sanity because they knew it was her plan, and, of course, there were some who did not come at all.

Les and the mayor hid, drinking. Each watched the other and thought that soon he would be alone, abandoned and forgotten by everyone.

—Just real sad, Les thought, and losin' a good boat, a real good business. He watched the mayor and it was pretty sure the mayor was gonna wink out soon because now when he lectured and preached you couldn't understand the words and if it hadn't been for that lousy timber jockin' . . . and Les turned from it.

While old Roza McKenzie hunched in the wind and the spit and speckle of occasional rain, clad in fading and ragged colors, and muttered past the roofed-over basement of the old recreation center which had shattered in the first blast.

—They was singin' in there. Hard as times was they din't have nothing to sing about, but sure as anything they were a-doin' it, and they wan't ever to catch her singin' and foolin' like that . . . and even if they did they'd only just swear she did it cause she stole something—old Roza walked near the sound for the warmth of it, then started toward where downtown used to be. There was still some stringy, ratty old froze up carrots and turnips in the ground. If folks was too dumb to take keer of their own and just go off talkin' and singin' . . . old Roza walked away, felt the cold, turned back. There was a garden right near, and they was singin', and nobody was going to be lookin' in that direction. Old Roza walked brisk. There was still some fire left in the old horse, praise God and damn Roosevelt and sweet Jesus and all the holy saints world without end in the blood a the lamb. Amen.

Epilogue

THE ROAD WAS LONG AND HAD BEEN. WHAT YOU MOSTLY HAD TO WATCH *for were the dog packs. People did not bother you much if you stayed clear of cities, but a lot of dogs were running.*

Mike's leg slowed him bad. It was never going to be all that good again. He had knocked off the walking cast in San Francisco. Had to. It hurt a lot, and it had even stopped him for a while. Now the leg was shorter, kinda, but good enough it carried him home.

The skies had stopped being so bad with sun after the first high pass in Oregon. He had felt the mist close in like a hand. The rain was in the mist, trying to get under the oilcloth he'd found on the kitchen table at an abandoned farm. There was real teeth in that rain, and you could not see far. The mist was as thick as he had ever seen it, and he felt like crying because the mist and rain told him he was getting on toward home. He actually had cried some, but there had been no one there to see.

Jake had been right. Killing was not the answer, but sure as hell there had to be an answer. Soon as he got there, soon as he got home, he told himself he better listen to Jake. Maybe between the two of them they could still do something.

The road wound out of scrub forest and over the top of a hill and then went in a long sweep toward the town. He paused to look, heart afraid, and Mike broke into a wobbling run that slowed to a walk. There were still some houses left on top of the hill.

They were bound to be alive. Just bound to be. Barrows and Jake and Jim and Penny and Julie and Dolores and that new guy, Max. All of them, because Barrows would not have it any other way. Still, the town was tore up worse than any of the others he had seen.

It was more than a half-mile but he walked it pretty good, he thought, and he ought to because he had already walked a thousand of them. The downtown wasn't there. It was like magic, or like your memory had built something that wasn't real and then you looked and didn't trust your mind.

Getting up the hill was worse, but he even did that good, now. Going to get to see everybody. See Penny and Jim. Their house was first . . .

They were still living here. He glanced around the rooms.

Nobody home. The rooms were still warm, though, or at least not as cold as outside. Where had everybody gone?

Mike walked down the street, past the broken library. Past shattered houses. There were still people here. He could tell that. There was bound to be somebody he could ask. The buildings had been busted up for a long time. He could tell that, too. There was actually grass growing on some of the torn up porches.

Then he heard sound, like voices from a good way off, and he walked in the direction of the recreation center. A spot of color was moving over there on the left. The ache in his leg was so familiar that he did not think of it. Somebody was in the garden at the old Johnson place. He moved closer.

It was crazy old Mrs. McKenzie, and she was hurt or something. She had to be, because she was whining and making a funny kind of sound. It made him feel better. If old lady McKenzie was alive, then they all ought to be around here someplace. He looked around, feeling the gusts, the spits of rain like occasional gray fingers from the strait. He got real close to her. She wasn't hurt at all. He slowed, listened. She was singing. Crazy old bat. He had better get her in out of this wind and wet. She could get sick being out here like this.

Mike walked toward her. She could tell him what had happened, and, God knows, she would, the way she always gossiped. But the first thing he had to do was get her in out of this rain.

Jack Cady (1932-2004) won *The Atlantic Monthly* "First" award in 1965 for his story, "The Burning." He continued writing and authored nearly a dozen novels, one book of critical analysis of American literature, and more than fifty short stories. Over the course of his literary career, he won the Iowa Prize for Short Fiction, the National Literary Anthology Award, the Washington State Governor's Award, the Nebula Award, the Bram Stoker Award, and the World Fantasy Award.

Prior to a lengthy career in education, Jack worked as a tree high climber, a Coast Guard seaman, an auctioneer, and a long-distance truck driver. He held teaching positions at the University of Washington, Clarion College, Knox College, the University of Alaska at Sitka, and Pacific Lutheran University. He spent many years living in Port Townsend, Washington.

Dale Bailey lives in North Carolina with his family, and has published three novels, *The Fallen*, *House of Bones*, and *Sleeping Policemen* (with Jack Slay, Jr.). He has been a four-time finalist for the International Horror Guild Award, a two-time finalist for the Nebula Award, a two-time finalist for the Shirley Jackson Award, and a finalist for the Bram Stoker Award. His International Horror Guild Award-winning novelette "Death and Suffrage" was adapted by director Joe Dante as part of Showtime Television's anthology series, *Masters of Horror*. His most recent novel was *The Subterranean Season*.